CW00860019

Valkyrie in Training

Laura Prior

Laura Prior

The Falling Series

Laura Prior

Laura Prior

Copyright © 2013 by Laura Prior

ISBN: 978-1494418342

All rights reserved. No part of this book may be reproduced or transmitted in any form or by any means, electrical or mechanical, including photocopying, recording or by any information storage and retrieval system, without permission in writing from the copyright owner.

This is a work of fiction. Names, characters, places and incidents either are the product of the author's imagination or are used fictitiously, and any resemblance to any persons, living or dead, events, or locales is entirely coincidental.

Dedication

Dedicated to my two granddads; Eric Lawrence and John Prior—both courageous soldiers in the Second World War.

As always, special thanks to my wonderful husband-to-be Simon, my beta readers Tanya, Sheree and my mam, and to Kyle for making wonderful front covers for the *Falling* series! A huge thank you to the fabulous Lauren McKellar who has edited Valkyrie in Training.

I would like to say a huge thank you to all of the fans of the *Falling* series. By continuing to invest your time and hearts in Jasmine's story and by sending in your messages of support I am able to continue writing.

Laura Prior

1

'Be in love with your life. Every minute of it.'

Jack Kerouac.

Zacharael

"Darling you look beautiful," Zacharael said, smiling at the beautiful black-haired woman before him. "And you are mine."

Zanaria laughed loudly, her white teeth sparkling. She twirled in front of him with her arms outstretched. She continued to spin, her bare feet flashing across the white marble floor. The light blue dress she had chosen was exquisite, not that Zacharael particularly noticed what anyone wore, but he couldn't help but admire how the material fitted to her body and fell to the floor softly, almost caressing her feet. One strap fitted closely across her chest diagonally, pulling the bodice in tight. Bangles were stacked from her wrists to her elbows, and her hair was loose, the silky black sheet adorned with hundreds of glittering diamonds. Though her wings were tucked away, she looked more angelic than any other angel he had ever laid eyes upon.

"But do I look trustworthy? Do I look strong and fearless? Do you think a human would believe in me?"

Zacharael stalked her around the hall, ducking behind a pillar. He was constantly awed by her ethereal beauty and couldn't help but to pause every now and again to analyze her. She didn't seem concerned by his silence and continued to spin, her eyes closed as she enjoyed the momentum.

The thought of her leaving this place took his breath away. To not be able to look upon her face every day was abhorrent to him, yet how could he naysay her? It was not his decision anyway, and she had accepted her new duties. But still . . . he felt mesmerized by the beauty of her form in the surroundings of the Heavenly Reception Hall.

The hall itself was otherworldly. It was cavernous—massive in length and width with ancient pillars on either side lined up like a row of trees. They were golden in color, thick and sturdy at the bottom, and thinned out as they reached their magnificent height. Ten meters up, they split into slivers, golden threads branching out, thousands of which gently touched the ceiling. Where they met, the golden color spread and faded into the white of the ceiling. The golden flecks reappeared, weaving between the mosaics, forming the clouds surrounding the angelic figures.

The gold of the architecture in the hall shone down on Zanaria, making her skin glow and shimmer as she continued to turn. The bangles chimed as they cast dots of light rotating around the room.

A grin spread over his face. He could feel his eyes shining with pride and love. She was a part of him. A part of his soul.

He smiled. “Zanaria, you will be the sweetest guardian angel there ever was. I promise you, your ward will trust in you, and will follow wherever you lead. How could they not?”

Zanaria grinned and laughed again, a melodic tune that echoed around the hall.

"Do you want to know who my human is?" she asked mischievously, her eyes shining.

Zacharael did, but he knew the rules. "It is not allowed. Only the principalities are aware of the protected humans."

She sighed. "I can't wait to get to the human plane. I am so excited to see the human moon and sun; to see the stars in the sky."

"Zanaria . . . " Zacharael warned.

She held her hands up. "I know, I know."

Zacharael sighed. "Being a guardian angel is an enormous responsibility. It is important you do not get enamored with the human world and lose focus. Our family descends from a line of Warriors and guardians, and you are well aware of the danger to us all in the humans' world. We have countless foes there just waiting for a young angel to kill - or worse."

She slid up to him and placed one delicate hand on his chest. He looked down at her small, feminine wrist, over her knuckles to her delicate fingers resting on him lightly.

"Zacharael, I am not afraid. Michael gave me this duty and I have embraced it. The warrior masters have ensured I am adequately prepared, and the principalities have taught me my mission well. My task is not a physical one, but a spiritual and emotional journey. It will take every ounce of persuasion and love I possess to ensure my ward follows my direction. I am confident in my abilities. I will succeed and make you proud of me, I swear it."

Zacharael instantly frowned, concern etched across his face. "I *am* proud of you. You are the most wonderful creature in all of the worlds and planes in existence. Your spirit is light, your generosity and love limitless; do not ever fear that I am not proud of you . . . know always that I love you." He trapped her hand on his chest and squeezed it to his heart, wanting her to feel his love with every word.

Zanaria smiled broadly, her white teeth sparkling like a million diamonds. For the hundredth time Zacharael wondered how such a miracle could exist.

She lifted her hand from his chest and laid her palm on his cheek. "As I love you."

A chatter of voices interrupted them. Stepping to the side, Zanaria lifted her dress slightly and turned to face the great doors at the end of the hall. One door was soon pushed open and a small crowd stepped through cautiously.

Zacharael watched with interest as the figures paused just inside, waiting for their guide—a cherubim angel named Java—as he pulled the door closed behind them. He stepped around them and gestured for them to follow him through the hall.

There were six human figures in total. Two held onto each other tightly—perhaps they were related in some way—while the others had the same stunned expression that he saw on most of the figures entering the heavenly realm. He glanced down at Zanaria, fully aware of the reason she loved the Heavenly Reception Hall so much. He, too, was enamored with the transformation that was about to take place here.

As the crowd continued through the hall, the transformation hit the eldest first. A human male who had obviously reached a ripe age began to unbend, his stride becoming longer and steadier. He lifted his chin and shrugged his shoulders as though a weight had been lifted.

The others only began to notice when the change hit them, too. Their forms repaired themselves; their skin tightening and lightening, their hair regaining color and thickness, their muscles beginning to tone and shape beneath the skin covering their body. As they continued to walk, they seemed to become lighter, happier, all worries and hurts dissipating. The youngest of them, a small boy with wide scared eyes ran forward and clutched Java's tunic. The cherubim stopped and turned to face him. He picked the boy up in his arms and gestured for the humans to march on, not giving them a chance to be distracted.

Zanaria sauntered down the hall behind the pillars, parallel to them, smiling serenely as she gazed upon the humans.

After some time had passed they approached the end of the hall. The humans were all now an equal size to the small boy, looking as young and fresh as he. They looked at each other and frowned in confusion before tilting their heads to search out another doorway. There was none. Their steps once again became hesitant and distracted, though they continued to follow the cherub to the wall.

Zanaria clasped her hands to her chest and gasped in adoration as the final transformation took place. The human figures were becoming transparent. They took on an icy blue glow as their bodies faded and only their soul was left—a blue transparent cloud, filled with light.

Java turned and raised his arm. The wall before them disappeared, leaving a cloud-filled space, golden light shooting through in beams. The souls hesitated for just one more second before rushing through the clouds and disappearing in their depths.

Zacharael turned to Zanaria. “When do you leave?”

“Soon. Within the day,” she replied absently, staring into the clouds.

2

'If you don't feel it, flee from it. Go where you are celebrated, not merely tolerated'.

Paul F. Davis.

In the days that followed, Zacharael went about his business as usual. He attended meetings, trained with his fellow warrior angels and learned of the wars and battles taking place in all of the realms. Though many creatures thought that warrior angels simply fought as ordered by the principalities, they were very wrong. Warrior angels were of the power class and held the strength of the heavenly realm in their bodies and thoughts. Warrior angels were not only brawn, but were honed weapons of knowledge. For thousands of years they'd studied every argument and every decision that led to every war. They'd planned alternatives to every situation, learned every technique in battle strategy and lent their strength and knowledge to their allies to strengthen their future battle prowess. Indeed angels of the power class were highly underestimated.

All angels were assigned to a class when they were born, normally dependent on their family line. The only exception to the rule was the dominions. As it was they who advised on the role the angel would play, they could not assign anyone to the dominion class. Instead, the archangels would pick a select few to learn the ways of the dominion.

Regardless of class, when each angel became of age, they were taught their duties gradually, and, after a hundred years or so when they were deemed capable, they were sent out on their first task. A task that Zanaria had been sent on a few days earlier.

Zacharael couldn't help but wish that she had been born to another class. There were three spheres of class, the first containing the seraphim, cherubim and thrones, the second with dominions, virtues and powers, and the third with principalities, archangels and angels. Then, there were the Grigori; the Fallen, who wanted to redeem themselves.

The seraphim were the angels of love. They found it among all creatures and nurtured and encouraged it until it bloomed, bringing happiness and wonder. Zacharael couldn't help but think that the seraphim class would have been a much better choice for Zanaria. The cherubim, like Java, were present at death, and escorted the humans to their judgment. Depending on the outcome, they then took them to one of the many planes of redemption, the heavenly plane or to the waiting room.

Thrones were the keepers of justice, and sentenced the souls the cherubim brought them. Dominions organized and gave out orders to the angels, including naming their class when they were born.

Both the virtue and the power class of angels were also known as warrior angels. They were sent to various planes, including the human one, and tasked with keeping peace between all creatures. Should one race of beings threaten the existence of another, they would be made to balance the fight. Principalities were specifically guardians of the human realm, making decisions based on variable outcomes and advising when another class of angel was needed.

Archangels were the chief angels, and angels were general messengers, also known as guardians.

It was rare that a young angel was chosen as a guardian, and Zacharael desperately wanted to question those behind the decision. He would have loved to know the details of her task but there were strict rules, and good reasons behind those them. If he had found out that she had been sent into a dangerous situation he would have been unable to stop himself from going there to help her, and that could jeopardize her entire mission. It was important to keep his faith, and trust that the principalities and dominions knew what they were doing.

Zacharael repeated this to himself every day. Each day brought new heartache, sadness and worry. Where was she? Was she safe? Had she found her ward? Questions poured through his mind, one after the other, none of which he could answer. Each day brought more loneliness than the last.

He soon found himself emerged in new tales of war and he tried his best to push thoughts of Zanaria to the side. A seasoned angel named Barius had brought news of a fallen angel targeting a small human child. The news had rocked the heavenly realm. As the norm, Fallen angels didn't care about humans. They were so far beneath their notice they might as well have been invisible. For a human to have been attacked and brutally murdered was incredibly bizarre, and no one could fathom the reason behind it. In fact, the general consensus seemed to be that Barius was incorrect and that it had been a vampire. *That* was believable. Vampires were a cruel race of beings, their only source of pleasure the draining of blood from a human and feeling their essence slip away while their fangs were biting deep. However, Barius refused to concede to this, insisting that his story was true.

Over the next few weeks, reports began to flood in of fallen angels targeting more human children. Hundreds were killed in just a few weeks. The human world was in panic, claiming terrorism was to blame. Friends and families turned on each other, countries sent their own warriors to fight each other, and battles raged across the human plane. The Heavenly Realm itself declared an emergency and sent warriors to calm the waters. It helped some, but there were many casualties. Unknown to the angels, the Fallen had tripled in number and outnumbered the warriors five to one. Still, the warriors fought on valiantly, killing the fallen one by one and sending them to their judgment.

Eventually, months later, a council was called. Angels from all factions were invited to sit in and listen to the tales of those recently home from the human plane.

It took place in the early hours of the morning outside in the soft white fields. Thousands of angels had gathered to listen to the stories and plan their next steps. Raphael—an archangel with incredible healing powers and a passion for teaching young angels their duties, stood up. He was well respected and loved, possibly more so than any of the other archangels. He was dressed as he often did: black material encased his legs, chest and arms, and a grey cloak swirled behind him, a slight breeze tossing it to the side. His long dark hair hung past his shoulders and his bronzed skin glowed, as though it had been painted a metallic gold.

He waited for a full minute until the angels waiting before him were completely silent.

“I have serious news to tell you all. It is undecided how we will proceed following the revelation of the catastrophic events we have discovered. Perhaps we will leave it to you to decide, or perhaps it would be wiser for the principalities to decide on a course of action.” He glanced over to where a group of principalities stood, each with a perplexed look on their face.

Raphael sighed and bent his head. “The angelic race has been compromised.”

A rush of gasps spread through the crowd, soon followed by angry voices. Zacharael frowned in disbelief and looked at his good friend Maion who’s eyebrows were raised, his mouth open in shock.

Again, Raphael waited for silence. “We have discovered humans who are able to do impossible things. They are worshipped among the humans. They use their abilities to further their wars, to kill and destroy those who stand in their path. These humans are liaising with the fallen and have attempted to cull our numbers. They are gifted, talented, and *not fully human.*”

What did he mean? This didn’t make sense. How could a human not be a human? Zacharael frowned in concentration, hanging onto every word that left Raphael’s lips.

“These humans descend from a human and an angel.” Roars and screams of horror spread through the crowd. Some angels shook their fists angrily at the sky, some fainted in shock, but still Raphael continued. “Some of us, some of *you* have lain with the human women and men, and created life where there should be none. They are an abomination. They should not exist. They lack the guidance and strength to control their abilities, and instead of using them to do good, they further their own causes.”

The crowd hushed when Gabriel stood beside Raphael. Raphael also fell silent. Gabriel was another archangel, but one so beautiful that to look upon her and to be in her presence was to feel as though you were touching Heaven itself. She was no warrior or healer, but it was said that she was the messenger of God. The words that she spoke were supposedly the very words He himself wanted to be spoken.

"Friends. Life has been created in a supposedly impossible situation. Does that not qualify as also being named a miracle? Do we not ask for these on a daily basis? Perhaps He has not answered in the way you expected but that does not mean it is not meant to be. Raphael speaks of lack of guidance, strength and control. What are *we*, if not all of those things? Do we not have guidance to spare for our wards? Do we not have strength aplenty—enough to protect them from those that would influence them in evil matters? Many of our guardians watch over these children as we speak, guiding them, loving them. Would you have them turn away from their duty?" Gabriel spoke softly, beseeching them all.

"My Lady," a principality named Roderer stepped forward. "May I ask if any of these . . . these . . . "

"Nephilim," she supplied.

From where Zacharael stood, he could see the gulp Roderer swallowed. "Have any of these *Nephilim* betrayed our race of their own accord? Perhaps that is the key to deciding what is to be done about them."

"Yes and no," she answered.

Raphael stepped forward again. "The Grigori report that the Nephilim have liaised with the Fallen in their efforts to open the Heavenly Gates. They have a number of options that they are considering. They seek a portal maker." At the disturbance in the crowd he quickly continued, "They have not found one yet, so they are trying to capture an angel and use him as leverage for entrance."

"They have not captured one, and our guardians are on full alert," Gabriel added.

"We stand before you with this information and ask for you to think and pray on it, and come to us with a decision. Do we destroy these Nephilim and the threat they pose to us?" Raphael bellowed.

After a roar of cheers had died down, Gabriel's dulcet tones were heard. "Or do we protect them, hide them from the Fallen, and teach them ourselves? Do not forget that these humans may be your own children, or the children of your dearest companions. Though they are unusual and unexpected, they may be *your* blood kin."

3

'The cure for anything is salt water—sweat, tears or the sea.'

Isak Dinesen

Throughout the day, angels were seen walking and flying with sad and confused looks upon their faces. Their auras were a mixture of greys and purples; confusion and sadness tinged with fear and anger, regret in some . . . and abhorrent horror in others. Zacharael went about his duties as usual then met his closest companions in the Library of Choices; a huge hall filled with books and tombs of every size. Musty old armchairs and tables were scattered around, open books laid out across tables and carpets, pored over by upset and puzzled angels. The library was much busier than usual, and for good reason. Angels absorbed every word in the books, hoping for an answer inside them of how to address the problem that had arisen. Gabriel and Raphael had given them until sundown to cast their vote. How did one go about making a choice between killing an entire race of beings or possibly making a decision that would result in the massacre of their own race?

Zacharael had meant to think hard and then ponder his decision with his friends, but found his concentration was firmly on Zanaria. Was her ward one of these Nephilim? He had not heard from her, so there was no way of knowing if she was safe or if she had been caught in the wars plaguing the human plane. Acid ate at his stomach at the thought that she could be dead even now. How would he go on without her? His life would be pointless, completely empty and devoid of her beauty.

“Zacharael!” Maion slapped him on the back, jerking him out of his reverie.

He blinked and looked around at his friends. He had found them where they had agreed to be, in the far corner by the little used books. They had pulled some chairs together around a small pool of water, and were already bathing their feet. Elijah, Maraibre and Varyerl gestured for him to join them. Maion quickly pulled off his boots and stuck his feet in beside theirs, closing his eyes as he tried to let the gently lapping water wash away his troubles. Zacharael sighed and joined him. The water felt good on his tired feet, but did little to soothe his aching heart.

“Fear not, friend, Zanaria will be safe,” Elijah said, regarding him closely.

“I simply do not like it. I cannot help the fear for her safety that overwhelms me with every second that passes,” Zacharael muttered quietly.

“Indeed, there is something quite peculiar about the whole situation. To have half-angels, or gifted humans, or these . . . *Nephilim* running around, it cannot be safe! I don’t know why the angels have not been pulled back to the safety of this realm while the fate of those poor creatures is being decided. As for the angels that had a hand in making them—I can only hope they are being punished. I simply cannot fathom this whole mess out!” Varyerl pondered loudly.

"I worry for Zanaria. I would be greatly relieved if the angels were pulled back immediately," Zacharael agreed.

"She should never have been sent. A warrior should have gone, not a guardian," Maion grumbled, sipping from a goblet that appeared in his hand. He rubbed his fingers over the engraved pattern of delicate leaves.

"Ah, that is what many of us thought, but the principalities assured us that the prophets appoint a guardian in many of these cases, not a warrior," Varyerl commented brightly. "What are we to do? Many of our dear ones have been sent to the human plane to serve as guardians. Surely not all of their wards are these odd creatures?"

"I, for one, do not trust these Nephilim. Though Gabriel claims they are kin to us, how do we know for certain they will be no threat once trained? They are unknown. We will be equipping them with the knowledge and strength that they may then use to kill us!" Maraibre exclaimed.

Maion laughed. "Easy, Maraibre—you'll have us scared of our own shadows," he teased his brother with a grin on his face. It earned him a thump on his shoulder.

"Regardless of what you think, Maion, I will stand by my opinion that these Nephilim are not to be trusted. There are only two options that should be considered. One: should they be left alone and monitored, with only these *portal makers* destroyed if they are found? Or, two: should they be rounded up and interrogated? We can then bring their angel makers to justice whilst studying their peculiarities," Maraibre suggested enthusiastically, clapping his hands together.

Varyerl splashed his foot in the water, spraying droplets over them all. “The principalities—”

“Forget the principalities, it isn’t Haamiah or Wendayer protecting the realms, is it? It is the warriors who integrate themselves in the planes of existence, and are forced to battle with evil beasts bent on destruction. The principalities sit on their chairs ordering everyone else around, playing games with any angel they like. I am through with games! The warriors must rise up and end this fight before it spreads like a disease to our realm,” Maraibre’s low voice growled out angrily.

Maion groaned in frustration. “These unknown creatures are children, Maraibre. They need to be protected and sheltered from the Fallen. Zanaria is perfectly capable of guiding her ward, Nephilim or not, and would likely be distraught at this conversation. Do you doubt her strength so much?”

“Of course not.” Maraibre refuted. He turned to Zacharael. “Tell me, do you agree? Would you not have preferred to go yourself? Right now, would you not prefer to take her place?”

Zacharael frowned in thought. “I trust fully in Zanaria’s skills as a guardian. If anyone can get through to a Nephilim, it will be her. Perhaps we think too harshly of all these creatures.”

“Do you wish to chance that when Zanaria’s life is at risk?” Elijah asked, glancing around furtively. The others leaned in to catch his words.

“These Nephilim are the sons and daughters of our own. Besides the fact that they are God’s creatures and should be protected for that alone, we should look to ensuring their survival and good fortune because we are, in essence, their soul family.” Zacharael sighed and rubbed his palm across his forehead. “My mind is conflicted, and my thoughts are torn into a million shreds. I think this, yet I feel a worry in my chest, a sickening scream in the pit of my stomach telling me that Zanaria should be recalled. It is my duty to protect her—”

“And mine,” Maion added.

“I am torn between ensuring her success in this mission, and therefore protecting her future as a guardian, while all I want to do is hold her close, and never again allow her to encounter danger,” he finished.

“The only way to ensure her safety is to destroy the Nephilim,” Maraibre proposed. “I vote to destroy them.”

“I think they should be protected,” Maion stated.

“I, too, believe they should be protected,” Elijah said.

Varyerl took a deep breath. “I think no good can come of these odd half-creatures. It will be better for them, and for us, if they are to be destroyed.”

They all looked to Zacharael. They had cast their votes, now it was his turn. He closed his eyes and allowed his feet to rub the smooth pebbles in the bottom of the pool. He thought of the way the water lapped at his calves, like kisses. He thought of Zanaria, her beautiful face, her smile, her golden aura that embraced everyone with love and warmth. What would *she* want? He shook his head ruefully. He *knew* what she would want.

“I think they should be protected.”

At sundown, the votes had been cast, and the angels once again met in the fields. Zacharael, Maion, Maraibre, Elijah and Varyerl stood together, side by side. The tension was palpable as they waited for the archangels to come forth. The crowd was silent, no whispers, no muttered conversations, not even a wisp of clothing made a sound to betray the gravity of what was about to happen. This was it. The fate of goodness knows how many people had already been decided. The angels gathered here had decided Zanaria's fate.

Gabriel and Raphael stood next to each other, no facial expressions giving their thoughts away. There was no introduction this time. Nothing else needed to be said. Zacharael closed his eyes and prayed that the decision made here would not be a mistake; that it would not cost him Zanaria. If they chose to destroy the Nephilim, a deadly force would soon sweep the earthly plane, destroying angel and Nephilim alike. He knew the Fallen. He knew what they were capable of. If the angels decided to destroy the Nephilim to prevent the Fallen from using them to attack the angels, he would have to find Zanaria with all of the speed he possessed.

Raphael stepped forward and lifted his head. "We will destroy them all."

4

'Kindness is a language that the deaf can hear and the blind can see.'

Mark Thain.

As the angels began to group together according to their rank, forming lines to enable an orderly departure, Zacharael slipped away. He slid down to the Heavenly Reception Hall and ran down the length of columns to the closed door at the end. He jumped when a figure stepped out from behind a pillar.

Gabriel regarded him carefully. She swept her dress behind her as she slowly circled him.

Zacharael bit his lip, desperate not to betray his decision, yet knowing full well he could not lie to her if she asked him where he was going.

“I will not,” she whispered.

His head jerked up, and his face flushed crimson. She smiled and stepped closer, placing one hand on his chest, reminiscent of Zanaria’s actions weeks earlier.

“I have something for you, Warrior.” She lifted her free hand and held out a silver dagger decorated with a small opal in the center. “Give this to your love when you see her.” She folded his fingers around it and stepped away, disappearing into a golden glow.

Unsure of the reason behind what had just taken place, Zacharael pushed the silver dagger into a sheath at his side and rushed forward to the door. As he placed his hand on the brass ring a hand touched his shoulder. He spun around.

Maion stood there. He was coated in armor, with metal cuffs attached to his forearms. Swords were strapped to his back where his wings had retreated. Except for his porcelain skin he looked like a mirror image of Zach. His black eyes stared into Zacharael's.

"Do not think to stop me Maion," he warned. "I love her; I *will* protect her."

Maion stared deep into his eyes. "As do I. I will come with you."

Zacharael nodded and pulled the door open. The two angels spread their wings and took flight.

They descended through the clouds, unable to see where they were going through the thick mist. They knew the direction by heart and flew unwaveringly, soaring through the wet mass that surrounded them and blocked the light from their eyes. They continued the downward spiral, knowing that eventually the black would lift, and they would reach the plane they were looking for.

Hours later they each breathed a sigh of relief as the heaviness lifted and the blackness ended abruptly. They stopped midflight, their wings beating just slightly to keep them afloat.

"Where to?" Maion called, his eyes focused on the blue and green mass tinged with grey before him.

Zacharael nodded. "The north. I sense that she is on the north side of this world. Follow me. We must continue carefully." He stretched his wings and beat out forcefully, rocketing through the sky with Maion following closely.

Eventually they entered the protective atmosphere: an almost tangible force that made their skin tingle when they touched it. Soon after, they were emerged in a dark grey sea that eventually faded to white. After a few minutes even the white faded, leaving large expanses of blue and green beneath them.

Zacharael closed his eyes and allowed his senses to guide him. He focused his entire soul on Zanaria. He bent his will to finding her aura, searching for her, *seeking* her among the millions of creatures on this plane.

They continued north and gradually swooped lower and lower near a city, noticing a number of fires burning brightly. They dropped onto a flat rooftop in the center of the city and were instantly sucked into the noise and chaos below.

Maion bent his knees and stretched his arms out, trying to rid himself of the cramps paining his arms. Zacharael ignored the ache in his body and folded his wings in, jumping off the edge of the roof onto a pathway. He began marching toward an alleyway he saw to their left. Maion grabbed him and spun him around forcefully.

"Wait! We should have a plan. Are you just going to march up to her and carry her off?" He asked.

Zacharael frowned. "If that is what it takes."

"Whoa! You know she will hate that. We need think this through. We need a strategy. There is obviously something happening here," he said.

"You may stand here and plan a strategy if you wish, but I will get to locating Zanaria first, then discuss a plan *with* her," Zacharael snapped. "She could be in danger even now!"

Maion held up his hands in defeat. "Then continue on, friend."

Zacharael marched on, ducking under a low overhang, and avoiding the street children running around his feet. They were lucky it was late evening so not many would have seen their descent. Maion was correct in that perhaps they should have thought of a plan first, but there simply wasn't time. If the Fallen were here merging with the Nephilim and the humans, it was imperative they get to Zanaria and ensure she was in no danger. Then they could decide what to do with her ward.

At the end of the shadowed alleyway they were able to run up a flight of crooked steps into an almost empty street. Hearing the sound of voices, Zacharael and Maion ran down the street and turned onto a much busier one. People bustled around with carts and wagons, women were screaming in doorways of homes, and children ran through the crowd, looking for their parents in the chaos.

"What has happened here?" Maion whispered.

"Nothing good, I fear," Zacharael answered solemnly.

A tall figure appeared before them in the shadows, halting them in their tracks. "What do you think you are doing?"

"Maraibre." Maion sighed. "Brother, you scared us. What are you doing here?"

"The question is, what are *you* doing here?" Maraibre asked anger flashing in his eyes. "You shouldn't be here. It is against the rules."

"Then why are *you* here?" Maion retorted.

"I followed you to ensure you did not get into trouble, *little brother*," he replied, his eyes flashing in return.

Zacharael pushed past him, turning at the last minute to grip his forearm. "I have no time to argue with you. I seek Zanaria."

"I understand you want to protect her and her ward, but you cannot go against the Heavenly Realm. It is already decided that the Nephilim are dangerous and should be destroyed," Maraibre pulled away.

Zacharael scowled, and leaned closer. "I will find her, and if she wishes to protect her ward then so be it, I will protect them both. The Nephilim are children to be saved, not persecuted because of their heritage."

Maraibre groaned. "The Nephilim are a species that should not exist. They will be the downfall of us all if they are not euthanized. Look what is happening here! The Nephilim have taken the city. The Fallen will descend at nightfall and kill everything still here."

Zacharael took two steps past him and turned his head. "Then we will be long gone—with Zanaria."

"Have you got her trail?" Maion asked, rushing past his brother.

Zacharael bit his lip and concentrated on storming through the crowd. "It is as I feared. I sense her fear, and if I can scent it—"

"So can the Fallen," Maion finished grimly.

They pushed on with inhuman speed and strength, approaching a large sand-colored building with a tall gate barring the way. Zacharael jumped, easily scaling the wall. Maion glanced around uneasily casting a tense filled look behind him at Maraibre before following.

As they sprinted up the steps to the door an explosion rocked the ground sending them reeling onto the stone steps. Screaming and shrieking sounded like sirens as further explosions shook their very souls. Maion sent one kick into the door, allowing it to fly off its hinges into the interior. They both barreled in.

"Zanaria!" Zacharael bellowed. He knew she was here. He could almost taste her fear - and sorrow.

"Zanaria!" Maion echoed his call.

Maraibre growled after them. "It is not wise to give away your presence, fools."

They ran down a large hallway and turned into another empty room. Zacharael shouted her name again as he spotted an open doorway at the back of the room. Jumping over a table he sprinted for it and slid through, grasping hold of the edge to turn around a corner into a kitchen. There he froze, relief surging through him.

"Zanaria! We found you." He let out a puff of relief, his heart beating in panic. He stepped forward, closely followed by Maion. He frowned as Zanaria continued to stare away from him, refusing to turn.

"Zanaria, it is us," Maion called, his relief evident in his voice. He stepped forward past Zacharael.

Zacharael's heart stopped beating for a long moment as he gazed upon her. She slowly sunk to her knees. The red line across her neck suddenly widened and her head slid to the floor. Her body began to disintegrate into a fine grey dust. One horrific moment of silence froze them.

When Zacharael could breathe he roared, a long cry of terror and heartbreak. He threw himself to his knees beside her, unable to comprehend what had happened.

The shrill ring of metal dragged his attention from the dust mound and he looked up, his expression remaining locked in horror. Maion stood with his sword ready as a young man stepped out of the shadows. Blood coated his forearms and a look of insanity stretched a smile across his face.

"You . . . did this," Maion bit out.

The man began to laugh manically. Zacharael lifted his hand to his face and touched the wetness on his cheeks. Tears . . . he had never cried before. He had never known such loss. He had never known such anger.

He focused his black eyes on the stranger and leaped forward. With his teeth, he ripped the stranger's head off and allowed the body to drop to the ground. Zacharael was coated in blood, his mouth full of the silky fluid.

He turned to Maion. Tears anew fell from his eyes as he took in the devastated expression on his friend's face, one he knew was mirrored on his own.

Maion sobbed as he fell to his knees beside Zanaria. He buried his fingers in the dust and brought handfuls to his mouth to kiss, whispering, "I'm sorry, I'm so sorry," over and over again.

If Zacharael's heart weren't already broken, it would have broken again. He didn't know what to think or what to do. His reason for existing, the only love in his life, the light of the heavens was gone—a pile of dust in her place. What was he supposed to do now? Shaking, he turned to Maraibre.

As Maraibre's head slid off in the same way Zanaria's had, Zacharael roared. The sound of his yell shook the building. Cracks appeared in the walls as a black aura soared out of his body. Fury, pure white hot fury spun around him as a Fallen angel stepped out from behind Maraibre's body, allowing it to drop to the floor as dust.

"Well that was . . . *fun*!" the Fallen angel drawled, smiling.

Zacharael leapt at him, ducking under the swing of a sword. He bit his white teeth into the bridge of his nose and ripped off the flesh there. Another scream signaled Zacharael to the fact that Maion now knew what had happened. He stepped back as Maion stabbed his dagger into the Fallen angel's chest again and again. He continued to stab even as the Fallen dropped to his knees, gasping.

Zacharael halted before him. He felt that he should say something. Perhaps he should ask him his reasons, or offer forgiveness? Wasn't that what angels were supposed to do?

He glanced down at the dust that was Maraibre, and then again at Zanaria. *No*. There would be no forgiveness. Ever. He stepped forward and stuck one hand just inside the Fallen angel's mouth, palm upwards, the second grasping his lower teeth. He heaved with all of his strength, a thrill of revenge rippling through him as the flesh ripped open at either side of his mouth. He tore the upper part of the Fallen angel's head off completely, leaving the mouth and lower jaw still attached.

It took Maion a second to realize that he was stabbing his dagger into dust. As he vomited over it, Zacharael turned and stood by Zanaria's remains, his mind completely still, not a single thought going through it.

Unsure if he had stood there for minutes or hours or days, he turned to Maion when he heard him speak.

"I will destroy every single Fallen angel and Nephilim. I swear it to the Heavens," Maion snarled.

Zacharael nodded his head and reached a shaky hand down to him, pulling him off the floor. "You have my word I will be there for every single one."

5

'Forgive yourself for the blindness that put you in the path of those that betrayed you.'

Unknown.

Years later

"Wait! I do not mean you harm." The hooded figure held up her hands and flinched, backing away from him.

"Then what business do you have here?" Zacharael snarled, slicing his sword through the air beside the hooded figure's head.

Maion entered the tent behind the figure and pulled back the hood, revealing a young woman with long dark hair and eyes of crystal white. She was beautiful, startlingly so, with old, soul deep eyes but an unlined, fresh face. "A witch," he muttered in disgust. "I will behead it this instant just to get its stench out of our camp."

"Wait! I am no witch. I am a sorceress, and I have come with a message for you," she pleaded.

Zacharael threw his sword down onto the ground and sat on a wooden chair near his desk. They had led their army to the south-east of the human plane in search of the Fallen and the Nephilim scum. They had obliterated thousands, bringing the realm back from the brink of devastation, earning themselves the titles of Captains of the Heavenly Army, but still they searched for more.

Any who encountered them trembled as they passed, praying for mercy. Zacharael and Maion would give none to their foes, and simply ignored anyone else as they were of absolutely no importance to them.

“I need no message from a sorceress,” he said. “Take her head.”

As Maion swung, the sorceress cried out. Her head dropped to the floor with a thud, her body closely following. Maion dropped his sword on the dirt floor and stepped over the blood that now pooled there.

“Now you have hopefully expended your anger, perhaps you will allow *me* to speak,” a high-pitched feminine voice called sweetly.

They spun around, gazes fixed on the entrance to their tent as another woman entered. With grey through her hair, and skin beginning to wrinkle around her eyes, she was much older than the first woman.

“What do you want?” Zacharael said.

“I am not here to talk about what I want, though, I admit that is a factor in my being here. I’m here to talk about you and your desire for death, destruction and . . . horror.” She stepped over the body and stood before the desk where Zacharael still sat. “If you wish to ever see your true love, you will need to cease this endless rampage of misery and hate.”

Zacharael stood, towering over the Sorceress. “Do not speak to me of my love. She is dead.”

“Yes, your love was destroyed by a Nephilim and a Fallen angel.” She quirked her eyebrow at him. “If you continue on this path you will never see your love again. End this now, and you will have an opportunity to do so. As will you.” She turned to include Maion in the conversation.

“What do I need to do?” Zacharael asked instantly. If there was a chance of seeing Zanaria again he would listen to anyone, even a sorceress.

“Zacharael, we will not barter with a sorceress. There is no bringing her back, you know that,” Maion argued.

Zacharael continued to stare at the old woman, daring her to answer him.

She smiled, her eyes twinkling with secrets. “The question is; what *would* you do? Would you die for her?”

Zacharael frowned. “Is this a prophecy, or a spell?”

The woman tutted at him, clasping her hands in front of her. “You didn’t answer my question.”

Zacharael loomed over her threateningly. “I would die for her,” he answered, threat lacing his voice with ice.

“And you?” she turned to Maion.

“I will die for no one. Least of all a sorceress. Keep your tricks and leave our camp, and you might be lucky enough to make the outskirts with your head still upon your shoulders,” he growled.

The Sorceress let a smirk lift up the corners of her lips even as she stared deep into Maion’s eyes with alarming intent. “I was not going to ask if you would die for her. I want to know . . . would you turn against everything you believed in for a chance to see your true love? Would you betray, steal and murder? Would you conspire with a creature you hate if it meant you would get the chance to kiss the soul you were destined to be with? Would you retrieve the Falchion of Tabbris and the Dagger of Lex?"

At that Zacharael glared at her. "What do you want with Tabbris and Lex?"

She smiled. "You've had your turn. I wish to hear Maion's answer."

Zacharael frowned, no longer sure he wanted to listen to her. The Dagger of Lex was a weapon imbued in myth and prophecy. Whether it actually existed was anyone's guess. But the Falchion...? How did she know about the Falchion of Tabbris? The curved sword, with magic imbued in the metal, was owned by Tabbris; an angel of the throne class who presided over free well, self-determination, choice and alternatives. He was always something of a question mark—eager to go his own way, never really toeing the line with the other Thrones. He certainly wasn't popular when it came to his judgments, often picking such obscure sentences that most thought him to be in league with a principality—most likely his soul mate, Bëyander.

Many myths surrounded his sword. Some told tales that it was the weapon of God, or that the reason he took such good care of it was that it was actually a living being. Zacharael had often thought that perhaps Tabbris had been told of a prophecy surrounding the use of his falchion.

The question was . . . why did this sorceress want it?

Zacharael slyly turned to watch Maion. Maion had clenched his teeth together and was refusing to answer.

The sorceress nodded her head and smiled again. "May I bring in a guest? There is someone here who has requested an audience with you many times, only to be denied. He was relentless in his demands that I bring him with me." She said.

"No," Zacharael said.

"Yes," Maion replied at exactly the same time.

The two angels glared at each other as the sorceress went to the tent flap and beckoned someone in. The newest visitor seemed to be an elderly man. A cloak too big for him hid him from scrutiny and he hobbled toward them, using a thin wooden staff for assistance.

He shuffled close to Zacharael. "Captain Zacharael of the Heavenly Army . . . I give you a gift." He held out a wrinkly, fragile hand and opened his palm. A small silver ring with an opal was there for him to see. "Take it. If you keep it safe, you will give it to your true love. If you refuse the ring or lose it, you will never see her."

Zacharael scowled. He hated bargains like this. How could he refuse now?

"What do you want in exchange for it?" he asked.

The old man continued to hold out the ring. "In exchange, I want you to send two angels to another realm. There is a war taking place in area seven-fifty-seven of the Lonely Planes." At Zacharael's scowl, his expression softened. "I assure you, Captain, I wish for only peace. I am on your side."

"Area seven-fifty-seven of the Lonely Planes is a werewolf plane," Maion put in.

"Indeed. Send your angels there to assist in the fight."

"Why do you care about werewolves?" Maion asked.

"What else do you require of me in exchange for the ring?" Zacharael interrupted, glaring down at the glittering ring.

The Sorceress took the ring from the seer and lifted it up, holding it out to Zacharael. "Take it. I care *not* about werewolves. The seer simply looks to the future and sees that they will be of some assistance to me. I have no time to hear his many reasons for wishing to meet you. As for what *I* require of you, firstly you must cease this war between the angels and the Nephilim then I want the Dagger of Lex found. I will tell you the rest in time."

Zacharael watched under heavy lids as the seer glanced up at the sorceress surreptitiously, covertly hiding his eyes under the fall of his hood.

After a moment's hesitation he picked up the ring and held it tightly in his palm. "Very well," he said.

Maion swore under his breath. "I do not agree to this!"

"It is done, Maion. Remember what I said, for my words will soon come back to you," she whispered.

As they stepped backwards out of the tent, Maion and Zacharael took a seat at the desk. Who knew if they had just made a deal with the devil? Only time would tell.

"No," Zacharael whispered, shaking his head. He would not bargain with creatures like these. *Scum*. *Filth*. He looked to Maion, seeing the same turbulence in his eyes. Together, at the speed of light they appeared behind them, slicing their swords through the air. The sorceress was beheaded, her blood splattering the floor around her remains. The sword that pieced the seer however, met only cloth, the material dropping to the ground while the old man disappeared.

6

'If you always do what interests you, at least one person is pleased.'

Katherine Hepburn.

Five hundred years later

At the words that came out of Commander Avrail's mouth—Zacharael and Maion's superior—Zacharael scowled. He felt his face screwing up with a black hatred.

"Zacharael we require you to join the team searching for the Nephilim," he had said casually. He stood a foot taller than Zacharel, with greying hair and a trimmed grey beard. Dressed in armor, he looked the part of Commander of the Heavenly Army.

Over the past five hundred years, Zacharael had made every effort to control his hatred for the Nephilim, had stepped aside and relinquished control of his senior position in the Heavenly Army. Maion had taken a bit more convincing, but he too had relinquished his duties and returned to the Heavenly Realm with him. The two said little to each other or to anyone. Maion seemed to seethe with anger below the surface, a boiling volcano ready to explode. It took little to set him off; a look, a word, sometimes even if another angel in the same room laughed or smiled he would bellow in rage and tear the room apart. Zacharael, on the other hand, found he had become a shadow of his former self. He could no longer summon a smile. He could no longer watch in the

Heavenly Reception Hall as new souls were admitted. He wished only to work.

Commander Avrail had initially refused all Zacharael's requests to be sent out on missions when he had relinquished his post. Something had changed his mind lately, though, and Zacharael found himself flying to the darkest corners of existence, hunting down monsters, demons, witches . . . everything but the Nephilim.

The angels themselves had come a full turn and had rescinded their declaration of war on the Nephilim. No reasoning was given; the angels were simply expected to follow. Furthermore, the warrior angels were being sent to *protect* them. Admittedly, it was better than sending the weaker angels to the human plane, but it was still an absurd turn around. And now this . . .

"I will go nowhere near those abominations! They should be destroyed, not cossetted and given the protection better suited to those of importance," he growled. He was angry enough that he had been ordered to meet him in this place where Zanaria haunted him without being ordered to return to the human plane to protect the very creatures that had killed her.

Avrail sighed. "I understand how you feel, and believe me, I feel our resources could be better used elsewhere. However it is the will of the principalities and we must obey."

"You obey then. I am a warrior. I hunt the Fallen and the demonic beasts that haunt the planes of existence. I am not a nurse maid sent to coddle children. But a few years ago we were declaring war on these creatures. Now we see them as kin. What caused this turn around?" he asked.

"Zacharael it matters not what the reasoning is. The principalities—"

Zacharael held his palm up and turned away.

"You cannot allow what happened to Zanaria color your view on the Nephilim forever. They are innocent, Zacharael!" Avrail called after him.

Within a second Zacharael had lifted him up, his fingers gripping his throat tightly. Avrail clutched at the hand around his neck, coughing and gurgling loudly. He struggled, unable to fight free.

"Stop!" a commanding voice shouted.

Recognizing the voice, Zacharael dropped Commander Avrail to his feet, watching dispassionately as he folded to his knees and continued to hack while stroking the painful skin on his neck.

Zacharael leaned in closely. "Do not speak to me of the Nephilim scum again. I ceased to kill them, and that is all you will ever get from me."

White wings shot out from his shoulder blades and launched him into the air, exiting the room by a roof tunnel.

The delicate, blonde-haired Gabriel reached down to Avrail and pulled him to his feet.

Avrail shook his head. "Have no fear, my Lady. Zacharael is a loyal warrior. He will change his mind."

Gabriel sighed sadly. "I do not think so. His anger and grief are so thick they penetrate the air around him so it is all he can see and breathe. He is much needed on the human plane, and could do much good in bridging the gap between the supernatural species.

I had hoped these last years would soften him and appease his sadness; alas, it seems to have had the opposite effect."

"Leave him to his anger for now. As the years pass, so will his grief," Avrail advised.

She shook her head. "No, his grief is so deep it will be stamped on his heart forever. I think we must look to others who will help our cause, Avrail, otherwise the flood Raphael has suggested may yet come to pass. If it comes to it, I will go to the human plane myself."

"As you wish, my Lady. As they have already agreed to this mission perhaps Haamiah and Elijah would provide us with some options." Avrail led the way from the room, Gabriel trailing behind. She turned to look around the empty chamber, its magnificent columns of gold, the branches touching the ceiling, the marble floors. It was a place of such beauty and such sad memories for poor Zacharael. Still, there was hope yet. She looked up to where Zacharael had departed and allowed a small smile to creep onto her face.

"You have not escaped me yet, Zacharael. I have another plan for you."

7

Your future is created by what you do today, not tomorrow.

Anonymous

One year later

"Do not do this Raphael," Gabriel pleaded.

He scowled. "It has been decided. You cannot resist this any longer. It has been agreed upon that the human plane must be cleansed. I will not back down."

Gabriel gulped. "Then give me ten days. My brother, I ask you for this."

He sighed. "What is it you wish to accomplish? You were able to talk Michael to your side. He gave you a year to prove the Nephilim could be rehabilitated, that they could be of use to our cause, but you have failed. Wars still rage on in the south of the human plane."

"But the north—"

"Yes you have accomplished what you wanted in the north, but the south is ruined. We have lost eighty-five angels there in this past year. If you had agreed to my plan they would be with us now. The weight of their death is on you," his voice boomed.

Gabriel held her chin up higher. "Give me ten days. That is all I ask. I will not stand in your way."

Raphael ran his hand over his face and groaned. "Very well. But hear me, the human plane will be underwater ten days from now."

Gabriel ran from him, her bare feet slapping on the floor until her wings lifted her up. She flew as though Hell's demons were behind her, not pausing to take a breath until she had landed in the Heavenly Reception . . . where her army awaited.

Commander Avrail, Elijah, Haamiah, Machidiel and a hundred more stood patiently, waiting for her. They knelt when she landed before them.

"Friends. We have ten days. Find as many trustworthy humans as you can, and tell them to build ships. Tell them to gather their families and friends, their animals and beasts, and pray to God that they will live out the flood that is about to rain down on them."

"What of our allies?" Haamiah asked.

She appraised him with sorrow. "Raphael thinks we have none. We do. I will tell Noah, and he will spread the word among the mystics."

"Are you sure he will listen? He is known to put his own interests first." Commander Avrail questioned. The warlock Noah was known to be somewhat of an eccentric, a loner, constantly questioning authority.

Gabriel nodded. "He will do this because he will be given the chance to save his own family."

* * * *

More than one thousand years later, in the dead of night on the human plane, Zacharael followed the sound of his wounded target through the dense forest on the outskirts of a small town far in the north.

The floods had come and gone. Life on the human plane had been destroyed, but much to the angels' surprise it had flourished again soon after. Zacharael was sure some trickery had been involved but Gabriel and Raphael had not spoken of anything.

It had taken a long time but as expected, the Fallen had risen again, angered by the angels continued refusal to allow them entrance to the Heavenly Planes. They had fallen silent in recent times, many begging for forgiveness by becoming Grigori—watchers. Others had seemingly melted out of existence. The warriors had still been sent out in search of them but few were ever found . . . until recently.

The Grigori reported alarming tales indicating that the Fallen were repeating their past follies. Thousands of children across the human plane were disappearing, all suspected Nephilim. The difference this time was that the Nephilim had not yet attacked the humans or angels. Neither had the Fallen. No wars had been started, no one had been proclaimed a God with their magical abilities—even the other creatures of the realm hadn't heard anything. The Nephilim had simply disappeared.

Every day, more and more angels approached the principalities to beg for their help in finding their missing children. At first they were arrested, and sent for judgment for fornicating with the humans, but the Heavenly Realm soon realized that, if this continued, too large a number of angels would be imprisoned . . . leaving too few to defend the Heavens.

Zacharael and Maion had repeatedly refused the calls to help. If they were going to spend their time finding the Nephilim it would be to destroy them, not to save them from the Fallen. Zacharael recalled the day Raphael had stepped back and allowed Gabriel to order the warriors to journey to the human plane to gather the Nephilim and take them to a place of safety. He had watched in amazement, waiting for Raphael to naysay her, but he had stood back, his head hanging down as Gabriel sent them on their way. It was not easy to refuse his commanding officers, but it was impossible to refuse the archangel. The constant battle between Gabriel and Raphael was confusing to say the least, but both Zacharael and Maion were firmly on Raphael's side. With the flood, they had felt relief for the first time, but now the tides had turned again and the angels were ordered to save the Nephilim that hadn't perished.

Zacharael and Maion had been sent with the others to find the Nephilim scum and deliver them to the safe houses that had been set up across the world. Thankfully, neither of them were expected to remain there as guards but were able to come and go, dropping off their finds. Other angels also played their part, providing warmth and safety, food, discipline, and security for the children. One of the principalities himself had elected to oversee one of the safe houses in the north; the one that was currently under attack.

An old, abandoned monastery had been used as the base for the safe house. It was located a decent distance away from the nearest town, ensuring privacy. The last thing they needed was to highlight their presence to the locals, who might witness angels flying in and out. The monastery was set in the hills surrounded by thick forests and deep lakes. It was a misty place, and thick clouds often shrouded the old building away from prying eyes. If any of the Fallen flew over the area there was little likelihood that they would spot anything suspicious.

As well as being in the ideal location, the monastery itself was perfect. Hundreds of chambers suited well to be made into bedrooms for the hundreds of children placed there. Larger rooms and halls were turned into classrooms when, after many disagreements, the angels acceded to Haamiah's wishes to teach the Nephilim of their angel heritage and gifts. Healers were present to aid with any medical issues that arose, and guardians provided the perfect companions. Some of the warrior angels prowled the interior and exterior of the monastery, but too few were available to search the surrounding forests.

A number of Fallen had attacked in recent weeks, managing to kill a handful of the half-angel children who had strayed too far from the safety of the monastery. Typically, the Fallen had hidden themselves away only to resurface when they thought it was safe. Only this time, Zacharael and Maion were waiting.

This was the sixth Fallen angel they had hunted down tonight. On previous nights, there had been perhaps one, or at the most, two of the Fallen stalking the area, but tonight something seemed to be happening. Zacharael couldn't help but think he was missing something. Why would so many come out at once? Perhaps it was in the hope that the warriors would be overcome by the numbers, and would be defeated.

Maion had taken the south side of the monastery while Zacharael had chosen to patrol the north. Zacharael began to wonder if it would have been safer to stick together.

Hearing a noise just ahead of him, he jumped, his wings catching the wind as he flew through the trees, hurtling toward a shadowy form fleeing. A blood-curdling scream rang out. Zacharael grinned—Maion had obviously made it in time.

He landed on the ground loudly, sticks and twigs cracking and snapping under his feet. He slid to a halt as a spray of blood coated his face. He spat a mouthful on the ground and swiped at his mouth as he stomped forward, watching as Maion sheathed his sword, smirking at the headless body disintegrating on the ground before him.

Maion looked up and smirked. “Sorry my friend, he looked to be getting away from you.”

“I had him exactly where I wanted him,” Zacharael replied. “Did you recognize him?”

Maion shook his head, “should I have?”

Zacharael shrugged. “Abanier; the younger brother of Zanaria’s friend, Ada. He was a good angel once.”

Maion’s face turned thunderous, his smile vanishing as his eyes pulled in tightly. “A betrayer deserves death. The Fallen and their puppets will receive no forgiveness from me. Do not tell me that you feel for this creature?”

Zacharael turned away and spread his wings, stretching them. “I feel nothing but anger, and a constant thirst for revenge. None shall receive forgiveness from me.”

Maion sighed, appeased by Zacharael's words. "Come, we should continue our patrol. I am not happy with the amount of Fallen present tonight."

Zacharael nodded his agreement and they took off together.

Flying up over the trees, the angels were almost in pitch black as they swooped low. The moon was covered over by thick clouds, so they needed to use their instincts to locate the Fallen. They sailed back toward the monastery, their eyes and ears searching for any hint of their enemy. Picking up speed as they scented them, the trail grew stronger and stronger as they neared the monastery.

An explosion rocked them. The air itself rushed up and knocked them out of the sky as the ground rushed up to meet them. They plummeted through the trees, the intense heat and force of the explosion allowing them no second to right themselves. They landed a few meters away from each other, covered in scratches from the fall through the thick forest. The ground rumbled like a thousand trombones—it shook as though an army walked over it. Zacharael rubbed his head deliriously, wondering if they were near a plate or a volcano.

He leapt to his feet and pulled Maion up by his forearm. Though Zach had suffered only a few scratches, Maion had come a little worse off; blood ran down his arm from a puncture wound in his left shoulder. He reached up and pulled the branch out of his flesh and shrugged off Zacharael's concern. Again, they spread their wings and raced toward the monastery.

As soon as they had cleared the trees they spotted the orange glow up ahead. The heat from the fire seemed to have fingers, licking at the angels as they neared. Screams and cries grew louder. Zacharael left Maion behind and sped faster, circling as he located his prey.

Haamiah—the principality that ran the safe house, stood at the north wall, a group of children cowering behind him. He was being attacked savagely by three of the Fallen as yet more swooped over him. Zacharael whipped out his sword and trailed those above the angel, beheading them. Their bodies rained down on the fight below, alerting the other Fallen that they had been found by the warrior.

The Fallen screeched their anger and leaped over Haamiah into the air. Zacharael kicked one to the ground and tackled another as he rushed at him. Snatching the third from the air he plummeted to the ground, stopping just meters away from the rock as the other two sailed into it. Zacharael landed beside them and made short work of beheading them.

He didn't wait to watch them dissolve as he normally did. Instead he whirled around and glared at Haamiah, who was leading the children to safety through the trees.

"Leave them," he said angrily. "We are under attack, Haamiah!"

Haamiah paid him no heed, instead picking up the smallest child and rushing into the trees.

Debating with himself for a second, he chose to leave Haamiah. If he wanted to risk his life for the half-human whelps then that was his decision. He would help the other angels still trapped. He ran and shot into the sky landing on top of the monastery where he had a better view. He heard a scream and spun, his eyes spotting a young black-haired angel being dragged into the forest by one of the Fallen. He stepped off the ledge and fell to the ground beside them, turning at the last minute to kick the Fallen away. He landed, sprawled twenty meters or so away from them.

Zacharael glanced at the angel weeping beside him and felt an ache through his heart. She looked just like . . . shutting down the emotions that surfaced, he scowled and stormed past her, pulling his sword out from the sheath at his back. He leaped onto the Fallen and stabbed his sword through the front of his throat, wiggling it until the creature's head simply pried off.

He turned around and swore under his breath as he saw the angel peering up at him, tears running down her face. He picked her up and leaped, locating Haamiah and depositing her at his feet. He could deal with her.

He snarled at her. Enough with these damn emotions! If he hadn't felt them before, Zanaria would still be alive now. No. Emotions equaled weakness. There would be none of that for him.

Zacharael sped back to his vantage point at the top of the monastery and similarly located a number of other angels, all guardians or messengers with no fighting skill between them. Where were the warriors who should have been defending the walls? He shook his head, furious at himself. He had known something odd was happening. He had killed too many Fallen tonight, more than any other night. He should have acted sooner but instead, annoyed by being sent here at all, he had brushed his suspicions aside. He would have to do what he could to rectify his oversight.

He spotted movement on the ground to his right. Leaning forward, he spotted a group of Fallen angels gathered around something. He dove off the ledge and allowed his body to fall through the sky, using his wings to pull him to a stop just before hitting the ground.

The Fallen spread out, facing him, leaving a small human male sitting on the ground behind them. Zacharael wrinkled his nose in disgust as he remembered this boy was no human, but a Nephilim freak.

Zacharael ignored him and concentrated on his enemies before him. One he recognized—a tall angel with a shaved head—a warrior, he was sure. Probably someone he had fought alongside in the past. *Betrayer*. The two others were slightly shorter but just as muscular, and well equipped with knives and swords. Regardless, he would see them dead.

Zacharael flew through the air and landed a punch to the shaven-haired angel's jaw, sending him spinning through the air to the ground. He turned and kicked high at the face of the second Fallen, attacking him from the right. Using his body as leverage, he jumped high and spun, catching the third in the face. He landed in a crouch and pulled out his sword, clashing immediately with a blade aimed at his neck. He knocked it away, as well as three more, and rolled to the floor to avoid a boulder aimed at his head. Dust rained down on him as the boulder shattered into pieces against the stone wall of the monastery.

He felt a hand grab his arm and turned, his fist ready to smash whatever beast held him. The small Nephilim stared up at him, the whites of his eyes sparkling in fear. He could feel a tremor running through him as the boy shook. A knife pierced Zacharael's shoulder and he snarled as he ripped it out, throwing it at the nearest Fallen. He surged to his feet, knocking the boy to the ground. *Typical Nephilim. They will be the downfall of us all,* he thought.

Standing in front of the young boy, Zacharael squared his shoulders, ignoring the blood running down his arm. He bared his teeth—a terrifying sight to most, and indeed two of the Fallen took a step back, allowing the warrior to charge forward. Zach raised his sword and met his attack with fury. The clang of metal echoed through the night.

When one of the Fallen knocked Zacharael's sword from his grasp he began to circle him to the right. He attacked furiously, his teeth snapping at Zacharael's throat. Zacharael met him blow for blow, knocking away each attempt to land a dagger. He punched the Fallen in the stomach, breathing deeply when he managed to knock him back a few meters. With the other Fallen just waiting for their opportunity, there was no time to relax and form a plan. The second Fallen—an angel with thick black dreadlocks—darted forward, swinging a mace as the two behind him snarled and growled. Zacharael dodged to the side and threw his arm up, catching the chain and allowing it to wrap around his arm. He yanked the angel closer and stabbed his second sword through his face. The angel screamed as Zacharael withdrew and plunged his sword into his chest, kicking him, hard.

Zacharael felt his body pushed back forcefully as he flew through the air and landed heavily against the stone wall. The wind was knocked out of him as the stone crumbled to dust beneath his body, leaving a gaping hole in the side of the monastery. He forced himself to his feet and gripped his remaining sword in his right hand. It was quickly knocked from his fingers as a hand gripped his throat halting any breath. He felt the blow to his jaw as the warrior punched him, releasing his hold. Zacharael shot forward to knock him off his feet, kicking him in his face as he scrambled to get to his feet.

A kick to the knee sent the Fallen to the ground again. Zacharael ran up the remaining wall and back flipped over the two Fallen angels attempting to grab him from behind. The third Fallen spun and snapped his fist up into Zach's jaw, sending him reeling backwards from the blow. Zacharael turned to the side, narrowly missing the second angel slashing with his sword. He ducked out of the way of another sword swing and jumped on the angel before him, his teeth sinking in as he tried to rip the neck open and rid himself of at least one of the Fallen. Two would be much easier to manage than three.

He felt a dull ache in his back but ignored it, reveling in the blood flowing down the Fallen angel's neck. As the pain grew more intense he lifted his teeth away and turned his head, dropping the angel to the floor. He looked down in confusion as he noticed the silver metal point protruding from his chest. The instant he realized he was looking at the tip of a sword the agony spread down to his abdomen as the Fallen angel behind him hacked the edge down his body.

He roared in pain as the sword was pulled out, the serrated edge slicing through organs and muscle. Bringing his hands to his chest, he felt the blood pour through his fingers. Sadness and regret filled his head as he looked upon the young boy quivering against the wall, barely a meter away with tears pouring down his face, and his mouth open in a silent cry of terror.

Zacharael felt a blow to his head and fell to the ground, his eyes still on the boy as blood ran into his eyes. *Oh well, it will be for the best. Without Zanaria I am nothing,* he thought, succumbing to the pain.

Fresh pain blossomed in his chest preceded by the stab of ice below his shoulder blades. He felt his essence slowly leave his body as his eyes closed, leaving him in darkness.

8

'A year from now you will wish you had started today.'

Karen Lamb.

Zacharael hissed in a breath as awareness flooded back through his body. The coldness seeping through his limbs told him immediately that his injuries were severe. He could hear the ringing of the clashing metal around him, of screams and roars as the Fallen met the Angelic. How long had he passed out for? He could only be thankful that his head remained on his shoulders and his soul present within his body, no matter how painful. Indeed he was lucky that others had found him before he'd been killed. If only they could continue to occupy the Fallen while he made his escape. Though the thought of running and hiding was a bitter one, he knew it was necessary.

Folding his arms underneath himself, he attempted to push his body up off the ground, groaning quietly as blood gushed from his chest with every small movement. He pulled his knees underneath his hips and righted himself slowly, holding his left hand up tightly to his body to stop the blood draining from him. He spat a mouthful of blood from his mouth and turned his head, dazedly looking around him. Dozens of Fallen fought with the angel warriors. They almost seemed to have encircled him, trapping him in the middle. He clearly needed to find a way through the fighting angels but injured as he was there didn't appear to be an easy or obvious route.

Besides, he thought, looking around one last time, *with no energy to stand, I will have to crawl through them all, and I can't see that being a successful mission.*

A shadow plunged the already dark night into pitch black. The fighting briefly paused, warriors ducking for cover. It passed quickly, and the fighting resumed for a second while Zach looked around in confusion.

A gust of wind akin to a tornado blasted Zacharael to the ground, dragging him toward the trees. Others cowered by the wall, ducked into the trees or were flung about by the strength of the wind. Zach dug his hands into the ground, clenching onto a thick root sticking out of the ground until the wind ceased. His wounds ached, his body begging for mercy.

A throaty scream echoed through the air, and soon after a body slammed into the ground in front of him, a look of terror and pain on the angel's face.

Zacharael recognized him. A noble guardian angel, Darius had been one of the first to volunteer for Gabriel's mad mission to save the Nephilim on the human plane. Deep furrows were gouged into Darius's abdomen while blood ran slowly from the tear in his shoulder where his arm no longer joined.

Zacharael fought against the concoction of emotions threatening to take him over. Nausea strangled him as he swallowed back the churning vomit. Profound sorrow threatened to moisten his eyes, the sadness and loss of a brother prominent in his mind. Darius was a good angel—he didn't deserve this. The pain Darius had suffered was plain to see as his face was stretched out in an open scream.

Zacharael felt bitterly angry that any of them were here in this realm facing danger on behalf of the half-breeds. He clenched his fists as he wondered who would be next. Maion? Varyerl? Haamiah? How could the archangels allow Gabriel to send them to their death like this? Was it possible that Gabriel had Fallen? Didn't Raphael see it? Didn't he see that this was utter madness?

Zacharael rested his forehead on the ground, misery threatening to consume him. It was too much, just too much to take. The sadness, the loss. *Zanaria*. How he missed her. The loneliness was eating him up. He couldn't watch this war kill everyone he loved. It wasn't possible to survive it. Perhaps it would be better to just give in now. Maybe it would be easier. It certainly couldn't be any harder.

"Dragon!" someone bellowed.

Zacharael covered his head with his arms as air pummeled him, and he heard the sound of beating. He gritted his teeth and kept his head down, unsure what he was wishing for. It soon passed, and Zacharael forced his wings out. Rocks and twigs sailed through the air, scratching and slicing him. He took the opportunity to rise to his feet and used his wings to propel him into the trees, half flying, half running for his life, instinct taking over again. Maybe he wanted to live after all. Relief surged through him as he felt the blackness enclose him, hiding him from his enemies.

He ran as fast as he could, using branches to propel him further. He leaped over logs and slid down ditches until he felt that he could run no more. He threw himself behind the thick trunk of a tree and assessed his injuries. His legs seemed bruised and cut but not broken; his arms were mostly okay, except for a deep cut on his right forearm. His hands stung from the lacerations caused by the branches and leaves that had whipped across him. His chest was still by far the worst of his injuries. Blood still ran out, albeit sluggish now.

He pulled himself upright as he heard the sound of feet pounding and branches snapping as someone hurtled through the forest toward him. He tested his wings and winced; even the shrug of his shoulders increased the throbbing pain in his chest. He breathed a sigh of relief and let his head fall back as he recognized Elijah.

Zacharael closed his eyes and thanked God he hadn't been found by an enemy. He had no weapon and he didn't have the strength to fly away, nor would he be able to fight and defend himself.

He gasped in alarm as something heavy slammed into his legs. He jumped up, groaning as his body protested. Looking down, he felt the blood drain from his head, a grey haze covering his vision. Elijah moaned and reached forward, his eyes begging for help, begging for mercy even as the Fallen angel standing over him pulled out the metal spear from his back.

Zacharael stared, disbelieving his eyes. He looked from Elijah to the Fallen angel and back again.

"Zacharael . . . " Elijah whispered hoarsely. He coughed, hacking up blood. "Run!"

"No," he said firmly. He wouldn't abandon his friend, even if it killed him. He glared at the Fallen angel and let out a snarl as he ran forward, grasping the spear and wrestling it from him and throwing it to the ground. He grabbed the Fallen angel by his throat. He squeezed as tight as he could, digging in his fingers. He bellowed in anger and used the last of his strength to rip away the Fallen's throat.

Blood gushed out of the gaping wound. The Fallen angel looked at him, in horror, before collapsing to the ground. Zacharael stepped closer and carefully placed one food on his chest. He leaned down slowly, trying desperately not to lose consciousness. He grabbed hold of the Fallen angel's head and pulled until it loosened with a loud rip. He dropped it to the floor and fell to his knees beside Elijah.

The angel was deathly pale. Blood ran from his eyes, ears and mouth as he stared up at Zacharael.

"The children . . . I need to save them," Elijah whispered.

Zacharael shook his head. He didn't know what to say. They were most likely dead, as Elijah would undoubtedly be soon. To go back now to try to find any survivors would be suicide. It would be a pointless mission that would only end in his death. No one would benefit from it even if he found a single Nephilim alive.

Elijah began to weep, pain and sorrow taking over.

"They're innocent Zacharael. They do not deserve to be torn apart by monsters. Some might have escaped. They could be lost and wounded in the forest. We have to save them," he sobbed.

"If any have survived it will be a miracle, Elijah. I will not go back there knowing there isn't even a sliver of a chance I will find one alive. I am wounded. The forest is teeming with the Fallen," Zacharael protested wearily.

"You don't understand. You must! I'll heal you, and then you will be able to go." Elijah moaned as he reached out to him, desperation allowing him that small movement.

Zacharael pulled away. "Do not! To heal me now will use all of your remaining strength—it will kill you. My injuries are grave but I will survive if we can get help before any more of the Fallen find us." He shook his head. "I will not do as you ask. I do not feel for the Nephilim. They shouldn't exist."

Elijah gasped and rested his head upon the ground at such an angle that he could still make eye contact with Zacharael. "My friend, I beg you to do this for me."

Zacharael frowned, his heart warring with his head. He simply couldn't understand the reasoning behind this insanity. "Why do you risk so much for these half-breeds? Why would you embrace certain death and risk *my* life for them when they are nothing to us? You have no responsibility for them."

Elijah moaned again, his body wracked with sobs. When he could once again draw a full breath, he closed his eyes. "One of them is my son."

9

'Love me when I least deserve it because that is when I most need it.'

Unknown.

Jasmine

As I screamed at Maion I felt as though my body liquefied. I felt as though the rage inside me had taken over and consumed me completely. I had become rage itself. I burned; my skin felt fiery hot. I could feel the smoke rising from my skin, causing my eyes to tear up. I tried to keep Maion in my sight, determined not to let him have his chance at me. I knew he would kill me the first opportunity he got, just as I would kill him. I forced my eyes open wide, almost blinded by the white light surrounding me.

Eventually the light hurt so badly I had to cover my face with my hands and clench my eyes closed tight. What *was* that? Was Maion using angel magic on me? I was so used to my grey haze that it rarely troubled me anymore, but this was different. This was so bright it was painful.

As panic set in, my mind went into overdrive. What had he done? Was I blind? Just as I began to hyperventilate, a fresh breeze began to cool me down. A cold chill bathed my skin, almost caressing me. I relaxed for a second, simply enjoying the relief before remembering Maion's face as he snarled those cruel words at me. He wanted me dead. I couldn't forget that.

I opened my eyes and gasped, my heart hammering at my chest. I was in the forest. The Never Ending Forest—the waiting room. I had been here many times before, so there was no way I could be mistaken. I was in the forest of spirits. Zach had told me last time I came here that this was a realm where non-human spirits were sent to await judgment by the angels of the Throne class. If they had committed a serious wrong against the angels they would be brought here and kept indefinitely, until the throne angels passed judgment on their souls. I had transported myself here by accident last time; had I done the same again?

I rubbed my forehead and groaned. I was so sick of all of this angel crap! What I wouldn't give to be a normal person instead of being dragged through all of this mess. Learning that I was a Nephilim had seriously messed me up. I had thought I had problems at the time—school, family, friends, *then* I discovered there were hundreds of evil creatures out there hunting me down. What a way to kill a girl's buzz!

My life had seriously become one huge drama. I felt as though I was in a television show—it was completely surreal, and I had contemplated more than once that I might actually be insane. Though I had refused to believe a word Zach said when I'd first met him, thinking he was a fellow patient of the nearest psych hospital—I had eventually had to learn an entire new history. If I'd thought human history was gory, I had changed my mind when I'd learned about the mystical world. Everything was so intertwined I was surprised I had ever gotten my head around it all.

The angel realm was bizarre, with their rules, classes and tasks. As expected, I had learned their history and memorized their lessons, but when their teachings clashed with what faced me in the real world it was confusing, and their teachings were contradictory.

Though they spoke of love and peace, the angels counted more species to be their enemies than any other in existence. The angels were on semi good terms with the sorceri but abhorred vampires, demons of any kind and witches. They were coming round to the idea of 'good' werewolves, but then that was a whole story in itself.

And then there was me . . . a Nephilim. Oh right, no I wasn't! Through all of my drama, Zach had continually told me that I had one angel parent and one human parent. That was all kinds of awful. I knew I had been adopted. My adoptive parents sucked big time, but I guess I had always hoped that my real parents hadn't willingly given me up. I figured that maybe they had been forced into it or . . . who knows—even abducted by aliens would have been better than the truth. I was led to believe that my biological mother was human and my father was an angel. The thought that my father was an angel and had allowed my adoptive parents to terrorize me was pretty terrible, but I still held on to the hope that I would one day find my mother.

Then a miracle seemed to occur. Haamiah, the leader of the Nephilim safe house, told me I had a brother. I raced across the other side of the world looking for him, ecstatic that I now had *actual* family, only to find out that he was a complete fucktard who was working for the Fallen angels, who were trying to kill me.

I still hadn't quite worked out my feelings on that one.

But, to finish off a long and drama-filled story . . . I then discovered that *actually* I wasn't a Nephilim. That's right—all of this crap I had gone through was for absolutely no reason at all. I was actually half *Fallen* angel and half valkyrie, and the angels seemed to think that my mother was actually Lilith—Queen of the Damned.

So there we go; I was now some kind of weird creature that no one had come across before and who no one seemed to know what to do with. Except Maion, of course. He thought I should be killed. Besides him, who were my enemies? Who were my allies? What on earth was a valkyrie? Even by Zach's admission they didn't really know anything about them, except his reassurance that they weren't evil—which I'm pretty sure was a load of rubbish he spouted just to make me feel better.

And here I was . . . back where it had all began in the Never Ending Forest. I still didn't know who I was, who my family was, who I could trust, or why the hell I was there. Only, I wasn't quite the same person. No, I was now twenty-four years old, nearly twenty-five. I had lost years and gained nothing.

I rubbed my forehead again and debated whether I should laugh or cry. I stood in the center of the same bedroom I had stood in five years ago; there was a large bed with white sheets tucked in neatly in the middle of the square room, wooden floorboards ran its length, and white walls surrounded me. At least, they surrounded me on three sides. The edge of the room before me simply ended a meter from the end of the bed. The forest had begun to creep in, with long branches and leaves falling to rest on the floorboards. Thankfully the daylight shone through the canopy, highlighting the otherwise creepy interior of the forest.

Last time I was here I'd met Emily, a witch who was awaiting her judgment. Before I had known that my ring made me immune to the rules of portal travel, she had tried to trick me into becoming trapped, like her. I could only pray that she had since been judged and sentenced to whatever fate awaited her. I wasn't so lucky.

"Hey there!" a southern American voice drawled loudly through the forest. The same slender, blond-haired woman appeared at the edge of the tree line. She wore the same green dress and brown leather ankle boots. She was just as beautiful as I'd remembered.

"Shit," I muttered. Realistically, I knew I could take her if she tried anything. I was seriously kick-ass, and a hell of a lot more of a threat now that I had developed my abilities. If she thought I was just another soul she could trick she would be in for a lesson.

As the witch came into view I saw her face drop into a scowl. She placed her hands on her hips.

"Ugh! What are *you* doing here? And where is that beast who followed you here last time? I hope you have him leashed," she spat.

"Maybe I came to kick your sorry ass all the way to the judgment room," I suggested.

A look of panic crossed her face before she masked it with a serene smile. "You could try."

I laughed. "Seriously, you shouldn't push me. I'm not the same girl you tried to trick before."

She raised her eyebrows mockingly with a confident smile and her arms folded casually across her chest. "Really?"

I laughed again, even as I began to feel the rage churning through me. That had to be the evil part of me stirring. I pushed it down, fighting to control it. I wasn't evil. *I wasn't.*

I'd always thought I just had a bad temper, but with the revelation that I was half Fallen angel I now attributed it to that. It had been kept under control by the ring Zach had given me, but now I imagined it was on the floor somewhere in the safe house where I'd dropped it.

Though I knew I shouldn't waste my time on the witch, I felt my pride nudge me. In fact, forget *nudge*, my pride practically opened my mouth for me and threw out the words.

"I've killed a witch stronger than you. I was entered into the Tournament of Ascension and survived fully intact," I boasted.

Emily instantly stepped back away from me. "No one leaves the tournament intact."

I frowned at her. I didn't need her judgment on top of everything else I knew I should be sorting out in my head.

"Whatever." I shrugged.

I was done. I needed to get out of here, pronto. I reached down for my power and felt it begin to coil and stretch as it became pliable. I smiled as my glittery shadow streaked out of my skin and whirled around me. I focused on the safe house, *willing* myself there. Nothing happened initially so I pulled harder and harder, creating a vortex of shadow around me. I closed my eyes tightly and wished, envisioning myself back in my room in the safe house.

I felt the ground shift and I smiled, letting the shadow dissipate.

To my horror I was still in the forest. It hadn't worked. I tried again, feeling my power swamp me, almost drown me. Again, nothing happened, and I remained in the bedroom in the forest.

I glared at Emily who just smirked at me in response.

"What's wrong honey? Neutered?"

Why couldn't I open a portal? What was wrong with my abilities here? I began to panic; I was going to be stuck here forever.

I shook my head to knock the panic out of it. Zach would find me. He always found me. As awful as constantly having to rely on someone else was, I certainly felt comforted knowing that he would come for me.

For the meantime I would simply have to occupy myself. Who knew how long it would take him to get here? Last time I had been here for hours before he had found me.

I stomped to the edge of the bedroom and dropped to my bottom, sliding off the floorboards to the forest floor. I smiled as the witch stepped off the muddy track back into the line of trees as I walked past her. My smile faded as I wondered silently if her fear was really what I wanted. I didn't like her, for sure, but did I really want someone to look at me and be afraid? Especially this wretched creature, stuck here until the angels decided to sentence her to an even worse existence. Sam, Trev or Gwen would have been capable of showing her that they weren't to be messed with, without her being frightened of them. All three of them were the type of people to inspire trust and loyalty. But then, they were actually Nephilim, whereas I was some kind of weird half-evil creature that probably shouldn't exist.

As I stomped through the forest following the mud track, I fought against the thoughts and emotions fighting for supremacy in my mind. Sadness and loss seemed to be winning, with my heart aching and my lips trembling

I could barely remember the girl I used to be. I had once been so desperate to find out who and what I was. I had been so sure that there was something out here for me. I had fought so hard to become who I was supposed to be, and to find my true family. Well, I had found out who and what I was. I was nothing, and I was no one. That naïve, stupid girl I had been had found nothing but rejection and disappointment. I had been rejected and refused by all of the family I thought I had found. The angels, my brother, even the other Nephilim in the safe house had begun to avoid me. Perhaps it would be better if I just let Zach go—I was just dragging him down with me.

I sighed. I would never be able to do that. Zach was the only good thing I had in my life, and it wasn't just the sex. He made me feel safe and loved, even if I didn't always believe it. Zach was so strong, and powerful. The other angels were nothing compared to him. No one else even came close.

I mentally slapped myself. I was getting teary for no reason. I needed to sort myself out and come up with a plan.

"Where are you going?" Emily called. She was closer than I had realized.

"Why are you following me?" I countered.

She ignored my question. "There's nothing out here."

"There has to be something," I said, continuing to hike onwards.

Truthfully, I had no idea what I was looking for. I wasn't sure if I was even looking for anything, or if I just needed a minute to breathe. I mean, really, how was I supposed to deal with any of this? One day I think I'm human, the next I'm Nephilim and have a whole species like me. I'm taken in and become part of something . . . the next minute, I'm some bizarre mixture of mythical creatures. How on earth was my brain supposed to accept that I was half Fallen angel and half valkyrie? I wasn't even a little bit human!

When my ears pricked at the crunching of leaves behind me, I spun around. I was prepared to kick her ass if I had to, but something made me pause when I read her expression. She reminded me of myself. She looked lonely.

I sighed again. "If you're just going to trail behind me then you might as well walk beside me. But I swear," I warned, my finger raised to a point, "if you even think of stabbing me in the back or tricking me in any way, I'll rip out your eyes and make you eat them."

Emily frowned, and then nodded her acquiescence. She trotted a little closer, leaving a safe distance between us, and waited for me to continue walking.

I lifted my knee up and stepped over a thick branch that had fallen over the track, then half turned to watch her gather up her dress and jump over. I rolled my eyes and tramped on, kicking a large stone out of the way. I kicked it harder than I had intended and scowled as it ricocheted off a tree, ripping it in half.

"You *have* changed," Emily muttered loudly.

"And you haven't changed one little bit," I retorted. "Aren't you sick of wearing the same clothes?" I winced after I said it, knowing how childish it sounded. I refused to look at her.

A few seconds later I heard her whisper, "I am."

I frowned, feeling guilty. I even felt guilty that I felt guilty. This was a witch, for goodness sake! A witch who had tried to get me trapped in this dimension by tricking me. Who knows how old she really was. Before she had been captured by the angels, she had probably been in league with all sorts of creatures. She probably had demons at her beck and call, and sorceresses on speed dial.

The light bulb in my brain clicked on.

"What do you know about valkyrie?" I asked.

Emily smiled at my request. She actually seemed delighted that I had given her a task. I certainly hoped that she didn't now think we were friends.

"My! The valkyrie. A mysterious species, if there ever was one! Why do you want to know about them?" she asked slyly, her eyes narrowing into slits.

"I should have known I couldn't just ask you a question," I retorted. "Are you planning on bargaining with me for information?"

She smiled. "Perhaps. What are the valkyrie to you?"

I shrugged. I certainly wasn't going to tell her I was part valkyrie. Who knew what kind of trouble that would get me in. I didn't know anything about them . . . about *me*. I didn't know who my enemies were, and I didn't know who I could trust so I certainly wasn't going to start telling my secrets to a witch condemned to wait in the judgment room until the Thrones decided on her punishment.

For the thousandth time I cursed Haamiah for not teaching me about other species. Who cared about the ways of the angelic and how to tend to an injured angel wing when I didn't even know who was likely to try to chop off my head?

"Forget it," I said, marching on.

10

'A girl should be two things - classy and fabulous.'

Coco Channel.

"Isn't there any sun in this bloody place? Do these trees ever stop?" I hissed as I glared up through the trees that seemed to touch the sky. The sky seemed to glow in a luminous swirl, though no heat penetrated the canopy. I was chilled to the bone, goose bumps covering my skin. I felt almost claustrophobic. All I could see were trees, logs, leaves and yet more trees. Occasionally there would be a slight alteration in the track we followed, which would bend a little, or curve upwards or downwards. Otherwise there were no significant marks to show us that we were even moving. It was almost as if we were walking on a treadmill; hours had passed, and my legs were beginning to tire, but it felt like we had gotten nowhere.

I stopped and turned to face Emily who trudged behind me silently, noticing her giving the sky a death stare. "Well?"

She shrugged. "We're awaiting judgment. We don't deserve sunshine." She pushed passed me. "At least the angels don't think we deserve to be lying in a clearing, baking in the sun, which is clearly what you have planned in this never ending trek."

I jerked my head up toward the canopy, realizing what she was saying. I stomped my foot in frustration. "You mean this forest literally lasts forever? We can walk and walk, and we'll never get anywhere? No clearing? Nowhere the sun will get through?"

Emily turned and raised her eyebrows. "You did get the name of this place, right?" she drawled sarcastically.

I scowled. The Never Ending Forest . . . I guess I had just presumed it was one of those depressing doomsday kind of names the Thrones had thought up. At the most, I had presumed it just meant that this was a forest of gigantic proportions, not that it meant that there were no clearings at all to let the sunlight in.

I pointed my finger at her, narrowing my eyes. "You had a house!"

"The hut?" She raised her eyes to mine.

"Yes! The hut! So why are we traipsing endlessly through the forest when we have somewhere to go?"

Emily held up her hands in mock surrender. "You're the one who wanted to follow the track. What is *with* you? You're so agitated! You never said you wanted to go anywhere in particular. You never even said you were looking for somewhere you could sit in the sun—I worked it out myself, from how you kept glaring at the sky as though you were going to somehow part the trees like Moses parted the sea!"

"Moses exists?" I let myself get sidetracked.

Emily continued to rant. "You were so much more pleasant last time when you were here, when your guardian tried to kill me!"

I glared at her, "You tried to trick me into being stuck here forever!"

"And? You deserved it for being such a needy, whiney, naïve—"

I flew at her, my rage quick to surface. I let my arm fly and punched her in the face. As she dropped to her knees on the ground I lifted my own and kneed her in the face before booting her in the side to send her sprawling across the track.

I could feel the power in my chest spinning, rolling, faster and faster, gathering the necessary speed to take over. Terror sent shivers running through me. There was no one here to stop me. Zach was nowhere near; what if it took over again? I felt bombarded by such a mixture of emotions, but pure, white-hot rage was the strongest, and seemed to be oozing through every cell in my body.

I blinked, trying to clear my eyes of the haze that had crept up before realizing that my glittery shadow had swamped me. Through the shadow I could still make out Emily, scowling at me, even as blood dripped from her lip. Each drop seemed like a catalyst for my anger.

As I leaped toward her I found myself stranded in the air, held there, immobile. I blasted my power out. I could feel shards of fire slicing through me, exploding as soon as they hit the air around my body. The heat was scorching, and my skin felt as though it were on fire.

The force holding me still abruptly loosened, and I dropped to the ground unexpectedly. I looked up to see Emily staring at me aghast.

"Look what you did!" she shrieked, her hand over her mouth.

From where I lay, I turned my head. All around us the trees were lit up with an orange glow, fire spreading from branch to branch with ash dropping to the ground and singeing the dead leaves there. As the fire picked up speed jumping from tree to tree, I surged to my feet and ran past Emily, grabbing her arm.

“Run!” I screamed.

I quickly let go of Emily’s arm as she began to run with me, picking up her dress so she could move unimpeded. I could feel my eyelashes and eyebrows smoke as the heat grew too much to bear. The smell of burning hair filled my nose. The crackle and roar of the fire terrified me. It was so loud, so all-consuming, I could have easily broken down and curled into a ball to cry. The only thing that stopped me was that I was 100 percent sure Zach didn’t know where I was. Most of the time I wanted to prove how strong I was, wanted to prove that I didn’t need anyone, but that was pure vanity. Right now, I could think of nothing better than for Zach, or anyone for that matter—even Maion would do, to swoop in and rescue me like a white knight in shining armor. Part of me thought that surely the Thrones would stop the fire, but somehow I knew they wouldn’t. What were we to them? We were nothing. If we died it would simply make their job easier. Unfortunately for me, being surrounded by this roaring fire was a thousand times more horrifying than anything Asmodeus had ever done. I was truly petrified.

I heard a whisper of sound behind me. Though I didn’t want to turn, I made myself check to see if Emily was still with me.

“We have to leave the track!” she screamed, though I could barely hear her over the sound of the fire.

When I nodded my agreement she grabbed my forearm and took off to the right, barreling through the thick branches, twigs snapping against us. She let go as the way grew narrow. I was about to knock her aside to leap in front when she lifted her hand

and pointed with her forefinger at the trees. With the heat at my back I barely caught it, but I saw her lips move as a blue sheen passed across her eyes just once.

I gasped as the branches blocking our way seemed to disintegrate before our eyes, taking on a jelly-like form, and dropping to the ground as we once again pushed on, sprinting for our lives.

If I hadn't been so caught up in running for my life with my mind still stuck on what Emily had just done I would have noticed sooner that the air began to drop a few degrees, affording us some time to rest.

Emily stopped, leaning against a tree, grimacing as she fell into a gooey mess the moment she touched it. She seemed to have as much control over her magic as I had over mine. I paused and turned to look behind me. Still seeing the orange glow in the distance, I judged that I had enough time to quiz Emily.

"What the hell was that?" I snapped.

She glared at me. "I was saving our asses, you ungrateful bitch."

"I'm not ungrateful! Obviously, I'm pleased you did whatever you did—but I want to know how," I said, feeling my rage resurface briefly noting that, in our mad rush to flee the fire, it had subsided.

"What? Just because we're stuck in here, you think we're incapable of using our powers?" she asked. "I'm just as strong and powerful as you. Your precious angels couldn't take that away if they tried."

"They're not *my* angels," I said without thinking.

She narrowed her eyes at me. I turned my back to her and stalked away, staring unseeingly into the forest. Her revelation had snapped me out of my anger, my focus completely on what she had said. Our powers hadn't been taken away?

"Then why couldn't I open the portal?"

She replied with a smarmy, "You obviously don't want it bad enough."

Before I had a second to reply, we were wiped off our feet by an explosion.

"I didn't do it that time, I swear!" I hissed through my teeth.

Looking at Emily's face and the unmistakable expression of terror, as well as feeling the heat prickling at my skin, I concluded we were once again in a flight for our lives. I jumped to my feet, pulling Emily up with me.

We ran, forcing our legs to go faster and faster. I concentrated on pushing my power into my limbs, forcing it to meld with my muscles and give me a boost of speed and energy. I bounded through the forest at an unmatchable speed. Except that it wasn't. I was beyond shocked to see that Emily was matching me step for step. She looked exhausted, yes, but seemed to be having absolutely no trouble keeping up with the pace I had set. I was perplexed by it, but pushed it out of my head as I narrowly missed being knocked out by a low branch.

I slid under it and followed Emily who had now passed by me. Another explosion behind us sent a thick cloud of grey smoke to envelop us. It pinched away any lead we had, but terrified us to new lengths until we were sprinting manically through the forest.

I glanced behind me to see how close the flames were. Emily screamed, and I whipped my head around. I held back my own scream as I found myself falling, plummeting. We flew through the air, off the edge of a gorge into the fast moving water beneath us. My stomach clenched and rolled, my shoulder blades scratched and itched, burnt skin flaking off, as I clamped my mouth shut to prevent the same terrified sound that was still coming from Emily's mouth, coming from my own.

We were high up, my mind guessed one hundred meters though my heart was sure it must be a thousand. If I had done what Zach and Haamiah had spent months teaching me, I should have been observing my surroundings, looking for hazards, looking for a way out of the water and for any dangers that could prevent our escape. But no, instead I stared in horror at the approaching water and the foam and spray that flew off it, all the while listening to Emily's high-pitched scream even as I congratulated myself on keeping my mouth shut.

I took a breath just before I sunk under the water. Clearly, it wasn't deep enough, as my lungs began to burn almost immediately. I found that I couldn't open my eyes, as the water beneath the surface rolled; the mud and the grit from the bottom of the river lashed at my skin.

I fought to the surface with great difficulty. The icy water threatened to numb my body while the noise deafened me. My clothes were stuck to me like glue. My lungs screamed for air while my legs and arms desperately propelled me through. By the time my head breached the surface I couldn't do anything but tuck my legs up against my body and suck the air through my painful throat while spreading my arms out on the surface, preparing myself to swim...as soon as I could breathe properly.

After quite a few gasps and wheezes, I looked around for Emily, my heart twisting painfully as I saw a dark shape in the water a few meters away, also being dragged around by the rolling current.

I took a deep breath and struck out, swimming for her. It took longer than expected but I eventually reached her and splashed around beside her dress, finding her head. I turned her to her back and pulled her face out of the water.

As soon as her head breached the surface she began to struggle and cough, spewing water out. Her struggles sent us both under, and I told her so sharply, forcing her back against me. I could feel the apprehension running through her, and I could sense her mistrust of me—or perhaps it was my own. I liked to think I was powerful and capable of looking after myself, but did I really trust myself to save both of us? Was I deluding myself? Probably.

I began to kick slowly, then, realizing I was making no headway, I kicked harder and harder, using every ounce of power I had, raging at myself. I was even relieved when the anger I usually tried so hard to repress surfaced, lending more strength to my efforts. Though Emily's dress caught in the water, threatening to pull us down, I used the anger that burned in me at her stupid dress to power us through the water until we began to near the edge.

The water still moved quickly, but it was slower here than it had been in the middle. I had to find a way to get us out of the water. I figured just crashing into the bank probably wasn't going to help as a steep rock walls coated the edge of the river. Short of rock climbing while dragging Emily up the cliff, I couldn't see any way out of this mess.

I turned my head down river, and noticed that, further on, the rock face dipped a little lower, allowing roots of the trees lining up on top of it to hang over the river edge. They were probably in reaching distance if I had both hands free. I glanced down at Emily. She glared at me with fury.

“Don’t even think of letting go of me or I swear I’ll cast a spell and turn you into a man,” she rasped.

“I won’t,” I found myself promising.

As we were swept downstream towards the roots I let go of Emily’s chest and wrapped my legs around her. I noted she restrained from cursing me when she realized I hadn’t technically let go of her. With difficulty I sat up in the water, perhaps pushing Emily a little lower, but I closed my eyes in relief as I managed to thrust myself clear of the water and wrap my arms around the branch.

“Don’t you dare turn this one into jelly,” I shouted over the roar of the water.

I began to pull our bodies out of the river with difficulty, sure that the ranting and raving I was doing in my head was the only thing that managed to get us out. As I sat on the thick root, I reached under Emily’s arms and heaved her out of the water, too. Almost ready to collapse, I knew I had to use my remaining strength to get us onto solid ground before I passed out. I stood with a limited amount of balance, and, hearing a loud crack as the branch snapped, I dragged Emily across the tangle of roots, dropped her onto the ground, and collapsed next to her.

11

'When the power of love overcomes the love of power, the world will know peace.'

Jimmy Hendrix.

Zach

"Where the hell is she?" Zach raged.

Haamiah stood by silently, occasionally staring at the ground as Zach ranted and raved. Zach paced the floor, occasionally punching the wall. Little, if anything, had survived Zach and Haamiah's journey here to the Heavenly Realm. Zach had wanted to immediately set out to find a Seer who would locate Jasmine, but instead Haamiah had insisted they travel here to seek the help of another Principality angel. Haamiah was keen on using up all of their angelic resources before turning to another kind for assistance, but judging by the disasters Jasmine had found herself in each time she travelled through portals, Zach was sure she would already be in danger. This time, at least, he wouldn't fail her. He couldn't live with himself if something happened to her. *Where was she?*

"I don't know," Haamiah answered warily.

"I'm right here boys," a sultry voice called out.

Zach and Haamiah swirled around to see a tall woman enter the meeting room. She had long brown hair that reached her waist, and she swayed with every step she took. She was hauntingly beautiful, with a little mole beside her lip making her look classically seductive.

She was nothing compared to Jasmine.

“Call me a boy again and you’ll not live to see another day,” Zach growled.

Haamiah hissed out his breath in annoyance. “Bëyander, you look lovely, as always.”

She smiled, her perfect white teeth sparkling. “Haamiah, you charmer. Zacharael . . . speak to me like that again, and I’ll have your wings to wear as a coat. I hear its cold this time of year on the Earthly plane; you may need those fine feathers of yours to keep warm on those *lonely* winter nights.”

Haamiah pushed Zach backwards as he lunged for her. “Stop! Both of you,” he warned.

Commander Avrail suddenly landed beside Bëyander, and pushed her behind him protectively. He glared at Zach.

“Zacharael, make threats again in these chambers and I will dismiss you from the Heavenly service, and you will spend your days as a Grigori instead,” he threatened. He ran a hand through his grey hair and stepped back. “Tell me what you are doing here.”

“It is none of your concern, Commander Avrail,” Zach spat. “This is a private matter.”

Commander Avrail snorted. “Anything done by one of my warriors involves me. Inform me of the problem.”

“One of our Nephilim is missing.” Haamiah spoke calmly and with authority. It had been his idea to come to Bëyander, and Zach could only be thankful that he had not hindered his search in any way. Yes, he had insisted on coming here, but at least it was a productive move. The angels of the principality class were usually playing by their own rules, moving the other angels around like chess pieces in order to get to their end game. He couldn’t blame Haamiah for any game he played, as, like all angels, he had his own rules to adhere to.

Commander Avrail glanced at Zach and back to Haamiah. “Why is this such a cause of contention? Nephilim go missing all the time, usually scooped back up by the human authorities or by their angel parent.”

Zach scowled and deferred to Haamiah.

Haamiah shook his head. “This particular Nephilim has no one among the human world she trusts, and is old enough to take care of herself. The problem is that she entered a portal, and Zach is unable to feel her essence and trace her to her location. We hoped for Bëyander’s assistance in locating her.”

Commander Avrail frowned at all three of them. “I fear you do not tell me the whole story. Firstly, a Nephilim capable of portal travel is a first. If such a creature existed, especially one known to the two of you, then of course you would have made me aware of her before now. Secondly, you have not explained why and how Zacharael is linked to this Nephilim, and is not where I ordered him to be—at his post in Australasia. Thirdly, this is no reason for Bëyander to be of any assistance to you.” He glared at them.

“Should I arrest you all now, and have you taken to the Thrones, or would you care to explain yourselves?”

Haamiah opened his mouth to reply, but Bëyander spoke.

“This creature is no ordinary Nephilim. In fact, she isn’t one at all,” she murmured. Zach’s eyes widened, as her words registered.

Within seconds Zach had her by her throat, his teeth snapping at her face. Before he had a chance to do any harm, Haamiah loosened his grip and flung him away.

“This will get us nowhere! Bëyander, what do you know?” he shouted.

Bëyander rubbed at her throat, scowling as Zach focused his deadly eyes on her. She sighed, and flicked her hair over her shoulder. “I am not entirely sure it’s in our best interests to tell you when our friend here is in such a . . . *rabid* state.”

“Bëyander . . . ” Commander Avrail hissed. “What do you mean this creature is not a Nephilim? What has been going on here?”

She frowned guiltily at him. “Zach was sent to be her guardian angel while Haamiah and I *watched* over her interests. In my defense, Zach was never supposed to get so close to her, and the plan we agreed upon is no longer relevant!”

Zach looked shocked. “You played a part in this?”

“It is quite a complex game, Zacharael. You cannot expect Haamiah to manage it all himself,” she argued.

Zacharael turned to Haamiah and glared at his friend. “You knew about this and you didn’t tell me? I am her guardian! I should have been told!”

"Tell me what is going on!" Commander Avrail bellowed, his face flustered and red.

Haamiah, Zach and Bëyander glared at each other.

"As even I clearly do not know the whole story, one of you is better off explaining," Zach said.

Haamiah took a deep breath. "Bëyander, Lawrence, Choo and I created the safe houses back at the beginning of the Nephilim war. We became aware of Jasmine's existence recently and I was closest geographically to her, so it made sense for the task of her future to fall to me. When we discovered more about this complex girl, Bëyander was also involved. Together we have watched over her."

"The two of you haven't done a very good job," Zach snapped.

Haamiah sighed. "I was given orders to ensure you became her guardian angel, to what end I am unsure, but I'm fairly certain falling in love with her was not part of the plan. It has become so complicated it is difficult to keep the end game in sight."

"And what is the end game?" Zach asked in a dangerous voice.

"Peace! Hasn't that always been the end we foresaw?" Haamiah shouted.

"Who gave the orders to remove *my* warrior from combat?" Commander Avrail questioned grimly. "*No one* commands my soldiers! *No one* has the authority to overrule my orders!"

"Michael has the authority," Haamiah said quietly.

The room fell silent.

As the archangel of battle and the defender of Heaven, Michael would certainly have the authority to overrule Commander Avrail. Michael was the archangel that all Warrior angels revered; the sound of his name silenced them all, and terrified Zach. What danger was Jasmine in for Michael to be involved? That it was the archangel who'd ordered him to be her guardian angel was a true honor, but he wished he knew the reason. It seemed as though there was a game going on all around him, with Jasmine as the centerpiece. He was doing his best to protect her, but how could he when no one was telling him the truth? Perhaps he could approach Michael himself? It was unheard of for an angel to approach an archangel though, and he had only seen him a handful of times in his long life.

"Why is Michael involved? What aren't you telling me?" Zach asked Haamiah, his heart feeling heavier than ever before.

Haamiah shook his head. "You know everything now. At least everything *I* know." He looked pointedly at Bëyander.

She raised her eyebrows and smiled. "All knowledge of Jasmine has come through Michael. I know nothing that Haamiah does not know."

"I need to find her. I *know* she is in danger," Zach persisted. "Tell me where to look for her. If you two are in league with Michael you must have some idea of where to start."

"We came to you in good faith, Bëyander," Haamiah said. "You are here and able to watch her more closely than I."

She tutted and smiled at them. "You do realize you will get nowhere with this. The Thrones are unhappy with the situation and have quarantined her until further notice. Your little . . . Valk-

Angel? Ange-yrie? Your little *creature* was watched closely by the Grigori, and her latest antics have ensured that the Thrones see her as a threat to our peace."

"What peace? We have *no* peace! We are at war!" Zach shouted, furious.

"Exactly, and your girlfriend is an unknown. She has proven that she is volatile in nature and completely unpredictable. If the Fallen get to her, or if the valkyrie sway her to their side there will be horrendous consequences." Bëyander scowled. "You risk all of us in this game you play, Zacharael."

"*Where is she*?"

Bëyander smiled coldly. "If she is your soul mate, shouldn't you be able to find her yourself?"

"She isn't there." Zach spat out. "She vanished. I should be able to sense her, but I can't. Even in another realm I should still be able to sense where she is, but her essence is being shielded."

Bëyander laughed. "Look at you—simpering after a Fallen angel. How unlike you! I have never known you to have fuzzy feelings for them; didn't you promise us you would destroy every single one you came across?"

"She's not like them," Zach hissed.

"But she will be. *All* Fallen angels are evil—you know this. Forget her!"

"Where is your compassion Bëyander?" Haamiah asked, astonished. "Tell us where she is, and if you have had contact with

Michael I need to know *exactly* what he has said. Why hasn't he stepped in and told the Thrones that he is involved with her?"

"Excuse me for not exactly caring about your little Fallen angel friend. *I* haven't forgotten what they did, and continue to do to our people. I haven't forgotten the sound of their laughter as they ripped my true love apart. Do not waste my time with talk of this creature. Do not waste *Michael's* time—he has more important things to deal with, and regrets ever showing an interest in her." She backed away slowly, her eyes narrowed at the angels before her. Commander Avrail glared at them all before deciding to follow her. They exited the room together and closed the door firmly.

Zach turned to Haamiah and glared. "Now we do things *my* way."

12

'Your vision will become clear only when you look inside your heart. Who looks outside, dreams. Who looks inside, awakens.'

Carl Jung.

Jasmine

I turned over onto my back and stared up at the trees, knowing I should get up and check how close the fire had come. There was every chance it would spread across the river or even come behind us, trapping us where we lay, and I really didn't want to get back into the water. I turned my head to see Emily panting beside me.

"Have you recovered yet?" I asked when she had grown quiet.

"From my near drowning?" she drawled. "I think so."

I turned my head so that I could see her where I lay. She sounded so subdued—not like the feisty witch I had come to know. I debated what to say. There was nothing I *could* say, really. We were stuck here. There was no looking on the bright side; all we could do was wait. I reached down for my power, feeling the coil and pulled, urging it to release the magic it held to open a portal. Nothing happened. It continued to coil around my abdomen uselessly.

“I need to go pee,” I muttered to Emily.

Without waiting for a reply I stood and forced myself to walk up the steep slope away from the river. I pushed on, deciding to climb a bit higher than necessary so that I could potentially see if the fire was spreading. I climbed over a log and shrieked wordlessly.

I ran toward the figure standing there, and wrapped my arms around him before jumping away.

“Aidan, what are you doing here?” I gasped, staring up in amazement at the blond-haired warrior.

“When I heard where you were I needed to come to see for myself that you were safe.” He leaned down and cupped my chin.

His touch warmed my skin, to the point where I thought it would melt. Every hair seemed to stand up, every follicle peaked as though to absorb more of his touch. For a fleeting moment I thought he was going to kiss me. Relief and consternation flooded through me when he sighed and dropped his hand. I had to restrain myself from falling into him.

I stared up at him, drinking him in. Besides the brief and awkward argument back in the safe house, I hadn’t seen him in months, and I hadn’t spoken to him properly for months before that. Though my heart belonged to Zach, a part of me still clung to the ideal of Aidan. Tall and muscular, with a beautifully soft, caring face framed with shaggy blond hair that fell to his shoulders, he was mesmerizing. I could look into his grey-green eyes forever, waiting for the shy, sweet smile he didn’t often show. Though he was a Fallen angel, he was a Healer, and more gentle and kind than many of the angels I had come to know. In fact, now I had more in common with him than before, being half Fallen angel myself. I would never have to worry that he was ashamed of me.

I coughed, breaking the tense emotion-filled silence. “How did you know I was here? I’ve only been gone a few hours.”

He grimaced. “Time moves differently in other realms, Jasmine, you know that.’

“Crap,” I swore. “How long this time?”

He looked down sheepishly. “Just under a week. I still have some friends in the underworld who were able to locate you. I just can’t believe they put you here.”

“A week?” I gasped. “Who put me here? I thought that this was the Throne’s waiting room? I was put here on purpose?”

He nodded. “So only *they* have the power to lock people in.”

“I thought I did it by accident.” I lifted my hand to my mouth in shock. “The *Thrones* did this? How can that be?”

He shrugged tensely. “I’m not sure. There are a number of possibilities. They could be protecting you . . . ”

“Or?”

“Punishing you for something you have done . . . for the tournament perhaps.”

“I haven’t done *anything,*” I denied in anger. “Surely they would prefer me to win, over the other contestants.” I glared at him, aware that he had mentioned “a number of possibilities.” I narrowed my eyes at him. What was he hiding from me? “*Or*?”

“Maybe because they know what you are?”

I stared at him, holding my breath. *"You know*?"

He nodded, lifting his face so that his eyes caught mine. I watched, my eyes trapped, my lungs unable to draw breath as he bit his lip and frowned.

"How do you know?" I whispered.

He shook his head, pressing his lips together tightly.

"I have a right to know who's talking about me," I hissed.

"A lot of people know . . . the *wrong* people," he answered tersely.

"*He* knows?" I questioned. I was referring to Asmodeus, the Lord of Castle Dantanian, one of the most powerful Fallen angels in existence, and my own personal nightmare. He had raped and brutally beaten me, up to the point where I hadn't known if I were even alive anymore. The memories of what he had done to me would haunt me for the rest of my life, and had changed me irrevocably. Because of him I was no longer the Jasmine I had once been. Nor would I ever be the Jasmine I could have been.

"How does what I am affect him? Why would he be interested?" I made myself say, knowing I needed it spoken out loud. Asmodeus had shown an unnatural interest in me because of my ability to open portals. I knew he wanted me to open the portal to Heaven so that he and his army could bring death and destruction to all who resided there, potentially taking over and ruling the Heavens. However there had always seemed to be more than just that. I was sure there was another reason for his brutal attack on me.

More than anything I needed Aidan to tell me what information he had, and quick. Surely by now the Thrones knew they had an intruder.

"He was interested in you before. No one escapes Castle Dantanian. It was a miracle," he replied.

"No, it was you," I said softly, remembering how he had helped Zach and I to escape.

"You would have escaped with or without me. You're special," he said quietly.

"*Don't* Aidan," I hushed. I shook my head. "We're getting off topic. I'll deal with Asmodeus *if—*" I rolled my eyes at the look Aidan gave me. "—or *when* he finds me. Tell me why the Thrones have locked me up here, and what they're planning on doing to me."

Aidan glanced around. "I don't know for certain but—"

I was suddenly catapulted through the air as the ground buckled and rolled. My body flew backwards against a tree within seconds. I fell to the ground in a heap, covering my head as the trees groaned and the ground cracked, branches falling all around me. As I grimaced, imagining the bruises that would soon begin to form all over my body, I looked around for Aidan to check that he was unhurt.

He was gone. With horror blossoming in my chest, I staggered to my feet and ran toward the river, where I'd left Emily.

13

'Life is too important to be taken seriously.'

Oscar Wilde.

When I reached the riverbank, Emily was already on her feet and she looked beyond furious.

"You left me," she shrieked.

We didn't have time for this nonsense, and I scowled at her to show my frustration. The Thrones had obviously found us, and could attack at any moment.

"We have to go . . . *now*," I ordered, marching away from her.

I presumed she would follow me, and I was right. I forced myself to slow down, trying not to take my emotional turmoil out on her. It wasn't her fault the Thrones had thrown me in here. The question infuriating me was *why* they had put me here. I couldn't believe that it was for my safety, after what had happened. What on earth did they hope to accomplish by this?

I felt myself get more and more worked up. I was so sick of meddling angels interfering and plotting. No doubt this had something to do with the attack on the safe house and *someone* up there had an endgame in sight. Well, I was done being their pawn. I let out a scream of infuriation, noting the lightning that slashed across the sky, briefly illuminating the forest interior. That was just great. A thunderstorm was all I needed right now.

"Okay, *psycho*. What's wrong with you now?" I heard Emily grumble. I turned my head to scowl at her, seeing her look up at the sky with worry. "Issues much?"

That really just summed everything up. I was stuck in a waiting room for the Thrones, who I'd never met, waiting to be judged for a crime that I hadn't known I'd committed, with an evil witch. My world was complete.

I debated whether or not to tell her what had happened with Aidan. What damage could it do? I huffed out my breath, my brain beginning to spin out of control. A thousand questions beat at me. Could I trust Emily? Why was she even following me? Did she have an ulterior motive? Would telling her about Aidan hinder or help me? If she knew I wasn't a Nephilim, would that affect our ally status? We certainly weren't friends, but I had saved her life, and I would like to think we had a sort of pact going on. Would that change if she knew I was part Fallen angel?

I stopped and whirled around to face her. "Why are you here?" I asked.

A look of surprise crossed her face. "I killed a man. Actually," she laughed, "I killed a few, but the one that got me caught was a new spell my coven was trying out—"

"No," I interrupted firmly. "Why are you *here*? Following me?"

I immediately saw the hurt flash in her eyes and regretted what I had said. Or, at least, I regretted saying it so harshly.

I sighed. "I didn't mean—"

"Oh quit it already!" she snapped. "If you had spent nearly a century stuck here, maybe you too would cling on to your only hope of escape."

"How can *I* help you escape?" I ground out. "Do you see me weaving any magic? Do you see me opening any portals? No! That's because I'm stuck here, just like you! I don't even know what the Thrones are punishing me for. I don't know what I'm accused of, or why I'm waiting for judgment and I can't use my abilities in this place—*you* have more power than I do."

"Well that's not exactly true now, is it?" Emily stalked close to me, her eyes flashing in fury. "What are you hiding from me? Why would the Thrones throw one of their own in here?"

She was getting dangerously close to the truth. Even though Aidan had said the underworld were aware of my new species status, that didn't mean anyone *here* knew. God, I didn't even know if being part valkyrie and part Fallen angel meant I had more enemies or less.

I sighed. "I honestly don't know the reason why I'm here - at least I'm not 100 percent sure."

"Is it something to do with the valkyrie?" Emily asked, startling me. "Because, honey, if you're in trouble with them, then you're beyond saving."

I swallowed, hard. "So you *do* know something about them."

She shrugged, her eyes glinting. "Perhaps. What is it worth to you?"

I bit my lip, anger surging through me. I warred with it for a second before realizing it didn't matter if it took over. It didn't matter if I unleashed the roiling fury that bit through my insides like acid . . . because I was *here*. I couldn't do anything here. The moment that sunk in I felt relief soothe me. I just needed to decide how much, if any, information I gave Emily. Was it important that I hear what she knew? I was unsure. Would it help me escape? Possibly. I knew I had to take the chance. Even if she could clarify who my enemies were, that could be information that could save my life.

I held onto my resolve tightly. I couldn't let myself get into any more trouble than I was already in.

"What do you want?"

"When you leave here, I want you to make sure you take me with you. Whatever it takes," she demanded.

"Why do you want to escape so badly?" I questioned, knowing it was a stupid question.

She raised her eyebrows at me. "Are you serious? Would *you* want to be stuck here forever?"

"Well, is it really better than the alternative?"

She raised her hands. "What is wrong with you? Of course the alternative is better! I could be at home with my coven."

I frowned, feeling completely bewildered. "Emily . . . " I didn't know how to phrase it, or if it was even an acceptable question to ask. "Aren't you dead?"

She froze. "Excuse me?"

I pursed my lips for a second then shook my head in confusion. "I thought everyone here was a spirit . . . you know . . . .waiting for judgment."

She rolled her eyes. "Oh my God! Are *you* dead?"

"No," I denied crossly, folding my arms.

"Well then, why would *I* be dead?"

I frowned. "I don't know. I was told that everyone here was a spirit, so that's what I believed."

As we stared at each other in silence, me with what I imagined was a confused, almost dazed look, and Emily's face painted with sheer outrage that I had thought she was dead, the oddest thing happened. We began to smile—begrudgingly at first, then grinning from ear to ear before progressing to hysterical laughter.

As tears poured from my eyes, I clutched my sides, unable to control the giggles that spewed from me.

"I'm sorry," I wheezed. "I just thought . . . I just thought . . . "

"That I was dead! Ha ha ha!" she choked. She raised her palm to her forehead and shook her head at me. "I can't believe you thought I was dead."

I shook my head, and blew out a breath. "Friends?"

She quirked her eyebrow. "I'm not sure I'd go that far just yet. Allies?"

I nodded. "Definitely."

She smiled then pushed past me, picking up her skirts to walk ahead. "Do we have a deal or not?"

I smiled. “We have a deal.”

14

'Not all who wander are lost.'

Unknown.

Emily began to say something but I lifted my hand up to silence her, ducking behind a tree.

"What was that?" I whispered. I glanced around. I had heard something; a low voice whispering ahead of us.

"What was *what*?" she asked irritably.

"There's something up there. I heard someone talking," I hissed.

Emily rolled her eyes. "Yeah, well there *are* other people here besides us, you know."

I frowned. I *had* actually forgotten that. But still, I wasn't keen on meeting any creature that needed judgment from the Thrones. What type of people would be here, in the Never Ending Forest? Vampires? Fallen angels? Murderers?

I turned to scowl at her. "Are you particularly *friendly* with anyone here?"

She scowled back at me. *"No."* She paused. "I didn't hear anyone though."

I turned back to peer between the trees. I had definitely heard a voice. "Well, I heard someone, and if you don't have any other allies out here then we can presume they're an enemy."

"Uh! Listen to you—all *enemies and allies*. You can tell the angels got to you. You're turning *into* one of them."

"I wish," I whispered, "and be quiet!"

As I watched for movement I wondered if it was true. Did the angels really think of everyone in terms of enemies and allies? The more I thought about it, the more I realized it was so. They did class everyone as one or the other, and that was probably why I felt so lonely now. I was no longer on their *ally* list.

Emily huffed out her breath and jumped out from behind the tree back onto the mud track. She cupped her hands around her mouth.

"Is anyone out there?" she called. Silence answered her. "See?" She turned around to face me with a grin. "You imagined it."

I opened my eyes wide in surprise as a shape stepped out of the shadows further up the track. This woman was dressed in clothing much more suitable for a forest than I was. She was wearing black trousers with thick brown boots laced up to her knees, a black tool belt slung low around her hips and a loose red shirt, covered up with a black leather jacket. Her brown hair was pulled away from her face in a ponytail. She clutched a knife in her hand.

"Oh shit," I muttered.

Emily swung round and immediately held up her palm to the stranger. Her hand began to glow green, the luminosity casting the forest with a weird magical glow. I stepped out from behind the tree and stood closer to Emily, unsure why I felt the need to. Was it because she was now my ally? I shook my head, and concentrated on the stranger.

I could hear her voice again, talking in my head. Random words broke through, but nothing that made any sense. I shook it off as I realized Emily and the stranger had begun to argue.

"Hit me with it and I'll scalp you, witch," the stranger threatened.

"You could try, honey, but it would be a little difficult if you're say . . . a worm," Emily threatened.

"Jesus! The two of you sound ridiculous." I stomped closer to Emily. "Put that down. And you! Put that away."

"Who the hell are you?" the stranger asked.

Emily drew herself up. "Emily. I hail from the Feral Witches of Longly. Who are you?"

I widened my eyes at that. *Feral* witches?

"Tanya, and I don't know you well enough to tell you where I'm from." Tanya smirked.

The green magic sitting in the palm of Emily's hand grew brighter and brighter.

Tanya scowled and ducked back. "I come from the Harpies of the Yuan plane." She stuck her dagger in her tool belt and lifted her hands up.

Emily gradually let her magic fade, allowing Tanya to step closer. She looked at me.

I shrugged. It wasn't as if I was actually going to confess to being what I was.

"I'm Jasmine—a Nephilim," I said.

Tanya laughed. "Oh, great. We've got one of the angelic with us. Now my torture is complete."

I rolled my eyes. "Fuck off. What do you want?"

She grinned at me. "Why would I want anything from you?"

I shrugged. "You tell me. You were spying on us."

Tanya shrugged. "Maybe I just wondered why the two of you were being so noisy when everyone knows the forest is teeming with creatures waiting to gut you?"

I scowled. "We wouldn't have seemed so noisy if you hadn't been following us, listening to every word we said."

Tanya smiled. "What are you doing?"

"The Thrones are interested in her for some reason," Emily supplied. "I'm sticking with her, if it means any chance of getting out."

"Getting out?" Tanya's eyes brightened. "Sign me up."

"Ugh! No one is going anywhere right now. And I don't even know *you*, so why would I agree to help you?"

Tanya whipped a sword out and twirled it in front of her. "Because you're going to need more than the witch's tricks to keep you alive in here once the other inmates know what you are."

That was that sorted, then.

15

'Go confidently in the direction of your dreams. Live the life you've imagined.'

Thoreau

Three days had passed, and Tanya had proven her worth on more than one occasion. While I was good at some things, hunting down animals and rodents to eat was not one of them. Emily foraged for fruit, roots and seeds and when put with the meat that Tanya caught and cooked, we did pretty well for ourselves. A sense of camaraderie seemed to have fallen on us, and despite my initial misgivings I found that I actually enjoyed the company of both her and Emily. Zach still hadn't appeared, and Aidan hadn't returned, much to my dismay.

Our pattern of living seemed to be walking until we had found somewhere Tanya deemed safe, only to be attacked before twenty-four hours was up, fighting for our lives, then moving on again. The harpy claimed that my angel smell was drawing them to us. Little did she know I wasn't exactly angel.

We had just settled in for the evening behind a thick clump of trees when I heard the sound of approaching footfalls. I jumped up and spun around, allowing room to defend myself as someone appeared to my left.

"Jesus, you scared the crap out of me," I exclaimed, pressing my hand to my chest to soothe my crazily beating heart. I turned to

Emily, a little startled to see how white she had become—and how far back she had ran. Tanya also seemed startled, though she held her blade out in front of her. I turned back to Zach.

Zach scowled and looked past me at Emily. “What are you doing here, witch?”

“Easy, it’s okay,” I soothed.

He raised his eyebrows sarcastically. Okay, maybe that was a little patronizing.

I shrugged. “She’s harmless.”

“She’s a witch. And she’s . . . here!” he gestured around incredulously. “Anyone waiting here to be judged for their sins is not harmless.”

I rolled my eyes, exasperated. “Then do tell me what I’m doing here.”

Zach paused, an odd expression appearing on his ruggedly handsome face.

“Zach . . . ” I narrowed my eyes at him. He knew something. “Do you know why I’m here?”

The mocking smirk was missing from his lips. His usually soul-deep eyes now contained a sharp edge of worry. I raked my eyes over him; there was something going on here I was missing. I glanced at his arms noticing for the first time what looked like a burn mark on his forearm. There even seemed to be blood seeping through his clothes. I stared at him, beginning to comprehend.

“Take your top off,” I ordered. “I want to see you.”

For the first time since I had known him, I could see uncertainty clouding his face. I couldn't stand that look on him. This was Zach. He was infallible, impervious, cheeky and charming. Even when he was leaving me high and dry, he had this intense emotion about him. He constantly flipped between dark and brooding and seductively charming. What on earth had happened to turn him into this solemn uncertain man?

When he didn't do as I had ordered, I ran to him and lifted my fingers to his jaw, sliding the length of my palm across the black stubble there.

"Zach, what happened?"

He took a deep breath and clasped his hand around my throat, rubbing gently with his thumb.

"Babe, don't freak out," he said hesitantly.

"Oh my God, what is it?" I stared up into his eyes, needing to trust him, needing him to tell me everything was fine.

He took a deep breath. "There was an attack on the safe house."

"Our safe house?" I whispered.

Zach nodded. "They set a fire in the night. Haamiah and Elijah got most of the kids out."

It took me a moment to respond. "Most of them?"

Zach nodded.

I struggled to focus. The faces of the Nephilim, young and old, raced through my mind. "Who set the fire?"

"We're not sure."

"Who . . . who didn't get out?" I whispered. The words came out muffled, as I had clamped my hand across my mouth.

Zach shook his head. "There were a few . . . " He cast his eyes downward as his words trailed off. "Some of the Nephilim are missing."

"Who?" Dread slithered through me.

"Gwen and Trev are missing. Sam was with the sorceress at the time, and she managed to get him out of there. Lilura thinks she knew who took them, but isn't 100 percent sure."

My eyes were full to the brim with tears, casting a kaleidoscope of light through my vision. My heart ached and my head felt so heavy and tight I thought it would explode. I couldn't speak, I couldn't open my mouth to push out the words; I simply stared at him in horror.

"She said Asmodeus took them. He hasn't left a message, or a ransom demand. The angels are hunting him. The Grigori are out there, as is Maion."

"Oh, well, thank the Lord that Maion is out there looking," I snapped.

"Jasmine," Zach sighed.

"Why am I here? If I'd been there I could have saved them. Who put me here?" I shrieked.

Zach flinched. "Babe, the Grigori were at the Tournament of Ascension. They saw you take the Star Mist."

I froze. "I didn't have a choice."

He spread his arms wide. “I know that. Haamiah knows it, but the Thrones aren’t convinced.”

“What are they going to do to me?” I asked, angry beyond belief.

“You’ll wait here until they judge you. They’ll hand out a punishment, and we’ll deal with it when it comes.”

“Emily’s been here for years! You expect me to wait here for years when my friends are missing?”

“There’s nothing I can do. This is the way it is,” he replied harshly, his lips setting into a firm line.

“You can take me back with you,” I suggested.

He shook his head. “I can’t do that. You’re here on order of the Thrones. I can’t go against them.”

I laughed bitterly and nodded. “Of course. Well, you’d best be off then. I wouldn’t want the Thrones to catch you being a naughty boy, sneaking in here to visit me.” I scowled at him. “Feel free to leave me here with the murderers and rapists while you go home and put your feet up.”

I knew I spoke coldly. I knew that, really, it wasn’t Zach’s fault I was here, but I was so sick of angels bossing me around, and manipulating me into situations I didn’t want to be in then abandoning me when I was in trouble. If it hadn’t been for angels telling me I was a Nephilim—something else they cocked up—then I wouldn’t even be here. Of course, I’d probably be dead, or addicted to drugs and booze, but the point was I was over being manipulated by beings who thought they were better than me.

Zach looked disgusted at my suggestion. "I wouldn't leave you here alone. I'm staying here with you. The Thrones have already agreed to it. After all, I'm still your Guardian."

I clenched my jaw. I stepped close to him and jabbed at his chest with my finger. "So you're leaving the search up to Maion? Haamiah and Elijah will be busy setting up a new safe house, so that only leaves you and Maion to look for Trev and Gwen. Tell me—who's going to actually look for them? You know Maion won't look for them. He doesn't give a shit about the Nephilim. Actually, no, correction - he wants us all dead!"

"You're not—" he began.

I cut him off with a furious glare. He seemed to get my meaning, as he quickly glanced at Emily then back at me.

Zach glowered. He hated it when I said anything negative about Maion, and he always defended him whenever he said anything bad about me. I never understood their friendship. They were completely different . . . kind of.

"We've sent word to Machidiel, but he hasn't heard anything from him yet. Regardless, Maion is not Fallen. He will do what is right."

I shook my head. I felt betrayed, humiliated that he always sided with Maion over me, and I felt so helpless. Zach may think that "sending word" to Machidiel was a big deal, but as I'd never met the guy before it meant bugger all to me. The fact that Zach was here, and Gwen and Trev were in the hands of Asmodeus was infuriating. I daren't even imagine where they were. I wouldn't be able to live with myself if the same thing that had happened to me happened to Gwen.

“Just go,” I said, turning away.

Zach grabbed my arm and swung me back to face him. I quickly knocked his arm away and glared at him, gritting my teeth. I could already feel my power on the rise.

“Leave me alone.”

“What the hell are you talking about?” he demanded, equally furious. He clenched his fists as he glared at me.

“I don’t need your help. If all you’re going to do is follow me around then you might as well just leave. If you want to do something, then look for Gwen and Trev. I can take care of myself but they will be helpless against any of our enemies - especially Asmodeus.”

“Jasmine, we don’t know for certain it’s Asmodeus,” Zach urged.

Irrationally I lashed out, back handing him across the face. “Don’t talk to me about him! Don’t even say his name. I don’t care who took them, I care that they could already be dead, or are being tortured while your precious Thrones have locked me in here. I could have saved them!”

Zach wiped the blood from his lip and glowered at me. “You don’t know that.”

I froze. That hurt more than any of the other crap he’d spouted. I knew I could have saved them, and I would have, or I would have died trying, happily. They were my only family, so for him to say I couldn’t or wouldn’t have kept them safe was repulsive to me.

All at once I felt like that young girl again; alone and miserable with no trust or confidence in anyone, betrayed at every turn, with no one to believe in me. I had worked damned hard to get away from her.

“Fuck you,” I said, turning from him to march back to Emily.

I listened, expecting to hear him stomp after me or shout my name . . . but he didn’t. I turned around after a few seconds and found that he had vanished. Was I glad about that? Was it what I wanted? I had no idea.

16

'Being a hero isn't about letting others know you've done the right thing, it's about you knowing you've done the right thing.'

Max Tennyson.

"I need to find them," I muttered hours later.

"You can't do anything from in here," Tanya said.

"I know," I muttered. I kicked a log, wincing as it flew through the trees, snapping off branches.

"Well actually . . . " Emily pressed her lips together, thinking.

"What?" I asked. "If you know something that can help . . . "

"Possibly." Emily held up her hands to shush me. "There is a spell we can do."

"Then let's do it." I bit my lip. "A spell to do what, exactly?"

"Well, we could create a trans-realm energy crystal to see them. Although that might not help with actually locating them, we'd only see them, like a photo. We could make a looking-map. It's difficult, but it could work."

“What use is that going to be from here?” Tanya rolled her eyes. “You need a spell that’s going to help someone on the outside find them.”

Emily turned to me with a blank look on her face.

I frowned. “Could we somehow send this map to the angels? Or to Sam?”

Emily drew her eyebrows in, deep in thought. “I couldn’t make a looking-map like that; it’s stationary from where it’s made. I could *direct* a finding spell at someone, but I can’t guarantee they’ll definitely see it. You have to know what you’re looking for to see the information in one of these spells. It’s not easy to pick a message out of thin air, and it definitely won’t work on a Nephilim. The recipient needs to have full magical knowledge.”

“Well, the angels must already be looking for them. Zach said Maion was leading the search.”

“Then he’s our best bet,” Emily said with a triumphant grin.

I groaned. “Are you serious? Maion . . . Maion is the *last* person I would want to trust with this.”

“If he’s already looking for them, he’ll see the signs of my magic. It won’t make the slightest impression on anyone else.”

“He’s *allegedly* looking,” I grumbled.

“Then he’s the one we need to send the spell to,” Emily finished with an air of finality, resolution stamped on her face.

I pulled at my hair, infuriated at my helplessness. “Fine. If it’s him we have to use then let’s just get started.”

"Okay. It's going to be difficult though," Emily warned.

"Are you sure you can do a spell from inside here?" I asked, uncertain. Surely the Thrones would zoom in on us the moment they saw what we were doing. I glanced around. They were probably listening in right now. Any second now they would send another fireball to incinerate us.

Emily nodded. "There's a way around it. I'm not actually doing a spell *in* here. I'm facilitating the magic, but the spell will be on the human plane with Maion."

I tilted my head. "Huh. That's quite sneaky. Are you sure even that much is allowed?"

She raised her eyebrows. "We'll see. It's a difficult spell, anyway. Add in the distance it needs to travel, and it will take a lot of energy. But first, we need to get all of the ingredients."

"What do you need?" Tanya asked. She was grinning like a cat. She looked excited to be a part of this, and I could understand why. Both her and Emily were stuck here, why wouldn't they jump at a chance to do something interesting—maybe even spit in the eye of the Thrones a little? It was great that they were excited, I just wished I could have said the same. Instead, I was a mess inside. My best friends were missing and I was stuck here, unable to do anything but possibly assist in a spell that may or may not work, and may or may not be heeded by an angel I hated. It was a frustrating and exasperating situation to be in.

"I need three dragonflies, a piece of silver, Mordal, Unakite crystal for balance and . . . " She reached toward Tanya and pulled out a single lock of hair. " . . . hair of Harpy."

"Ow." Tanya glared at her.

"Can we find the other things here?" I asked. It sounded as though there were a lot of things on the list and I wasn't convinced we'd find the ingredients for a witch's spell in an angelic realm. Wasn't that the point? We were in isolation because we'd been bad. Why would the Thrones allow the existence of such things in their realm?

"Sure, I know I've seen dragonflies down near the lake. It's a bit of a walk from here, but I can definitely get them and *silver*—" Emily held out her arm to show a multitude of silver bangles sliding out from under her sleeve. "—we have right here. Mordal we can dig up from around the base of one of the trees, it's everywhere. The most difficult thing to get will be the Unakite. It grows near mermaid swarms; the beautiful shimmering green and pink comes from their scales. We can only hope that there's a naughty mermaid in here somewhere. Otherwise we'll have to make do with something else, but it won't be as effective."

"Mermaids exist?" I gasped.

Emily and Tanya laughed in response.

"Fine. I don't know anything . . . blah, blah, blah. As for your crystal, I'm sure these forests are just teeming with naughty mermaids." I groaned. I felt so exasperated. Was this just going to be a waste of time? If she needed this Unakite for the spell to work then why didn't she come up with something else? Maybe a spell that we *could* find all the ingredients for? It wasn't as if there was a magic shop nearby.

"I've seen mermaids here," Tanya said, smiling in glee.

I snapped my head up. "Are you serious? There are mermaids, *here*?"

Emily and Tanya laughed and turned in the same direction, marching off through the trees, leaving me to lag behind.

When we camped for the night, if you could call it camping with no tent or sleeping bag, Emily lit a small fire with a quiet mutter and a wave of her hands after I had gathered some twigs and branches. Tanya crawled closer and lifted her hands to warm them.

“That’s really cool,” I told Emily, envious of her fire-making ability.

She smiled. “Thanks.”Tanya rolled her eyes. “Lighting a fire is all it takes to get you revved up?”

“Well, you know—she made fire out of nothing” I mimicked what Emily had done.

“It doesn’t exactly work like that.” Emily laughed.

“It doesn’t?” I shook my head. “Seriously, this is so infuriating. I’m told nothing! I can’t even count the number of times I’ve been thrown into something, and because the angels didn’t think it was an appropriate subject to teach us, I’ve nearly lost my life! How am I supposed to know how a witch casts spells? I don’t even know what a harpy is! How is a dragon killed? That would have been useful knowledge when I was attacked by one.”

“Left forelimb,” Tanya and Emily shouted out, bursting into laughter.

“What?” I asked grimly.

“Beneath the left forelimb is a small soft area—no scales,” Emily explained.

Tanya nodded. “You stab a sword in there far enough, and that’s how you kill it.”

I glared at them. “Exactly my point. Don’t you think that is something that I should have been told? I’m part of this mystical world, and all I’m ever taught is angel stuff, which, quite frankly, is both boring and unhelpful!”

“Well, yeah. Angels have always been like that. They’ll never change. Take vamps, for example; they’re taught how to hunt their prey from a really young age,” Tanya said with sympathy in her expressive eyes. She shook her head slowly.

“Tanya, that’s a terrible example,” Emily chastised. She turned fully to me. “Witches are taught the very essence of magic from when they are children. Yes, ethics and morals are important, but power comes with the very existence of being a witch, and needs to be nourished. We would never send our children into the world without knowing every facet of our power—curses, transmutation, enchantments, exploitation-”

“Exploitation?” My jaw dropped.

“Sure,” Emily gushed. “As if we would send out our baby witches without first teaching them how to disarm and kill their enemies?”

“That’s a fair point,” I mused. “Although . . . you teach ‘baby witches’ to kill?”

“Not just witches.” Tanya joined in, turning her back to the fire. “We would never send our harpies out without knowing every weakness of likely assailants, and how to use them to their advantage.”

“That’s the difference between angels and the rest of the otherworldly factions.” Emily sighed sadly, as though it were tragic news.

Tanya nodded, grunting her agreement.

“What do you mean?” I asked. Were the angels really so different to everyone else?

“Well, besides abandoning their Nephilim children, which is definitely unusual in the mystical realm, even their fully-fledged angels don’t know about other species. They put everyone in a box, and decide this person will know this, and this person will know something else. They never give all of the information to everyone.”

“They work as a team,” I heard myself saying.

Tanya waved her hand. “Isn’t a team much stronger when all of the players know the rules?”

I stared at her blankly. I was torn. Tanya was definitely right, but I could still see the other side of it. “What about humans? They all have different jobs and different duties. They don’t all know the same information.”

“That’s humans! Their whole society is completely different to ours,” Tanya argued.

“Maybe the angels are emulating them,” I offered.

She shrugged. “it wouldn’t surprise me!”

“It’s not right, though,” Emily added. “Angel children are wrapped up in the clouds and protected by warriors. They’re rarely even allowed out of the Heavenly Realm, and could you even imagine if they dared to make friends with someone not angelic? It's strange and sad that they don't get to experience the world."

"The world is dangerous. Maybe they're just trying to protect them," I mumbled.

"Why would they protect the angels and not the Nephilim? It's very contradictory," Emily said.

I scowled. When put like that it did seem quite odd. Yes, the angels had eventually provided some semblance of safety in the likes of Haamiah and Elijah, and the provision of the safe houses, but we had all been abandoned initially. It was as though we were an embarrassing relation they tried to ignore. No, not *we*—I wasn't even a Nephilim. I was something else. Not that I would ever tell a witch and a harpy that.

"So teach me," I said. I belatedly wondered if it would have been better not to show my ignorance. I sighed; if I didn't ask anyone for assistance then how would I ever get the help I needed? Emily and Tanya were staring at me, speculation in their eyes.

"You want us to teach you *what* exactly?" Tanya asked.

I stretched my legs out in front of me. "Everything. Pretend I know nothing." *Which was pretty accurate*. "Tell me about witches and harpies, tell me how to cast spells, channel power, how to kill vampires and about the different factions of demons. Tell me which sorceresses can be trusted—"

"None," they both muttered.

"None?" I echoed, frowning. That wasn't right. The angels were in alliance with the Sorceress of Ice, and her family.

"No! *No one* can trust a sorceress. They're manipulative bitches who deserve to have their eyes ripped out and their kidneys fed to dogs," Tanya said, as Emily and I exchanged a shocked look. Tanya grimaced. "My soul mate was killed by a sorceress over a hundred years ago, so I might be a little biased, but I'm still telling the truth."

"You don't ever want to go up against a sorceress, and you don't ever want to make the mistake of trusting one," Emily said solemnly. She ran her fingers through her blond hair, detangling the long strands.

"The angels I'm with . . . they're in alliance with the Sorceress of Ice." I looked from Emily to Tanya.

"The Sorceress of Ice isn't in alliance with anyone," Tanya said.

"I swear it! I was there, I saw her." I scowled.

"Then she has some other ulterior motive. Ask anyone in the mystical world who the most untrustworthy species is and they'll tell you the sorceri."

I gulped, thinking of Sam. He'd gone with Lilura when the attack on the safe house had happened. Surely she hadn't had anything to do with it? I felt paranoid even letting myself think that. I knew her. I had seen her and Sam together, and they were mad for each other.

Oblivious to my silent conversation with myself, Tanya laughed, and said, "And the most untrusting species would be the Fallen!"

Emily laughed. "Yes! Definitely the Fallen."

"The Fallen?" My attention zeroed in again. "Why would you say that?"

"Because, just as no one can trust a Sorceress, the Fallen trust no one. Not each other, not their leaders, their children or their god—that's why they're Fallen. Fallen from grace, fallen out of their family heaven."

"You're saying they're Fallen because they don't trust anyone?" I asked.

"Yeah. So the story goes." Emily leaned in closer. "Among the witches it was told that Lucifer and a few of the others had risen up against the angelic god, and were obviously sent to Hell." She chuckled. "But all those others who had wavered in their trust of your god were sent to the human plane as Fallen Angels. They had wavered in their trust, so they were no longer welcome on the heavenly plane."

"Is that true?" I gasped. "I heard a slightly different version of events."

Emily let out a peal of laughter.

Tanya rolled her eyes. "One thing you need to learn about the otherworldly: everyone has a different version of events about everything. You'll rarely get the whole truth, but you will often get little bits and pieces—enough to come to your own conclusion. But it is true that the Fallen are the most untrusting of the otherworldly. If you ever get out of here I imagine you'll see it for yourself one day."

I thought to Aidan; he was so sweet and loving, unfailingly gentle, yet I hadn't broken his heart when I had gone back to Zach, and he hadn't even needed an explanation or an apology. *He didn't trust me*, I realized. He never thought I would stay with him. I felt incredibly guilty about that. I had proven him right. I had proven that he shouldn't done so.

Another equally, if not more important, factor was that *I* was half Fallen angel. Did I trust? No. I didn't, at least not easily. Sam, Gwen and Trev had somehow wormed their way into my heart, but I didn't trust them enough to tell them that I wasn't a Nephilim. Actually, I had no plans whatsoever to tell them, even if I ever got out of here. I wouldn't have told Haamiah, either, if he hadn't already known, and I certainly wouldn't have told that dickhead Maion.

I wouldn't tell Emily or Tanya either. As much as I felt we had camaraderie, I was sure they would somehow use it to their advantage. Or was that just my Fallen angel instinct revealing itself? I had never trusted anyone easily, always thinking the worst of people, but I had presumed and blamed it on my childhood, and on the people surrounding me. Maybe it wasn't them. Maybe it was all me. Maybe this was my wake-up call to look around and figure out that I had run out of things to blame my bad luck on, and needed to look at myself instead.

I looked up, realizing the conversation had lapsed again while I'd zoned out. I bit my lip.

"What about the valkyrie?" I asked.

"The valkyrie again?" Emily narrowed her eyes at me.

I shrugged. "I'm just curious. I didn't know they existed until a while ago, and I'm interested."

"Ugh!" Tanya grumbled. "If a harpy's existence depends on his or her ability to steal, then a valkyrie's depends on their ability to harvest. They harvest the souls of warriors to increase the strength of their God in preparation for the end of time and the final war."

"When will the final war happen?" I asked.

"Probably never." Emily laughed. "You don't see any other factions harvesting powers, do you? They probably only do it to give their odd little lives some meaning."

"I'm not following you."

"The route of all of their strength lies in their ability to harvest. Besides harvesting souls, they harvest *abilities*." Emily leaned in closer, hissing the words at me as though they were venom.

Tanya crawled closer, lowering her voice like she was telling me a ghost story. "They get close to someone and suck in their abilities. Providing they have been able to expose themselves for long enough, they then possess the same strength or ability. For that reason they are one of the most formidable enemies to have in the mystical world. You think you've got one up on them—" Tanya clapped her hands together. "—then *bam*! They can match you, strength for strength."

"So they use another person's power against them . . . that sounds kind of evil," I mumbled, thinking back to Zach's reassurances that the valkyrie weren't evil. If I remembered correctly, he had described them as sexy and mischievous, but definitely not evil. Was he just completely full of it? I watched Tanya and Emily glance at each other.

"No, they're not really evil. You can't just categorize everyone like that. You need to get out of the angel way of thinking," Tanya advised.

Emily nodded. “All species in the mystical world straddle the two boundaries. Certain elements of their powers seem evil, but they’re not,” she said. She gestured to Tanya. “Harpies steal. They lie, and cheat and steal. They would take the food right out of your hand if they could. It’s in their nature. So, if that’s all you know about them, based on your categorization you would class them as bad people. The thing is, they have to steal. The drawback of their powers is not being able to willingly take anything for themselves if it’s offered. If they didn’t steal food, they wouldn’t be able to eat it. They’d just starve to death.”

I looked at Tanya, unintentionally running my eyes over her shapely body. She didn’t look as though she was starving, and she hadn’t stolen from us . . . that I was aware of.

She smirked. “I learned the loop holes quickly.”

I blushed and turned to Emily, silently urging her on.

“The same with witches; we don’t set out to curse people, most of the time, but a girls gotta make some money to live.” She shrugged. “Most of us sell potions and spells, wards and charms, and it’s not really our business how they’re used.”

“Even if they’re used for evil? Like if someone came to you and asked for a spell to bring someone back from the dead, or to kill their enemy, would you do it?”

Emily shrugged again. “Sure, I’d warn them of the risks of it, as is my moral duty, but I’d do the spell, and charge them a hell of a lot of money for it.”

“So witches are sort of like mercenaries,” I said, uncertain if I was about to offend her.

She let out a squeal of laughter. "Yes! That is exactly it."

I smiled. "But what about the really bad witches? I met one on a werewolf plane last year. She was all with the killing and torturing. She'd held two angels prisoner for centuries."

Emily sighed and looked at me in mock sadness. "Alas, they do our reputation some damage." She grinned. "You get your rogue witches, of course, but that's the same in any faction. With angels you get the Fallen, with witches you get those few who take their magic to extremes. With valkyrie, you get one or two who go out of their way to bring down their enemies."

"Seriously, though," Tanya said, "not a lot is known about the valkyrie, they're really secretive. I doubt you'll ever even see one. I never have."

I smiled to cover my awkwardness. I was so torn. I wanted to tell them what I was, to get the inside scoop on everything to do with my heritage and powers, but at the same time, could I trust them not to turn on me?

I sighed and changed the direction of the conversation. "What about other species? Werewolves, for example."

"Ooh, sneaky four-legged fur balls," Emily hissed.

"What? I met some lovely werewolves!" I said. I grimaced and amended. "Okay, I met *one* lovely werewolf."

"Nuh-uh." Tanya shook her head. "I'm with the witch on this one. Werewolves are sly. And always with the sex! I accidentally on purpose attended one of their *gatherings*, only to find a giant orgy. It was disgusting. Now lycae . . . I could totally get on that," she purred with a sly smile and a wink.

“Lycae?” I thought back to the lycae in the Tournament. She had seemed . . . *creepy*. You know, before I beheaded her. “Aren’t they the same as werewolves, but a different breed?”

“No way! Werewolves are arrogant, selfish dogs. They turn into actual furry creatures, for heaven’s sakes. They’re total slaves to their wolfy-selves,” Tanya said. She winked. “But lycae are completely different; from their wicked cool personalities to their wolf manifestations.”

“Lycae don’t turn into soft, cuddly little wolves. They turn into ferocious beasts. Their eyes glow orange, and their bodies grow large, their fangs elongating. When their beast rises, they’re no longer in charge - the lycan is. They have two separate entities living in the same body, both with the same goal,” Emily said.

“Which is?”

“To find and protect their mate,” she answered.

“No orgies for the lycae. If any other beast dared to lay a paw on their mate they would rip them to shreds.” Tanya licked her lips. “There is no contest between a werewolf and a lycae.”

“Can lycae be trusted?’

Tanya nodded. “Definitely. When a lycae makes a promise, it’s forever. Lycae make the best allies.” Tanya nodded.

“And the best lovers.” Emily grinned wickedly.

“Okay, I hear you!” I laughed.

17

'We can't become what we want to become by remaining who we are.'

Oprah.

"So who is this Miss Elda character? She sounds suspicious," Emily said around a mouthful of apple.

For the past hour she and Tanya had been quizzing me about my past, namely before I had been told I was Nephilim. They seemed to find the whole concept of school bizarre, and my druggy problems perfectly acceptable. It certainly put a new spin on things.

In particular they thought my appointments with Miss Elda, the School Guidance Counselor, to be odd.

"She was . . . nice," I said, in response to Emily's question. "Out of everyone there, she was the only one who offered me hope that I would get out of the mess I was in."

Tanya snorted. "If that had been me, I would have told you to get rid of your parents and go have fun."

"Yeah, you should have just got rid of them," Emily agreed.

I had to know. "And by 'get rid of' you mean . . .?"

"Kill," they both said simultaneously.

I nodded, unable to hide my grin.

"You could have chopped their heads off, set them on fire. You know, stabbing them through the head would have had a poetic charm," Tanya said.

Emily took over with enthusiasm. "Yeah, honey, you could have mixed up all those potions you had."

"Drugs," I corrected.

She shrugged and continued. "You could have poisoned them, turned them into familiars, made them eat each other—although the spell for that is a little tricky, and you have to be pretty careful they don't make a try for you . . . if you know what I mean."

I watched Emily and Tanya chuckle, amazed at how different people were. In particular, the people in *my* life. I couldn't help but compare; what if Emily and Tanya had been the ones to find me and tell me about the hidden worlds? Or Aidan? Would I have been more likely to believe them? Would I have trusted them?

Actually, I surmised, I probably *would* have. I'd probably have gotten so caught up and influenced by them I would have killed my mother and Colin, left school, and never looked back. Of course I would have undoubtedly ended up here, awaiting judgment for murder. I glanced around with a sigh. It looked like, either way, I was destined to be here.

"She's not even listening." I heard. I looked up to see Emily and Tanya laughing at me.

I gave them a mock scowl. "What?"

"We were laughing at you hooking up with that angel." Tanya laughed throatily. "Bad luck that *he* found you."

I shrugged. "I'm happy he found me. It could have been a lot worse for me if he hadn't."

"Not really," Tanya refuted. "He told you what you were, dragged you away from the human world, and boom! Now you're caught up in a war between the angels and the Fallen." She shrugged. "It could have been so much better for you—imagine if the harpies had found you first, or the valkyrie, or the elves."

"Or the witches," Emily added.

Imagine indeed. I would have been so different. What if the valkyrie had found me first? Or the Fallen? Would I be somewhere, harvesting souls? Or would I be randomly killing people off, hunting down Nephilim to butcher? I would like to think that I would still be on the non-evil side of this odd world I lived in. I might not be particularly religious, but I believed in good and evil. Did I believe in God? And in that respect, if so, which one did I believe in? The valkyrie had their own god, the Fallen worshiped Lucifer, and the angels worshipped the regular one. If only I could see for myself if they existed I might be able to figure things out. Just because I was half valkyrie and half Fallen angel, did that make me evil? I wished I could meet this angelic god and ask him . . . or her, all of the questions I wanted to ask. Were beings classified as good or evil depending on what they were, or on their deeds? Now that the Thrones had locked me up for being what I was, I would have thought God thought the same—ergo throwing me firmly in the evil category.

I knew I had my faults; I could be selfish, I was impulsive, the no-sex-before-marriage thing was definitely out of the window, but was I *evil*? I wished I could ask all my questions, but never being one of those people who prayed regularly or had visions, I guessed my questions would remain unanswered. Did God even speak english? Did He speak at all? What was His purpose? Just to raise those who fell, and forgive them? The Fallen certainly weren't enjoying any of that much talked about forgiveness. Was my fate wrapped around His finger? If so, and we were actually all just following a script, then why the troublemakers—the beasts, demons and Fallen?

None of it made any sense to me. I could only hope that one day I would work out my place in this world.

18

'Inside all of us is a wild thing.'

Unknown

Aidan

"If you came to beg for our Lady's assistance in the hopeless fight for your life, you are wasting your time."

"Our Lady is not interested."

Aidan sighed. This would be more difficult than he had anticipated. It had taken days to find this place, and a lot of debts would now be owed thanks to the information he had been given leading him here. However, judging by these two arrogant beasts guarding the door, this apartment in the center of New York City was apparently exactly where he wanted to be.

As the twins turned to leave, Aidan snarled. "I have not come to beg your Lady for anything," he spat. "I have information that will be valuable to her."

The twins glared at each other, suspicion and dislike very much evident on their faces.

The first stepped forward. "What would you know that would be of any interest to our most glorious one?"

Aidan leaned in, inviting the twins to come closer. They frowned and stepped forward, turning their faces to catch his whispered words. He opened his mouth to speak then hurtled forward, cracking both of their skulls with his own. With a kick, he sent one spinning into the door, smiling as he slid to the floor. The other jumped on his back and pummeled him until he managed to shake him free.

Aidan spun around and let his fists fly, pounding the twin's face until blood spurted from his nose. Leaning forward, he sank his sharp teeth into the delicate flesh of his neck, ripping away the veins and arteries.

"What is going on out here?"

A tall, blonde Fallen angel stepped over the werewolves' unconscious bodies and strode toward Aidan. *Lilith.* She pointed to him.

"You! Who the hell are you?"

Aidan stepped forward. "I have information for you."

She smiled at him sweetly. "Really? Do tell."

Aidan glanced at the werewolves on the floor, his resolve wavering.

"Speak up, little mouse! You came here and bloodied my wolves, so you better have something interesting for me or I'll castrate you." She leaned in, grabbing his balls with an iron fist.

Aidan flinched, grimacing as she tightened her fingers.

"Your daughter's in trouble. She's being held prisoner in the Never Ending Forest." He gasped.

For a second Lilith looked surprised, something Aidan was not expecting. He was about to say something when she let go and clicked her fingers at him.

"My daughter . . . the Nephilim."

Aidan nodded quickly.

"And the Thrones have her, you say?" She narrowed her eyes at him.

Again he nodded. "Will you help her? The angels will repay you well."

She laughed throatily. "Which angels will repay a Fallen angel for saving a half Fallen hybrid?" She paused and scowled at him. "Which angels has my lusty little daughter made friends with?"

Aidan spoke quickly. "Haamiah, Elijah, Zacharael . . . I would be greatly indebted to you if you would go to her."

She cocked her eyebrow at his comment before dismissing it. "Such powerful angels. Why have they not gone to her aid?"

"They know where she is, but don't want to go against the Thrones. I imagine Zach simply wants to keep her out of Asmodeus's clutches," he said bitterly. He rubbed his forehead and sighed. "Truthfully, I do not know why they have left her there, but she's trapped with no way out. As her mother . . . will you help her?"

Lilith smiled slowly. "As her mother, it would be my duty to go to her aid."

19

'Get on your knees and pray. Then get on your feet and work.'

Gordan B. Hinckley.

Jasmine

As soon as it was light again we continued on our way to the lake. Last night's conversation had given me bad dreams, and I couldn't help the grim mood I was in now. I had followed behind Emily and Tanya silently, while they had chatted merrily, getting along well. If I weren't mistaken I would have said they were firmly BFFs now. It was nice being around them, certainly different to being in the company of the Nephilim.

"We're here," Tanya hissed.

I flinched, leaving my thoughts, and jogged over to them.

"We are?" I asked.

Tanya gestured for me to look through the branches. I leaned forward and peered through, seeing a dark, murky pool on the other side. It looked empty.

"Are you sure this is it?" I whispered.

Tanya nodded. Together we stepped carefully around the trees and approached the water's edge.

A splash made me jump. Goosebumps trailed up my arms and a shiver ran through me. I glanced at Emily, who looked terrified, and at Tanya, who merely looked apprehensive. When I looked back, a girl had appeared in the water.

The girl was beautiful; I mean jaw-droppingly, exquisitely haunting. Her eyes were crystal blue, the lightest sky with diamonds twinkling in their depths. Thick black eyelashes framed them, and strongly arched brows—she looked like a glamour model. Long blonde hair framed her face, the lengths swirling in the water beside her shoulders. Somehow the strands dried, the color lightening from a dark blond to almost golden, as soon as they left the water.

As I stared she stretched her bare, slender arms to the bank and pulled herself through the water to it. She began to rise from the water, draping her upper body across the grass, pursing her lips together with a secret smile.

As she lifted herself up, the tops of her breasts were bared—the most seductive pose I could imagine. I could only be thankful that Zach wasn't here to see this. I felt drawn to her in a way that didn't seem quite real. I almost felt as though I were dreaming; a surreal aura seemed to surround me, and the air had a shiny, barely visible glow to it.

"Jasmine!" Emily shrieked.

I blinked and looked around, shocked to realize I stood just a step away from the woman. She opened her mouth to smile, a cunning look in her eyes. I felt my eyes widen painfully as my gaze was transfixed by the glimpse of little white fangs.

I leaped back, my otherworldly strength enabling me to clear the distance I had unknowingly travelled, and I landed in a crouch just in front of Emily and Tanya, noting the girl was even further out of the water than she had been. I frowned as I took in the shimmering pink and gold of what appeared to be scales around her legs.

I spun around and gasped. “Is she . . . ?”

Tanya laughed at my expression. “A siren. Jasmine, you nearly got shredded by a *siren*!”

I nodded absently. “A siren . . . like a mermaid?”

Emily rolled her eyes. “They decided they wanted to be called mermaids because it sounds less threatening. What you’re looking at is one vicious bitch of a siren.”

I turned to look at the siren again. This time her beauty faded into the background as I properly took in the muscles in her arms, the deadly focus in her eyes as she locked onto me, and the flash of her fangs as she laughed at us before slithering silently back into the water. She sunk below the surface, her hair pooling on the watery ripples for a moment before following her into the depths.

“How are we going to get it?” I hissed out the corner of my mouth.

Emily frowned. “I don’t know.”

“We need to create a distraction,” Tanya whispered.

“Like what?” I asked. A thought occurred to me. “I could make a fire.”

Tanya grinned. “Do it.”

"Where should I aim for?"

"The bank, just there. That will make her and the rest of her them under the water, move away from us," Emily suggested.

I shook my head. "Are you planning on walking through fire to get to your crystal, then?"

She grimaced. "Maybe not."

"We can't make one on the opposite bank or either of the sides, because that will make them move closer to us."

Tanya frowned. "We need to scatter them. Can't we chuck a load of branches into the water and light it up?"

I bit my lip. "But then they would be wet. I can't make a fire out of wet branches." I looked at Emily.

She shook her head. "Not me. I can make tiny flames, one at a time—enough to make a spell or light a campfire, but not the type of explosion we need. Maybe you can do it if we stick a few branches together and make a raft."

"That might work," I agreed.

We quickly gathered up four semi-straight branches and a pile of smaller ones. Emily whispered her magic words, leaving us speechless when she somehow melded the wood together. We lay the other branches on top and carried it to the water's edge a little further round the pool. Not seeing any mermaids, we dropped the raft gently into the water, then scampered further back to where Emily had said there would be Unakite.

Emily knelt on the floor and trailed her fingers through the air in front of her. Her eyes immediately began to glow as she whispered softly. The breeze seemed to pick up at the sound of her voice, whirling around us. It seemed to locate the raft, and within no time had pushed it toward the middle of the pond.

I sighed, feeling a little nervous. I glanced around expecting the Thrones to kill me at any second. Where they watching us right now? The moment I let my magic loose, would they kill us all?

I pushed any thoughts of the Thrones and failure away, knowing that no matter what happened, I needed to do this. I concentrated on Gwen and Trev. I pulled up my power, letting it trickle down my fingertips. It stung a little, felt prickly and eager to fire off. I released it, focusing on the branches floating out ahead of us. I spotted the flicker of a flame and immediately relaxed as it traveled down the branch, jumping to each of the smaller sticks, lighting them up. Smiling now, I fed the fire little by little, not wanting it to burn up too quickly.

I let my eyes wander away from the flames, pleased when I saw the water splashing as the mermaids dived deeper away from us.

Emily knelt by the water's edge and plunged her arm in. She felt along the edge, crawling along the grassy bank until she forcibly heaved a piece of crystal out of the water and fell back. She quickly scrambled up and skipped back to us, gleefully holding out the Unakite.

It wasn't quite what I had imagined. It was a softly muddled pink and green color, no bigger than her palm. It didn't glow, it wasn't particularly sparkly, yet there it was—the missing ingredient for our spell.

I grinned at Emily, her smile infectious. Feeling deliriously happy for some reason, I followed as she and the harpy ran away from the pool and weaved their way through the trees. When they had decided we were a safe distance away they dropped to the floor. I sat beside Emily, curious how she would proceed.

Emily used her fingers to brush the leaves aside and dig a small hole in the mud, not too deep or wide. She pulled a handful of a green, mossy herb out of her bag—the Mordal—and smoothed it between her palms before laying it down like a sheet at the bottom of the hole. She whispered quietly and a flame popped up in the middle, lightly burning it, sending up a soft and unexpectedly sweet and minty smell from the herb.

She shook her bangles down her arm and stared at them for a second before slipping them all off, selecting one and returning the others to her wrist. She carefully placed it in the middle of the tiny fire. She looked up at me.

"In case they are separated you need to pick just one of them to locate."

How could I choose between Gwen and Trev? I could only pray they were together, but just in case... who had more to lose?

"Gwen," I said quietly.

Emily nodded. "We will open a pathway so we can see her first, then we'll send the directions. Maion will get clues to find her. Whether he understands them or not is out of my control."

I swore under my breath. Wasn't there anyone else I could send the directions to? Zach had said he was working on a way to have me released, Aidan didn't know anything about Gwen and Trev being missing, and I didn't know what Haamiah was doing . . . so that left Maion. He was the only one I knew for certain that was actively looking for them. Surely, he would be open to signs.

I nodded my agreement and crossed my fingers.

"*Incendia . . . creare*. Flame . . . create," she whispered.

I couldn't help but feel surprised that the spell was in Latin. Was this the reason we had been taught Latin in the safe house? Were they secretly teaching us about other species?

All three of us stared into the fire, watching the silver bangle melt quickly, creating a shiny pool on top of the Mordal. Emily picked up one dragonfly.

"*Ostensus*." Reveal. She dropped the first dragonfly onto the silver. It was quickly absorbed by the liquid.

"*Locus.*" Location. She dropped the next dragonfly in.

She dropped in the last dragonfly. "Gwen."

She picked up the Unakite and placed it where the three dragonflies had sunk into the silver, then quickly placed a strand of hair Tanya held out into the fire. Curiously, she placed just the end in, leaving the length sticking out sideways.

Emily held out her hands to us both. I watched Tanya gleefully take her hand and hold out her other hand to me. I bit my lip and took a deep breath, joining hands with them. Emily closed her eyes and inhaled the smoke drifting up from the fire, so I did the same.

When nothing happened immediately, I opened my eyes again to glance at Emily. She remained still, her eyes closed. I chewed on my lip and stared into the fire. The pink and green of the Unakite seemed to glow, luminous, changing the hue of the smoke to pink and green wisps.

As I stared, my eyes stinging, the forest seemed to fade, the colors in the fire becoming everything to me. I slowly turned my head, struggling under the weight of it, to see that Emily and Tanya were also glowing pink and green. I sucked in a breath, my chest feeling tight, and stared into the fire again, hoping I would see Gwen's location before I passed out.

I blinked, and when I opened my eyes a thick grey fog had encompassed me. I could feel my breath heavy and rasping in my head. A loud whirring noise made me feel both dizzy and sick, as though I were under water.

I forced my eyes open wide and lifted my hands to push aside the fog. I tentatively took a step forward, now seeing that Emily and Tanya stood beside me, doing the same. I refused to cower behind them and strode forward more purposefully. Gwen had to be here . . . somewhere. Would the spell take us directly to her, or would it show us on some kind of map?

My question was answered when the fog cleared somewhat and I saw Gwen, just feet away from me. She sat on the floor with her back to a thick, grey wall. She clutched her knees to her chest and she was screaming, only I couldn't hear anything besides the whirring.

My heart ached so badly for her. Gwen . . . my Gwen was so frightened. I had never seen her like this. She was so fearless and strong. Out of all of us, she seemed the only one who was confident in who she was. She was *Gwen*!

I dropped to my knees in front of her and tried to touch her. Could she see me?

"Gwen!" I shouted, my voice sounding hollow to my own ears.

There was no response. She stared right through me, almost cowering away. Emily placed her hand on my shoulder to get my attention. I looked up to see her pointing further away with a question on her face.

What I saw horrified me. The fog where Emily had pointed had cleared, and I immediately recognized the tunnels, the stone floor, the gothic archways. Gwen was in Castle Dantanian.

20

'Have no fear of perfection, for you'll never reach it.'

Salvadore Dali

I turned back to Gwen. I felt frozen. Even being here in a vision was beyond terrifying for me. The realization made me want to scream and threaten Emily, ask her to end the spell and return to the forest. The other part of me, a part that I hadn't really realized existed, wanted to desperately switch places with Gwen. I didn't want her to go through this. I knew what would happen here, and I couldn't bear the thought of the pain and terror she would have to endure.

If I hadn't been so completely devastated perhaps I would have been surprised and proud at how much I had changed. Though I had battled to change myself and change other people's perceptions of me, I still thought of myself as that girl: unworthy of anyone, unworthy of consideration. Yet here I was, wishing there was a way to exchange myself for a girl I loved.

The hand on my shoulder increased its pressure, pulling me away. I scowled at Emily, even as I realized she was concentrating on something else. She held in her palm a glowing orb. It was yellow, like a little ball of sunshine. I frowned at her, wondering what this was. She hadn't told me anything about this.

Emily blew on the orb and it fluttered, splitting into tiny yellow balls before vanishing completely. Emily mouthed something at me. I stared at her lips trying to lip read. I shook my head, saying that I couldn't understand her. As I muttered the words my gravity shifted. I fell backwards, shrieking wordlessly.

My eyes fluttered open as I crashed back onto the leaves and twigs. I gasped for breath, still feeling as if the fog was choking me. I scrambled to my feet, almost falling over Emily in the process.

"What happened?" I gasped.

Emily sat up, grinning she stretched out her arms. "The spell is complete." She pointed at the fire.

When I looked, I saw that the hair strand was completely burned. Had it acted as a timer of sorts? We only had a certain amount of time in the vision before we were kicked out?

"Did you have time to send the directions?" Tanya asked, rubbing her back.

Emily nodded and smiled. "Yep. Spell complete."

"What do we do now?" I asked.

They both looked at me in confusion.

"What do you mean?" Emily asked.

"We can't leave her there! You know where we were, right?" I said.

I flinched as lightning struck above us, my emotions rocketing high.

“It was a vision. We weren’t really there,” Tanya said, jumping to her feet. She reached down and pulled Emily up.

“We can’t leave her there,” I shrieked again.

I could feel the familiar feel of my power rotating, churning through my chest. My arms and legs felt energized and alive, ready to explode. I fidgeted, rubbing my fingers against each other even as I paced.

“We can’t leave her there,” I repeated.

“Easy.” Tanya held up her hand, shooting a worried glance at Emily.

“We did what we set out to do. We sent the directions to Maion. He’ll find her, I’m sure of it,” Emily soothed.

I laughed throatily. “Maion? Maion will find her? He wouldn’t help his own mother. He’s an evil son of a bitch, and if I ever see him again I’m going to rip him apart.”

Flashes of his mouth smirking at me, his eyes scowling and ridiculing me, the way he frowned at Zach in disapproval whenever he saw us together all zoomed through my mind, demanding attention. It was just fuel to the fire. I screamed in anger, building my power higher and higher until the ground shook, trembling beneath me. Wind whipped around us, throwing up the leaves and branches, toppling the trees. I shrieked louder, clasping my head in my hands as the sky split over and over, seeming to be influenced by my mood.

Tanya reached me first, grabbing my shoulders, screaming something at me. I snarled and punched her, knocking her to her knees before kicking as hard as I could, sending her flying through the air, through the trees. I turned to Emily who was approaching me. She held her hands up as her eyes glowed green. The air around me suddenly felt thick, like I was trying to walk through jelly. I couldn't move.

I thrashed and screamed, bellowing my revenge. My revenge made me hot, hotter than ever before, and I felt the smoke encompass me as I tried to burn a hole through the spell Emily was casting.

Sense was slow in coming, but when I realized what I was doing I tried to rein the rage in, sucking it back inside where I could leash it. If only I had my ring this wouldn't have happened. No, I couldn't rely on a ring forever. This was my fault. The rage and anger was already inside me, and I had let it out without thinking.

I stopped struggling, and when the spell lapsed I fell to my knees, swaying as I stared up at Emily and Tanya as they approached me cautiously. I wouldn't stop them. I knew what they would do now.

I closed my eyes, and waited for them to end me.

"Get up stresshead." Tanya laughed.

I opened my eyes, one at a time, and frowned at them as they towered over me, smiling.

"What are you doing?" I whispered hoarsely.

"It's late; we need to find somewhere to sleep. I'm thinking we want to move on from here, seeing as these trees are likely to collapse any second now." Emily grinned.

"I tried to kill you," I gasped. I couldn't understand it. Any time I had done something like this before, everyone had gone running for the hills.

"So?" Tanya asked, shrugging. "Everyone has a few murderous moments in their lifetime."

I stared at Emily, openmouthed.

She tilted her head toward me. "Don't worry about it, Jasmine. Actually, it was quite fun."

"I hit you," I snapped at Tanya. "I hit you and kicked you, and you're seriously going to stand there and tell me it's fine?"

Tanya groaned. "Party police alert! You can tell you've been living with the angels too long. So what if you let rip a little?"

"My letting rip means you two almost died," I screeched. I couldn't understand it. Why were they reacting like this?

Tanya snorted. "Yeah, right. As if you could take us both. And that kick . . . pfft! That was just a love tap!"

I paused. Was she being serious?

"We can argue about who could take who later. For now, we need to find somewhere safe to camp." Emily turned away and began to plod through the trees. She called over her shoulder, "And neither of you could have taken me."

I staggered to my feet and mindlessly followed the witch, Tanya trailing behind me. I felt *lost*. They genuinely didn't care that I had just attacked them. This was different. Instead of being angry and casting me off they simply argued over who could have beaten who. I couldn't help but compare it to my friends, who would have been appalled at my behavior. My letting rip like that was akin to having a toddler tantrum. The angels would have been cross, Zach would probably have been embarrassed, and Maion would have used it as a reason to kill me. Yet a witch and a harpy, two beings that were supposed to be my enemies, didn't think twice about it. It was a non-issue for them. How could that be possible? Could a witch and a harpy be more understanding than angels? Or was it just the different lifestyle? Emily and Tanya had lived among other species for so long they were used to it—but then, so had the angels, so why didn't they feel the same? It was just too much for my brain to figure out.

I grimaced and let it slide from my mind for now. I concentrated on feeling relieved that the spell had worked, and refused to consider the possibility that Maion wouldn't find Gwen. He would find her and Trev, and Zach would find a way to get me out of here, and then everything would be fine.

I listened to Emily and Tanya banter about who would kill who until they found a place to stop for the night, then I curled up nearby, feeling like I had found where I belonged for the first time in my life, here among two people I was supposed to abhor.

21

'There is something beautiful about having the chance to rewrite your future.'

Crystal Gentilello.

I woke up with a jump. The weirdest feeling came over me, as though someone was watching me, as though there were eyes peering at me through the dark. I pulled myself into a sitting position and glanced at Tanya and Emily. It was so dark I could only make out the faint outline of their bodies.

I blew out my breath and grumbled to myself as I realized my need for a toilet. What I wouldn't give for an actual bathroom. Or a shower, and a change of clothes, for that matter. It was a good job I suited the grunge look, as I seemed to spend a lot of my time dirty.

I stood up and quietly tiptoed away from the others, looking for a sheltered place. I breathed a sigh of relief as I peed and quickly pulled my jeans up afterward, heading back toward our campsite.

I whipped out my dagger as I made out a shadowy figure sitting against a tree trunk only a couple of meters away. The dark figure remained relaxed, uncaring that I was pointing my weapon at it. I could make out its legs, stretched out in front and crossed at the ankles. As I peered closer I noticed it also holding a dagger, tossing it from one hand to the other, while the moonlight jumped off in glints.

"Well, Sleeping Beauty finally woke up . . . and might I say, what an interesting conversation! Aren't you just full of surprises?" a male voice asked in a soft, lilting accent.

"What are you talking about?" I hissed. I allowed my eyes to leave him and search the shadows around us, looking for someone else.

"Your *mother*, dear," he said, the trace of a smile playing on his lips.

I began to feel sick. What had he heard? "What do you know of my mother?"

"Only what you told me," he whispered, as if confiding a secret.

"I didn't tell you anything," I said, my voice shaking. Nausea threatened to choke me. No one could know who I was. I didn't want *anyone* to know.

Black eyes flashed in front of me, deep, commanding and angry.

"Run," Zach's voice echoed through my mind.

I blinked quickly, and continued to stare at the creature in front of me. I placed one food behind me gently, testing him, unsure if I could get away. I could try to fight him. I would probably win. If I unleashed my rage, I could kill him. Only, would I also kill myself? I had no control over anything when I did that. I wasn't even myself then. Jasmine ceased to exist and some evil, horrible creature took over my actions.

"Ah—ah—ah," he warned, noticing my movement. "I wouldn't do anything so silly as try to run from me. You'll just get me . . . *excited*."

"Who *are* you?" I demanded. I reached down for my power, feeling comforted by the familiar surge as it began to flood my veins.

The creature jumped to his feet and held up his hand to stop me as I stepped back. "My apologies. My name is Salvatore." He bowed at the waist, his eyes never leaving mine. "And you are . . . ?"

"Nobody," I replied instantly.

Now that Salvatore was standing out of the shadows I could make him out a little clearer. He had the same tall, broad build that the angels had, with masses of tattoos covering his body. Symbols, pictures and words coated every inch of skin I could see. His hair seemed to be dark in color, and hung loose around his face.

"That's not true though, is it?" He chuckled.

"What are you?" I questioned. The list of creatures he could be ran through my mind, one after the other; Fallen angel, vampire, elf, warlock, berserker . . . with his carefree attitude and dangerous demeanor, I was betting vampire.

"Well that's a little personal, don't you think?" He laughed.

I scowled at him. "You seem to know personal things about me."

"Ah, yes! I know your mother's name . . . " he said slowly, his eyes seeming to narrow on me, waiting for a reaction.

"I don't know what you're talking about," I said angrily, more than a little bit terrified. *"What are you?"*

He sighed. "I'll humor you, for now. I'm Grigori," he answered, stepping forward.

"You can't be," I breathed, shocked.

A million things raced through my mind. How could someone like him be an angel? Grigori were the watchers, the observers of the realms who reported any concerns back to the Principalities. This angel felt *evil*...he felt like one of the Fallen. If the likes of him were Grigori then how could I ever trust in the angels again?

"You're Fallen," I whispered, the tremor in my voice evident.

I was aware that some Fallen angels became Grigori to repent for their sins and to earn forgiveness by being the angelic lackeys, but evil seeped from him. If he had been chosen to be a Grigori then what was he doing here in the waiting room? What had he done to be sent *here*, among the vampires and witches, while awaiting his judgment? Was there another reason for his presence in the Never Ending Forest? Had someone sent him? Asmodeus?

I was suddenly very aware of being alone with him. I stepped back once, gauging his reaction then whirled around and bounded through the trees, shouting at the top of my voice for Emily and Tanya. Screw being quiet; we had clearly already been found.

I felt a blow to my back and screamed as I flew forward, landing on my face in a wet, sticky mess. My cheek stung as I felt blood dribble down my cheek. I scrambled to my knees, desperately trying to get my feet under me even as the world was spinning. I needed to be upright to protect myself, and I needed to locate my dagger from wherever I had dropped it. I groaned as Salvatore planted one boot in the middle of my back and forced me to the ground again with a sickening thud. I heard something crack, and agony spread through my sternum. In the split second that followed I thanked God for my supernatural ability to heal quickly.

"What do you want?" I screamed. I tried to move again, but felt as though my body would snap in half from the weight of his foot bearing down on me. The pressure he exerted was so excruciating, white flecks mixed with the grey in my eyes, making the little I could see one mass of grey.

I spun onto my back as a kick to my side flipped me over. Another kick to my head rendered me useless. My stomach heaved as I fought to remain conscious. Another slap across my face and I felt my eyes roll back, leaving me helpless and clinging on to the very edge of consciousness. I cringed as I felt the thud of Salvatore dropping to his knees beside me. I felt the sickly sweet smell of his breath as he leaned close to my face, trailing his fingers down my cut cheek.

As his fingers left my cheek and ran down my jaw to my neck, I began to shake in terror. This couldn't be happening. I was strong. I was powerful. No one could hurt me. I had sworn it to myself. I tried to move, only succeeding in turning my head, which again threatened to knock me over the edge into nothingness. I trembled as he ran his fingers down across my chest, gently squeezing my breast. I heard him chuckle to himself as he ran his hands along the bottom of my T-shirt and freed my breast from the cup of my bra, tweaking my nipple into a point.

I was desperate to kill him. I needed his hands off me. I coughed and spluttered, the only answer to my efforts blood running freely from my mouth.

His hands left my chest and began to caress me through my jeans. I groaned and rolled my eyes back, almost praying to fall unconscious so that I wouldn't have to go through this again. The pressure as his fingers worked me was sickening. Each touch made me want to scream and rage, as much from the disgust of having him touch me as the thought of being helpless once again. After Asmodeus, I had promised myself that I would never again be at someone's mercy.

Salvatore stripped my jeans down to my knees, and the jolt set off agony through my ribs again. He gripped the side of my panties and ripped, instantly sliding his hand in between my thighs and forcing too many fingers inside.

I was crying openly now; sobbing, wordlessly for Emily and Tanya. I didn't even care if someone saw me in such a compromising position. Before, I would have been disgusted if anyone saw me so weak and helpless, but now I just wanted it to stop.

Salvatore leaned close to me, his weight pressing me into the dirt, rocks digging into my back.

"Your friends are dead. I ripped them apart before they even knew what was happening," he whispered, his voice laden with glee.

The fingers inside of me were suddenly ripped away. The cool air touched me as a savage snarl filled my ears. I closed my eyes and held myself still, certain this would be the end. He was going to kill me. I was so certain I would never see Zach again. I hadn't achieved anything in my short life, only failures, again and again. Instead of the strong, confident warrior woman I pictured myself to be, here I was; trembling, crying like a coward with my eyes pinched shut, as though I were afraid of the dark. There were so many things I had yet to do. So many things I hadn't asked, and hadn't said. I wanted to know who my father was. I wanted to know if I had family out there looking for me. I wanted to know if Sam would end up with Lilura, and if Gwen and Trev would be safe. I wanted to know if Maion regretted what he had said. I wanted to know if Zach really loved me. *Zach.* I even wanted to know what Pete, Nate, Abbey and Pricilla were doing, and if anyone had taught Jayden a lesson yet. I wanted to know where my fake-mother and Colin were.

Nothing happened. I forced my eyes open, as wide as I could make them. Even the slight movement of my head made me quickly shut my eyes again, as the world spun above me.

When the nausea passed, I looked around. I pulled myself into a sitting position, and, swaying, I reached to the side, dragging my body across the mud. I winced as I slid over rocks and sharp sticks. All the while I could hear sheer savagery just steps away. Ripping, cracking, snarls; I had no idea what was happening, but I knew that I needed to get far away from both the Fallen angel and from whatever he was fighting with. I presumed he had lied about Tanya and Emily being dead and I hoped that we would be able to escape while the beast he fought with hopefully killed him.

I had barely moved a couple of meters when the noises stopped. I knew I was in trouble when I heard the thump of footsteps moving toward me. As a figure emerged from the darkness and loomed over me, I ignored the agony in my body and lurched forward, striking out with my fists. I lunged closer, biting down hard on what I thought was an arm as it crossed over me.

I screamed around the flesh then sunk my teeth deep, trying to imitate a crocodile clamp. I felt blood fill my mouth but I guzzled it, determined to inflict as much pain as I could. A finger slipped between my lips and pried my mouth open, dislodging the grip my teeth had on the flesh.

“Jasmine, stop,” a familiar voice said urgently.

I looked up, finally recognizing the shadowy face before me. *Zach*. My angel. *The love of my life*. Relief flooded through me with such intensity it bordered on pain, mingling with the aches already present in my body. It was closely followed by shame and humiliation.

"I'm sorry," I sobbed, shaking as I rested my head on his chest. "I'm sorry, I'm sorry, I'm sorry."

Zach slid his arms around me and lifted me off the ground, safely cocooned in his arms. He turned with me and headed through the trees. Each step he took jolted me just enough to make my ribs throb.

"Why are you sorry?" he asked softly.

I pressed my face into his neck, inhaling his fresh, manly smell. "For everything."

"You have nothing to be sorry for. This wasn't your fault. I should have been here," he replied.

"No!" I argued. I wanted to lift my head and look into his eyes so he would know that I'd meant what I said. "This is my fault. Everything I do just turns into a mess."

"Like what?"

"*Everything*." I sniffed. "Right from the very beginning. Opening portals, getting so angry I don't know what I'm doing, never thinking about the consequences. I'm still the girl you hated, right back at the beginning of all of this. I haven't changed."

Zach stopped and nudged me gently so that I faced him. "I *love* the girl I first met. I just didn't understand her at the time. I don't want you to change or be anyone other than who you are. I fell in love with *you*, not some fantasy girl you've made up."

"I'm no good for you," I whispered against his cheek. "When they find out what I am . . . "

He turned his face so that his lips weren't even a centimeter away from my own. "They can't do anything. I love you. You love me. No matter what anyone else says—that is the truth. So you can be as angry as you want. You can level cities with your rage, or open a thousand portals if you need, but I'll still find you every time."

22

'You can do anything but not everything.'

David Allen.

Zach held me for only a few minutes then told me he had to leave before the Thrones zoned in on him. I didn't ask him to take me with him. I knew what the answer would be. I simply bit the inside of my cheek and kissed him goodbye.

I forced myself back to where Tanya, Emily and I had camped. By now I knew they were dead. They had to be. I had screamed, shouted and begged for help and they hadn't come. If they had been able to, they would have.

Now I was alone. Completely alone.

Seeing their motionless shapes on the ground side by side, I stepped closer, dropping to my knees between them. Emily's glassy eyes stared up at me, unseeing. Her throat was slit, the ground soaked with her blood. My heart turning to stone, I looked at Tanya, noticing the same red line across her neck. As my mind began to spiral in to despair, an overwhelming urge to scream swelling in my throat, I closed my fingers into my hands tightly, digging my nails deep enough to draw blood. The pain seemed to center me, giving me something to hold to, to feel.

Keeping my body taught and my mind blank I stooped to pick up the bag of nuts and seeds Emily had collected, and the dagger

Tanya still held in her fist. I couldn't stay there long as the smell of blood would undoubtedly attract any demons for miles around. Though I hated leaving their bodies there uncovered, I knew that the Thrones would take care of them at some point. They would clean up the mess and pretend it had never happened.

When I thought of the years the two of them had wasted here, just waiting . . . I wanted to weep. I wanted to scream and shout and rage, but I knew if I let my anger go I wouldn't come back from it. So I bottled it up, kept swallowing the lumps in my throat with every curse that came through my mind. I took Emily's bangles and the long thin necklace she wore, and I pulled a plain gold band from Tanya's finger, determined that if I ever got back to the human plane I would find their families and return them. I had to do something, here where I was so helpless and trapped; I needed to focus on something I could do.

I swore as I pushed too closely through a patch of thick trees and scratched a layer of skin off my arm. I pushed the strap of the bag further up my arm and took a deep breath, ignoring the anger that already swirled inside me.

What was I doing? Was I now doomed to live like Emily? Alone, here for a hundred years? Was that my fate? Surely not. Surely, someone would get me out of here.

I scowled and kicked a rock, sending it flying through the trees. No, I wasn't the type of girl to rely on someone else to save her. Not anymore. I would save myself. I would. Yes I had won the tournament, I had trained and sparred and learned everything I could. I followed their rules and toed the line, but they still didn't trust me, as evidenced by my being here.

I was trapped because the angels that were supposed to look after me didn't think I could handle the abilities I had been given. I would never forget the look that Haamiah and Maion had given me when they'd found out I had taken the Star Mist. They were horrified at the thought that I had even more power. The thought of messed-up Jasmine, all juiced up and ready to go, was apparently worse than facing an army of Fallen angels. Were they right? Maybe then. Maybe even a long time ago, but I was different now, and none of them could see it. They couldn't see the girl who had gone from nothing, from less than nothing, to a warrior, a force to be reckoned with. As much as I had wanted them to see an ally to help fight in the war against evil, a fellow fighter to knock back the Fallen . . . they only saw what they expected to see.

I used to bite my tongue and hold in my words when I was around any of them, too scared to make a mess of things and have them deny me the home I had become used to. I was so scared of being alone again I had done my best to embrace my brother, only to have him throw my help back in my face. I had let them push me so far as to risk my life just in the hope that they would see me, and give me some appreciation for who I was and what I had become, but each time I did anything it seemed to set me further and further apart from everyone. I stood for nothing and no one stood for me. Even Zach was on the fence. I knew he loved me, but I also knew that given the choice between me, or his friends, he would choose them. In my head I could even forgive that; they had been around a lot longer than I had, that was for sure, and it wouldn't be so bad if they all liked me. But Maion was the problem. He was the big fat rock sitting right in my way. His opinion counted a lot to Zach, probably more than anyone else's, definitely more than mine. Was it wrong for me to want someone to put me up higher than anyone else? Was that what I had unknowingly signed up for by agreeing to marry an angel?

Did I have a choice now, and even if I did, would I change my decision? If only I knew more about him. He was so reticent to tell me anything deep about his life. He had been alive for a thousand years, there had to be some dark secrets he was hiding. There was so much I wanted to know. So much that would let me really know him. We had an intense connection and I could tell that our souls craved each other. Our hearts were already entwined, but what about our heads? Logically he certainly wouldn't be gaining anything by loving me. As a half valkyrie and half Fallen angel I shouldn't want anything to do with him—I should be running in the opposite direction.

Would telling me his secrets really change anything? Would it make me feel more wanted or more connected to him? I had always wanted to know why he hated me so much when we had first met. He had loathed me. I freely admit I wasn't the most wonderful of people back then, but he had hated me. Why? When he didn't even know me, why would he hate me? Unless it wasn't me he hated but the fact he thought I was a Nephilim? He hadn't been the friendliest angel toward any of the Nephilim, but what had they done to him? Had some Nephilim broken his heart a long time ago? Had someone betrayed him?

I shook my head, I was sure I was going along the right track, but I just didn't have it. A thought came zinging into my brain. I could see his past if I wanted to. I could see the answer to the secrets he hid from me.

I grinned, elation flooding through me. I knew the ingredients for the spell. Why couldn't I just change the focus? Emily had completed the spell to send Maion the directions to find Gwen and Trev. She had said to do that she had to see into the past and follow their tracks. She had seen their past. Couldn't I do the same to Zach, and see his past?

I mentally brushed the dust off myself, now having a goal set out in front of me. I needed to get more ingredients. I had the silver and I had a supply of Mordal in the bag, but I needed more Unakite, harpy hair and dragonflies. With nerves fluttering in my stomach I turned and ran back to where I had left Emily and Tanya. I reached them just in time. As I leaned down and swiped some strands of hair from the Harpy, their bodies began to shimmer. I leaped back, my heart in my mouth as I threw myself behind a tree, peeping out to see what magic was happening.

To my shock their bodies grew brighter and brighter, as though stars were glittering away inside of them . . . until they disappeared. I bit my lip and choked back a sob, more determined than ever to get their jewelry back to their families, sans one silver bracelet, and I rushed off through the forest toward the lake.

I ran as fast as I could, sprinting through the trees. My sense of direction steered me well, and before the day was through I had skidded to a halt at the edge of the lake. I dropped to my knees and concentrated. I could hear the light buzzing all around me, I could tell my prey were everywhere. I sat still and concentrated on slowing my breathing, drawing my fire to me. I could feel the tingling at the tips of my fingers and kept it there, waiting.

I quickly sent a spark out, smiling victoriously when one small blue dragonfly dropped into the water just at the edge where I sat. I quickly scooped it out and set it on the ground next to me, concentrating on the next one. Before long I had all three dragonflies packed away in the bag and I was jogging off towards the mermaid pool. This would be the most difficult part.

I arrived at the pool just before nightfall, though I certainly wouldn't get a beautiful sunset. The sky had dimmed, leaving the forest in cold shadows. I tried to follow the exact route Tanya had taken us and managed to do pretty well not to fall in. By the time I reached the water's edge I was shivering, and wracked with nerves.

I peered down into the water, looking for ripples or changes in the flow of the water, or for the sound of waves. It seemed to be still, the water calm. I squatted down by the edge and slowly slid my hand in, feeling around the edge until I touched the cold crystal. I ran the tips of my fingers over it, trying to find something to hold on to so I could heave it out of the water.

I shrieked as something cold clamped onto my wrist, trying to drag me in. Thankfully the bank held firm when I lunged back with the Unakite trapped between my fingers, pulling my attacker out of the water with me. I set my skin alight, forcing the flames to scorch the hand that held on despite the water running down my arm in little streams. With a scream the mermaid dropped down, back into the water with a splash.

I gasped, panting, my heart so panicked it send shards of pain through me with each beat.

"What do you want, creature?" a voice snarled from further back in the pool, somewhere in the deeper shadows.

I sucked in a breath and lifted my chin up high. "Nothing," I said. I let myself smirk as I opened my fist. "I've already got what I came for."

I staggered away from the pool and forced myself to jog for a good couple of hours afterwards. Those mermaids . . . they were a thousand times more spine-chilling than any of the other demons I had come across. It could be because they were so beautiful, so innocent looking. Or maybe because in my human life I had always thought of them as good, sweet and friendly mystical creatures, not evil beasts that tried to hypnotize you then drag you down into their murky pool so they could drown you and eat you.

I shuddered at the thought. *Creepy.*

By the time I felt safe enough to stop running it was so dark I couldn't see a thing. I knelt down by the base of a tree and leaned back, catching my breath. I arched my back, feeling my bones crack, leaving me numb. I briefly considered putting off the spell until morning, but the same part of me that was bitterly angry about the mistrust that the angels had shown persuaded me to set out the ingredients and begin.

As Emily had done, I dug a little hole in the dry dirt in front of me, pushing aside dry leaves and twigs. I pulled out the Mordal and spread it flat. Pulling up my power, I cupped a small flame in the palm of my hand, nudging it until it travelled down my index finger to jump on to the herb. It caught fire slowly, sending out a gorgeous, minty aroma. I dropped one of Emily's silver bangles into the center.

"*Incendia . . . creare*. Flame . . . create," I whispered, sending power into the flames.

I watched the silver begin to melt, shiny droplets dribbling down the edge of the bangle to form a small pool on the Mordal. It took some time, perhaps a little slower than when Emily had done the spell, but eventually the bangle melted completely and the small pool of silver took on a cloudy, sparkling sheen. The sparkle was new . . . but I shrugged it off, presuming it had come from the difference between Emily's and my power.

I picked up one slightly singed dragonfly. This would be the most difficult bit. I needed to pick the right combination of words, and my Latin was limited to the few lessons the angels had given us in the safe house. Which three would get me the result I needed? I couldn't do this spell again. Just the thought of going back to the mermaid swarm made me nauseas.

I blew out a long breath to calm my nerves.

"*Ostensus*." Reveal. I dropped the first dragonfly onto the silver, watching as it began to sink as it was sucked under.

"*Apsconditum*." Secrets, I hissed, dropping the next dragonfly.

I paused for a second, searching my memory for the word I needed. I had two options on the tip of my tongue. What would get me the best answer? What would make the biggest difference? I closed my eyes and thought of Zach with desperation. Was he loyal to me? Though he had secrets, was he still mine? Was he lying about something to protect me, or was he working on his own agenda?

"*Amor*," I whispered quietly. Love . . . I needed to see any secrets he had that affected our love. I had no doubt that he loved me, so I was certain it would show me what I wanted.

I reached into the fire with the Unakite and placed it on top of the three dragonflies on the silver, then placed the end of one single strand into the fire and lay it sideways.

"*Patefeci*," I said, quite calm now.

I leaned forward, inhaling the herbal smoke that spiraled up toward me. The flames dimmed sharply, glowing red. I stared down, ready to accept whatever I saw.

At first the red flames were simply reflected in the cloudy silver platter now forming. The colors from the dragonflies had set a green and blue hue to the silver, while the Unakite glittered in the middle. I continued to stare, knowing it would happen soon. I took normal breaths, determined not to overdo it.

The world was gone, and I felt naked. I looked down at my hands, seeing that my body now existed in a ball of pure energy. There was no flesh, no bones or clothes, only a dense, shimmering shadow where my body should be. My head felt swirly, as though I was drunk, or maybe high. I fought down the nausea that caused an acid burn in my stomach and forced my tilting body to stand straight, looking ahead. I narrowed my eyes, unable to see clearly through the white cloud I seemed to be in. It was difficult to make out any shapes at all, let alone reveal Zach's secrets. Had I done the spell wrong? I had imitated Emily's actions. Maybe she was just better at this than I was.

I took a step forward, the ground rolling beneath my feet. I reached out and parted the cloud, distracted by the white wisps that trailed through my fingers, barely tangible. I took a shallow breath. It sounded so loud in my head. I could hear everything, from the pounding of my heart, to the movement of each individual hair on my arm, the soft squishing noise when I blinked, and the roar as I took a breath.

I heard whispers ahead, and my resolve cemented. I strode forward, as quick as I could on this unsteady ground. I stopped when I saw Zach. He was . . . Zach. Everything else melted away. I could barely sense the cloud, and the rolling floor was no longer a problem for my balance. I stared at him, taking too long to realize he was embracing someone. A woman. *Not me.*

She was exquisite. She pulled away from him and began to spin, dancing around him slowly. She looked like a princess . . . like an angel. She wore a fitted light blue dress that touched the floor and swirled around her as she turned. Sparkling black hair shot out all around her.

She could be anyone, I reminded myself as jealousy crept up on me. I focused on listening to what they were saying.

“Darling you look beautiful, and you are mine,” I heard him say.

My stomach dropped and I heaved, my body protesting what I was seeing. How could this be? He had sworn that I was his soul mate. Was this what I had felt all along? Was this the secret I had known existed but had been too scared to ask him about? How long ago was this? Was this recent? Zach didn’t look any different, but then, he would never age.

Who was she?

I could do nothing but stare as she laughed and spun around him, their words blurring into the fog. I crushed my hands to my face, trying to regain my focus. Love. I had wanted the spell to show me secrets of Zach’s love, only I had thought it would show me secrets involving me . . . not another woman Zach loved.

The vision pulled away from me.

"No!" I shouted. "It's not finished. I need to see more!"

My voice was thin and wavering. I sounded as though I was speaking underwater. My voice seemed to echo around my head, and I knew they couldn't hear me. I swayed as the ground rolled and I lost my step, falling to the floor. I kneeled on all fours, closing my eyes tightly until the wave stopped.

I looked up. This time, the cloud was less prominent. I could see much more clearly. I could see Zach. I stepped forward, my feet taking me to him this time. I frowned as I got closer, seeing the blood all across his bare chest. He had wounds, two great cuts across his stomach, but there was too much blood on him for it to just be from them.

I turned around, only now realizing there was an army at my back. I shivered as I surveyed the host of warrior angels. Holding swords, axes and maces, up high, they bellowed at something in the distance, screaming their defiance. Each one was similarly coated in blood. What had they killed? What had they been fighting for?

I frowned up at Zach, sad that he couldn't see me, and turned away, walking as though in a trance toward the other angels. I slid past them, surprised that not a single warrior jostled me, and stopped when I reached the last one. I took a side step and stared, transfixed on the sight before me.

People . . . hundreds, no thousands of people lay dead or dying on the grass. Their blood seeped out on the seemingly endless fields in front of me.

Nephilim.

I froze. Even my heart seemed to stop beating. I felt nothing. I didn't know what to think. I turned and ran through the crowd, all of the angels seeming to conveniently move out of the way so that I didn't touch them. I reached Zach, howling in frustration as I recognized Maion standing beside him. I slid in between them, touching Zach's face, begging him to see me. Whatever was happening, he needed to stop. I needed to know if this was the past, present or future.

"Zach!" I wailed. My voice echoed. Nothing.

Zach leaned right through me and clasped Maion to him. I shuddered and stepped aside.

"We'll kill every last one, friend," Zach said.

Maion nodded, seeming as furious and vicious as always. "We will rid every realm of these Nephilim scum."

As my blood turned to ice, Zach nodded. "I promise, brother . . . every last one will die."

I heaved again as the cloud rushed to the fore, hiding them from view. Yet again I was ensconced in white mist. I staggered, and looked down at the floor in the hope it would stop the ground from reeling.

This time, the vision that was revealed was of Zach and Haamiah talking with someone. Another beautiful angel. I rolled my eyes. The clouds parted further and another male angel was revealed. They were talking . . . no, arguing. I smiled with relief when I saw Zach catch the woman by the throat. At least he wasn't embracing this one. I leaned in and focused on his words, the wisps of sound just reaching me.

“Where is she?” Zach yelled. I prayed he was talking about me, and not the black-haired beauty I had seen him with in the first vision.

The woman smiled at him. The smile on her lips didn’t reach her eyes, however. My instinct told me immediately she wasn’t to be trusted. “If she is your soul mate, shouldn’t you be able to find her yourself?”

Their words faded in and out, making it impossible to understand. I saw Haamiah open his mouth, seeming to also argue with the female angel. That surprised me; what could she be saying to shock the annoyingly chilled out Haamiah?

“But she will be. All Fallen angels are evil—you know this. Forget her.” I heard the female hiss.

I shuddered. They must be talking about me. Did this mean Zach was on my side? That he was looking for a way to help me?

Zach turned to Haamiah and glared. “Now we do things my way.”

I was knocked back off my feet. I screamed as the vision seemed to shake, throwing me from side to side. All of a sudden another one appeared, shooting toward me through the cloud.

I gasped and kneeled up. Aidan. Aidan was there, fighting with two werewolves. The fight seemed to be on high speed—it was over in seconds. A moment later I could see the faint outline of a woman. I had no trouble in seeing her grasp Aidan by the balls. I cringed, flinching as I saw the grimace on his face.

“She’s being held prisoner in the Never Ending Forest,” I heard him say weakly.

Their voices faded in and out. I groaned in frustration. What was Aidan doing?

“Which angels will repay a Fallen angel for saving a half Fallen hybrid.” I heard the soft words.

I saw the pain in Aidan’s eyes as he begged, “Will you help her?”

I was thrown backwards with such force I thought I would be sick. Hitting the ground, I heard cracking of the rocks beneath me, the rustle and crack as leaves and twigs were pulverized.

I opened my eyes and sucked in a deep breath. I was back in the forest. I scrambled to my feet to look at the red fire that had begun the spell. The hair strand was fully seared, now no more than a little line of ash. The fire was no longer red, but had died down until barely an ember glowed.

I sat back and stared at it. What should I do now?

23

'You have one life in which to do everything you'll ever do. Act accordingly.'

Colin Wright.

I had passed out by the embers, waking up in the early morning feeling groggy and despondent. Zach hated Nephilim. Zach had another woman. I just didn't know what to think. There was too much going on. All I could think was that I shouldn't have done the spell. Was that cowardly?

Twigs cracked behind me. I leaped up from the ground and turned.

"Oh my God!" I screamed, my heart pounding in a heady mixture of relief and excitement. "What the hell are you doing here?"

Gwen's chocolate brown eyes closed for a brief second before she ran to me, throwing herself in my arms. Almost suffocating me, she wrapped her arms around my shoulders and buried her face in my neck. Her body trembled as she squeezed.

I glanced over her shoulder. I couldn't see Trev anywhere. If they had disappeared or been taken together shouldn't he be here with her? What had happened to them?

Anxiety began to course through my veins and I stroked Gwen's hair, shushing her.

"Gwen, what happened? Tell me," I pleaded.

She pulled back from me and ran her hands across her face, wiping away the tears that soaked her cheeks. I could barely believe this was the same person. She seemed . . . *changed*. Her usually thick, glossy dark brown mane hung in lank unwashed strands down her back. An ugly purple bruise covered her jaw and what appeared to be purple finger marks dotted her neck. She wore her own clothes, but they were ruined beyond repair, only fit for burning.

Wide eyed, I asked again, "What happened to you?"

Silent, she turned her back to me and staggered away, falling to her knees a near the trunk of a tree. She began to sob anew.

I froze in place. My emotions were warring with my mind. I couldn't form one complete thought. The name Asmodeus kept flashing in front of me. It had to have been him; it just had to. What had he done to Gwen? If she had survived what I had gone through, would she be changed like I was? Was she damaged irrevocably? Never to be the same fierce yet sensual Gwen? And what of Trev? The fact that he wasn't here could only be bad news. If Gwen had escaped or been rescued then Trev should have been right there alongside her. They were inseparable, best friends . . . and more?

A cold shiver ran through me. What if Gwen was here as a spirit? I shook the thought away uneasily. What would Gwen ever have to atone for, to be judged for? She was the sweetest, kindest girl I had ever met . . . if she was dead she would go . . . elsewhere.

In my heart I could only presume that Trev was dead, and Gwen had somehow been rescued. After all, as Maion had said, "No one escapes from Dantanian." The thought that I would never see Trev again blew me away. How could his angel mother allow him to be harmed?

I forced myself to crouch beside her as she curled herself over, her face buried in her knees as she keened softly.

"Gwen, I don't know for certain what happened to you, but you have to tell me where Trev is. I need to know," I whispered, my voice shaking.

She took some deep breaths in and lifted her chocolate gaze to mine. "I don't know. I was trying to escape, I ran into the tunnels . . ."

My mind blanched at the memory of those tunnels, where I had found Zach half-dead, tortured and hanging from chains. The stench of blood and death and rot.

"We were separated early on," she continued. "He was somewhere else, and I was . . . " Her breath hitched. "There was something going on up in the castle, and they were distracted. They left me alone and I ran. I remember you telling me about the dungeons where you found Zach, and I thought that if I could find my way there then I could find him."

"Did you?" I asked when she paused.

She shook her head. "I did, and I didn't. It wasn't *him,*" she whispered.

"What do you mean?"

Her face crumbled, tears beginning to streak down her cheeks again. I lifted her chin and demanded with a glare that she tell me.

“He was different. He looked cruel,” she said.

“How can that be?” I wondered in horror. “Could they turn him? Can the Fallen *turn* a Nephilim into another Fallen?”

She shrugged. “I don’t know, but I swear it wasn’t him.” She touched her neck lightly.

“He did that?” I inhaled.

She nodded, terror imbued on her face. I couldn’t believe it. Trev was so quiet, and sweet, and kind. He was the voice of reason. The careful one among us. What had happened to make him do that to Gwen?

“How did you get here?” I asked absently.

She looked at me with child’s eyes; innocent, scared, and begging to be saved. “I don’t know where we are.”

“We’re in the waiting room.”

She looked at me in horror, her expression saying it all.

“No! I’m not dead. I swear it,” I reassured her.

“Am I?” she asked in a trembling voice.

I grimaced. That was something I would love to know the answer to.

“I don’t know,” I said unsurely. “I’m not, so I don’t see why you would be. Remember I’ve been here before and I wasn’t dead then either. And there are others here who are still alive too.”

Her brow crinkled in confusion. “How is that possible? The waiting room is where spirits go. Where they wait until they’re judged by the Thrones,” she rambled, reciting one of Haamiah’s lessons.

“I know,” I cut in. “I know all of that, but it’s not true. I am continually finding out new things, things that go against everything we were told. Something’s wrong here. Creatures are put here against their will, some alive and some dead.”

“So? They’re evil! They’re here for judgment.”

“You think it’s fair to be kept imprisoned here for a hundred years waiting for judgment, even though you’re still alive?”

She paused. “Well . . . they must have done something really bad.”

I shook my head. “There’s something going on, Gwen. Something bigger than us.”

She cocked an eyebrow. “You think the angels are plotting against us?”

“Maybe,” I said miserably.

“Then why would Maion rescue me?”

Maion? Well, there went that theory.

I frowned at her. “Maion rescued you?”

She nodded. “He just appeared in front of me in the tunnel. He flung Trev off of me and grabbed hold of me, then . . . ” She gestured around us. “I was here.”

I stood up and took a step back from her, my eyes searching for a sign of the warrior angel.

"Where is he?" I asked.

Gwen slowly got to her feet beside me. "I don't know. When I opened my eyes I was just *here*, on my own. I heard someone and started walking towards the noise, and it was you."

"Why would he bring you here?" I frowned in confusion.

"I thought you must have been involved," she said.

My heart twisted. I turned to her. "I wanted to," I said, pleading for her to believe me. "I heard you were missing, and that Asmodeus had you."

"Why didn't you come?" Gwen asked sorrowfully. She took a small step back, her face scrunching up as she tried not to cry.

Tears filled my eyes even as I swallowed, fighting back the distress. I tried to smile. "I wanted to, so badly . . . I couldn't open a portal." I shrugged. "I'm stuck here, maybe forever."

"Why? Why are you in the waiting room, anyway? And why can't you open a portal? You've done it before."

For a second I debated telling her the truth. I was here because the angels were so full of shit that they would abandon me and judge me for drinking the Star Mist when they had led me to the tournament in the first place. I knew I certainly couldn't confess what I was. After seeing the way she shook when telling me that Trev was no longer *himself*, how could I break the news that I was no longer a Nephilim either?

"All good questions," I replied, evading her eyes.

"What about Zach? Does he know where you are?" She began to sound more and more like herself, outraged that I was stuck.

"He knows. He's been here to see me. He's . . . working on it," I answered.

"Have you been here on your own?" she asked. I could see her heart breaking for me.

"Don't Gwen," I stomped away from her.

"What?" she asked, startled.

"Don't feel sorry for me."

"You've been here on your own for God knows how long, and I'm not allowed to feel bad? What gives?" She scowled.

I swung around to face her. "I know where you've been. *I've been there.* Don't pretend to me that you're fine. Don't pity me for being here when you've been . . . *there*."

Gwen blanched. "I don't want to talk about it."

"You don't need to. Not to me, because I already know," I said through clenched teeth.

This all just brought me back to that terrible place I was in when I had first escaped. Over the years since, everyone had tried to make me talk about it: Gwen, Trev, Sam, Zach, even Valentina had questioned me, using a multitude of tactics. But I didn't want to *talk* about it. At first I hadn't even wanted to deal with it, I had just wanted to pretend it had never happened. Piece by piece I had put myself back together. I certainly wasn't the same person I was then, and never would be again, but I was no longer in that place . . . I wanted revenge, and one day I would have it.

I didn't need to hear Gwen's story. In truth, I didn't want to know. I had only recently managed to sleep without nightmares. The training I had done in the safe house had finally enabled me to feel safe again. I finally believed in myself, that I could defend myself, that I was strong enough. It was clear that she felt the same way I had, not wanting anyone else to know what she had gone through.

Gwen pursed her lips and looked up at me. “Then we’re in agreement.”

I nodded. “Come on. We need to get out of here.”

24

'Decide that you want it more than you are afraid of it.'

Bill Cosby.

Gwen and I walked on in silence for a few minutes.

"Where are we going?" she asked.

I immediately felt guilty for not telling her, and just expecting her to follow me.

"I'm looking for the hut that Em—the witch lived in," I amended, swallowing down the lump that threatened to choke me.

"Whoa!" Gwen exclaimed. She grabbed my arm and swung me around to face her. "What if she's there? Didn't you tell us she was evil?"

"She's not evil," I denied sharply. I stretched my arms out in front of me, not wanting to have this conversation at all. I could see by the look on Gwen's face that there was no way she was going to let it drop. "She's not evil," I repeated.

"Yet she tried to trick you into being stuck here for the rest of your life . . . " Gwen narrowed her eyes at me.

"She was lonely," I whispered. My eyes filled with tears for what now seemed like the hundredth time today.

"Jasmine, what happened?" Gwen pulled me closer.

I let her hug me for just a few seconds, taking comfort in her warmth. I stepped back and took in a deep breath. "Emily—the witch—was stuck here for like, a hundred years. She wasn't dead. She wasn't a spirit. She had been condemned to wait for her judgment for a century, all alone."

"What had she done?"

I shrugged. "She hadn't exactly been good, but no one deserves this fate. I don't think the Thrones had any plans to actually judge her, this *was* her punishment. Anyway, she and I kind of became allies . . . friends." I sucked in a deep breath. "She was killed. Both her and a harpy we had become friends with."

"By who?"

"This plane isn't safe. These forests are teeming with lycae, vampires, demons . . . the angels aren't in control at all - or maybe they are but they just don't care."

"Then why have you been put here?" Gwen asked angrily.

There was that question again. The one I couldn't answer. I just shrugged in reply.

"Back to your original question, no one will be there. It's the only place we can be assured of safety . . . if I can find it."

"How do you know that someone else won't be living in it by now?"

I put my hand into my back pocket and pulled out the large metal key that Emily had carried around her neck. I had seen it before, and had known immediately what it was when I saw it on the ground beside her body.

"She was a witch, she put hexes on her hut as security, but the key will remove them." I smiled bravely. "We just need to find the damn hut before it gets too dark, or we'll be camping out under a tree again."

"Won't it be easier to find by air?" she suggested with the briefest of smiles.

I grinned at her, ridiculing myself for not thinking of it sooner. "Can you carry me?"

She smiled openly, "if I can carry . . . " Her smile dimmed. "I can carry you."

Within minutes we had taken off; me clutched between her legs, and Gwen with her beautiful purple wings spread out above us. We stared at the trees below us and kept a watch out for anything that broke the pattern of the green treetops.

A good number of hours later we had landed and were standing before Emily's hut. It stood partially obscured between the trees, shrouded in darkness. It looked exactly the same as it had previously, and I could only wish that I were here in different circumstances. At least now I no longer had the eerie feeling as I approached it, knowing that today it would be a sanctuary.

We approached the door slowly. Placing the key in the lock I turned to Gwen, hesitant. She put her hand on mine and together we turned the key and pushed the door open smoothly.

I stepped in and grabbed a candle off the nearest table. Cupping my hand over the wick, I allowed my power to stream through my palm and heat it until a flame sparked. I held the candle in one hand and pushed the door closed behind Gwen at the last minute, catching the frozen look on her face.

Oops.

“What did you just do?” she asked slowly.

I smiled wistfully. “Yeah, that’s something new I picked up.”

She raised her eyebrows and stepped further into the one room hut. I lifted the wooden plank and barred the door, wondering if there was any way I could avoid telling her my new species status. I followed her to where the logs were piled up in the fireplace.

“It’s probably best not to start a fire . . . not that lighting one would be a problem for you, evidently.” Gwen let her words hang in the air between us.

I bit my lip and glanced at the fireplace where a black cooking pot hung on a metal pole above the logs. As much as I longed to be warm, I knew she was right. We couldn’t afford to alert anyone to our presence. Emily was able to cast spells to keep herself concealed and safe here, unfortunately we were one Wiccan short.

Gwen lay down on the pallet near the wall, pulling the sheets over her. She mumbled something that sounded like an apology and was asleep within seconds. I hesitated a moment before realizing that I, too, was exhausted. There was no point in staying awake, and this was as safe as we were going to get. I hadn’t slept for more than a few hours at a time since I had arrived here so I might as well grab a few hours while I was in relative safety. I glanced around the room, noting the small table and stools, the baskets filled with vegetables, and the thick black trunk pushed against the wall.

I sighed, my heart aching. For a second I closed my eyes and allowed myself to wallow in misery, pitying myself thoroughly. For a moment I let myself think about everyone and everything that I had lost, everything I could have had but that fate had snatched away from me.

I opened my eyes again and pushed all of those thoughts away with a deep slow breath, and slipped under the sheet next to Gwen. Closing my eyes, I drifted off quickly, the faces of all the dead Nephilim haunting my dreams.

* * * *

I woke up when Gwen started to scream and thrash in her sleep. I woke her and hugged her, letting her cry her fill. When she had calmed down, she slipped off the pallet and stormed out of the hut. I followed to find her staring out at the trees.

“Do you want to talk about it?” I asked hesitantly.

Gwen shook her head and turned away to cast her gaze over the forest.

I sighed deeply. "Can you at least tell me what happened to Trev?”

I shivered as Gwen turned to face me, looking shell-shocked. “What happened to him to make him act like that? He can’t be Fallen” I whispered.

She shook her head stiffly. “I didn’t say he was Fallen. He was different. He wasn’t . . . *him*.”

"What are you talking about? How could he not be him?"

She blinked rapidly, her voice wavering. "We were separated . . . someone helped me find the tunnels—I remembered that's where you found Zach, and I thought I would find Trev there."

A shiver ran down my spine as I was drawn back into my memories of Castle Dantanian. "Keep going—though don't think I missed the part about *someone* helping you." I took a deep breath. "Trev was in the tunnels..."

She nodded, trembling. I reached out and gripped her hand, wanting to show my support, needing her to know that I knew what she'd been through—that I had lived it too.

"I found him there. He was just sitting there."

"He wasn't chained?"

"No. He just sat on a chair. When he looked up there was blood all around his mouth." She lifted her hand to her mouth. "There was a dead body on the floor next to him. God, Jasmine—he had fangs! And his eyes . . . they weren't human. They had a red ring around them."

"How? What? How?" I gasped. I couldn't stand this slow, drawn out story. I needed to know what had happened to Trev *now*.

"I don't know!" Gwen wailed. "I think he was turned."

"Into what?"

"I think . . . I mean, he looked . . . like a vampire," she breathed.

As she stared at me her skin began to fade paler and paler while her eyes grew wider and lost focus. I had to fight to keep from panicking. I pulled her to me and let her squeeze me tight, even as my mind began to spin out of control. I had to fight to control the power churning through me. It demanded that I go to him and save him from whatever miserable fate he was sucked into.

How was this possible? Could a Nephilim be turned into a vampire? If so, did that make Trev a vampire, or was he a half and half like me? Would he be evil? I had never met a good vampire—any I had met had tried to kill me shortly afterwards. Would Trev still be *Trev*? The thought of him turning into an evil bloodsucking monster seemed ridiculous. Trev was sweet and kind, the kind of goofy, laughing guy that everyone wanted to be friends with. He was our best friend and though I hadn't gotten to the bottom of it, I had thought he and Gwen had gotten pretty close.

Another thought occurred to me. What had happened to Trev's angelic mother? She had always been present whenever he had been in trouble. She had even sent down Heavenly fire when we had been attacked by a dragon recently. Surely there was no way she would let Trev be turned into an evil beast? I just wouldn't believe it. There had to be some other explanation, or maybe Gwen was mistaken.

Just as I was about to voice my thoughts, a thump nearby sent shivers down my spine. I spun around, not expecting who appeared before me.

25

'You were born an original, don't die a copy.'

John Mason.

"Maion." I scowled. Though I now had mixed feelings about the Warrior—after all, he did save Gwen's life—I still detested the sight of him. I would never forget the cold, heartless way he had suggested putting me down, as though I were a mongrel no one wanted. I suppose, if I was being honest with myself, I hated how he had made me feel because that was how I felt most of the time. It was as if he had unearthed my biggest weakness and flaunted it in front of those I wanted to impress.

I was unsurprised when Maion did little more than acknowledge my presence with a scowl and push past me into the hut.

"Maion!" Gwen cried out. I watched with a heavy feeling in my stomach as she ran into his arms, hugging him tightly for a second before stepping back and gazing up at him with adoration. *Like a puppy.*

She was rewarded with a small smile. *Ugh*, it was enough to make me puke.

Maion steered her past where I stood and wrapped his arms around her. My heart clenched, knowing what was about to happen.

"Wait!" Gwen objected, reaching out towards me. "We're taking Jas with us . . . *right*?" She spun back to the angel beside her.

Maion paused, hesitantly glancing at me then back at Gwen.

"We can't take her with us," he muttered.

"What?" Gwen screeched. "You *are* joking?"

Maion growled, "She is not permitted to leave this plane."

I *knew* it. However, having it in my mind and having it said out loud was a little different. I felt frozen, as though I wasn't really there, but was watching from far away. Perhaps it was just my self-preservation kicking in but I said nothing, just kept my mouth shut and my head held high. I wouldn't beg. I wouldn't scream and let my anger overtake me. Zach wasn't able to help me escape, and apparently neither was Maion, even if he had wanted to. In his case, it would be futile even to ask. No, I would have to think on this some more. I would have to find my own way out of here.

I watched as Gwen continued to rail at Maion, waiting for him to snap. He didn't; he remained his usual calm, aloof, sneering self, an arrogant prick made of stone.

"It's fine," I said, shrugging nonchalantly when Gwen stopped to take a breath. "Gwen, just go with Maion. Someone needs to be back there to find a way to rescue Trev and make sure Sam's okay."

Gwen looked from me to Maion in amazement. Eventually she backed down, seeming to regretfully accept that there was no possible way for me to go with them. She grabbed me tightly, pressing my body to hers before kissing my hair.

“Promise me you’ll stay safe. Promise you’ll find a way back,” she whispered with tears in her eyes.

I nodded, a lump in my throat. “I will. Promise you’ll make them find Trev and Sam. Zach said that Sam was with Lilura.”

She nodded and stepped back slowly into Maion’s arms. She held on to him tightly as he wrapped his arms around her and his wings carried them up to the sky.

Just as I was about to feel sorry for myself, warm arms encircled me from behind.

26

'It makes me happy to know that none of us get a how-to guide. We're all just kind of winging it.'

Unknown.

I glanced up at him, knowing immediately that I wouldn't say anything about what I had seen. That was then, this was now. It was cowardly and probably selfish but anything I said about it would end in an argument and I needed him close to me now.

Zach held my hand and tugged, pulling me up next to him as we began to walk through the forest. I kept looking up at him, continuously awed by his sexual prowess. I could look at just one part of him and immediately feel turned on. For example, his eyebrow piercing—who would have thought that a little piece of metal could be so . . . delicious? His thick shoulders that begged to be scratched led down to bulging arms that could destroy and kill, or hold me tenderly. His legs were strongly built with a core of steel, and were used to launch him up into the air with his wings outstretched, or lay across me as we slept.

"What are you smiling at?"

I looked up at him again, blushing, feeling the heat in my cheeks. I covered it by raising my eyebrows and smiling coyly.

"Looking at me, were you?" I asked with a grin.

His smile widened, his white teeth flashing at me. “Maybe.”

I shrugged then turned to him, pulling at his arm to make him stop and face me. I reached up to his shoulders and wrapped my arms around his neck, turning my face up to his.

A movement in the corner of my eye caught my attention. It was fast, dark and coming right at us.

“Zach!” I screamed.

Not the outcome I had intended. Zach threw me to the ground and turned around, taking the brunt of the force head on. He had thrown me a little further than necessary and I lay, sprawled out ungracefully on my back on top of the dry leaves. Seeing Zach hurtle to the ground, I flipped up onto my feet and jumped forward, my fists up and ready for action.

Bemoaning the lack of a weapon I took in the demon’s size. He was at least seven feet tall, monstrous in size, with dirty-green colored scales covering his entire body. His eyes looked a mixture of black and yellow, in an oval shape with a second eyelid, similar to a reptile. It too, was ready for fight, half crouched with a thick sharp spike protruding from each of its palms—as though the length had come from within its arms.

I glanced at Zach as he rolled to the side and stood up next to me, a blade in his hands. He exchanged a look with me that I understood immediately. It was a playful yet deadly look, almost a dare. When the briefest of smiles touched his mouth, together we ran toward the demon.

I reached it first and kicked out with my right leg, knocking it to the side. I quickly switched legs, and with a high kick sent it reeling backwards. I spun around and used the build up of speed to kick out again, returning to my fighter's crouch with my fists held up.

Zach stepped forward, his blade zinging past my face, blood shooting from the demon as it ducked away too slowly. The demon roared and leaped for Zach, easily knocked aside by Zach's powerful blows to the chest with his legs. The creature fell forward, knocked off balance, and was kneed in the chest and tossed back into the leaves.

As it surged to its feet I lunged forward and smashed its head with a right hook before spinning my shoulders to power through with a punch from the left. The demon returned the punch, catching me in the jaw, but I held on to consciousness, shaking the hit off, and returned the blow with my magic powering through of its own accord.

My magic began to seep out delicately, as though it were toying with the demon as much as I wanted to. It fizzled as it came into contact with the demon's skin with each hit I made, sending a thrilled reaction through my skin, almost like a little electric tickle.

Zach ran behind the monster and sunk the blade in through its shoulder blades. The demon shrieked, a deafening screech that would have woken the dead, and spun to face him, trading blow for blow. Zach had kept hold of his sword but had to drop it to the floor as the demon set upon him with renewed fervor, blocking the expert punches Zach was aiming. They each managed to score bone-shattering hits, and I desperately looked for a way to jump back in the game.

When the demon smashed its huge arm across Zach's face, he fell back onto the ground. I could sense the victorious glee emanating from it. I grinned mischievously and leaped into the air, kicking out with my right foot to belt it away from Zach. It fell backwards but caught its balance, rushing at me again. I narrowed my eyes, excitement powering me with every heartbeat.

It threw out its arm, the spike glistening with blood, and swung in an arch around its body, trying to slice me in half. I ducked under the first swipe and blocked the second with my own arm, using the momentum to boot the demon in the abdomen before returning to knee it in the face and knock it away. It drew toward me again, teeth snapping inches away from my face. I threw myself to the side and flipped up onto my feet again, launching myself at it with punches and kicks while running around it, dodging and ducking any retaliation. I drew in a deep breath as I stepped back after I had made a particularly impressive blow to its head to see Zach blasting in with his blade, slicing the demon's head off completely.

Panting, I waited for Zach to turn around to face me, watching the body fall to the floor. As he turned, I saw the glisten of sweat on his forehead and a savage look in his eyes.

"So?" I asked, gasping for breath as I drank the sight of him in. "What do you want to do now?"

We came together in a rush, kissing. His lips devoured mine, over and over again, pressing onto my own, biting and licking, sometimes nipping so savagely I wondered if he had drawn blood. His hands started off in my hair, his fingers seeming to massage my scalp even as he pressed my face tightly to his. My own hands clutched at him, my arms around his neck, feeling the strength there and the determination that ran through him in the ripples of his muscles. I felt energized and freshly awakened with each movement he made as his shoulders rolled under my arms. I turned my face up to suck in a breath, and though he allowed it he soon returned to my lips, his tongue stroking mine incessantly, relentlessly taking over. He ran his hand down my jaw, stroking my neck, before slipping his hands down my back to pull up my T-shirt and trail his fingertips across the skin on my lower back, tracing my spine up and down. Shivers of ice fired through me, heightening everything. I could no longer think logically; in fact, I could no longer think about *anything* other than his lips taking mine by force, and his hands touching me everywhere.

He left my mouth and trailed kisses down my neck, sucking and biting as he continued to stroke and rub my skin, massaging me. It was almost like a dream; I could almost hear the tense, thriller-like music surrounding us as our passionate embrace deepened. It was as though what we had just done had set off a chain of emotions and events that we had no control of. My body was its own entity and his matched mine speed for speed, action for action.

I closed my eyes and rubbed my cheek on his shoulder and he pulled my T-shirt up higher, his mouth working on my neck. Zach's huge hands seemed to encompass my whole back, sliding up and down, heightening my senses.

He wrapped his arms around me and squeezed tight, as our mouths continued to slaughter each other. He took a few steps away from the carcass below and put me on my feet gently before pushing me to the floor. I lay on my back, supported by my arms, as he pulled my boots off one by one, running his hands down my calves. He leaned in to bite my ankles, licking my skin with his tongue as he ran his hands roughly up my inner thigh. He loosened the button at my waist and without pausing to play, dragged the pants off me in one go. He hooked his hand under my knees and dragged the material over my feet before crawling up my body and pulling me into a sitting position.

He kissed my mouth again, completely dominating me. He reached for the bottom of my T-shirt and pulled it over my head roughly, grabbing me by the throat after to suck and bite at my neck again.

I placed both hands on his chest and used my power to push him away forcefully, only able to savor the confused look on his face for a second before I reached for the bottom of his T-shirt and worked it up over his chest. He lifted his arms and I dragged it over his head, dropping it to the ground beside us as I fell onto his lips again.

I pulled my mouth from his and narrowed my eyes, commanding him silently to be still and allow me to have my way. I bent my head to his and began to kiss my way down from his collarbone. Somehow, the sweat beading on his skin created an almighty aphrodisiac, making me rub my lips and tongue over his skin to taste him. He held his arms away from his body even as I nipped at his nipples, my tongue flicking to soothe them afterwards. I rubbed my face against each muscle ridge; the difficulty I faced restraining myself from biting too hard was evident in the way I shook, and the way my power batted at me from the inside like a sledgehammer demanding me to let go and take over.

Zach had evidently decided he was going to battle me for supremacy, turning me quickly so that my back was to him. He held my throat against his shoulder and kissed my shoulder as he dipped his free hand around me, touching, squeezing and massaging. Being so much larger than me, he had no trouble in the position I was in to delve deeply inside of me with his fingers, completely taking possession of my body. I turned my face to his, invigorated when he dueled his tongue with mine again, his hand running down my throat possessively. He pushed me to the ground and turned me over so that I was facing him. Staring at me intently, he followed me down, sinking into my body even as I arched into him.

He refused to kiss me, instead holding my gaze in his as he pulled out and slid in slowly, as deep as he could go. With a savage glint in his eyes he began to pound into me, his strength making my eyes water as I opened my legs wider to cradle his hips, my fingernails sinking into the muscles of his bottom to drag him in harder and harder.

As I neared my release, I pulled my power up through my body and forced him off of me to lie next to me. Shock registered on his face as I quickly leaped on top of him and slid his hard, wet cock inside of me again, riding him to the hilt. I picked up speed as he reached up and squeezed my nipples tightly, growling as he began to feel the same urgency as I did.

Losing ourselves completely, he dragged me down to him and we exploded into a million pieces, wrapped in each other's arms, sparks of fire and ice singeing every nerve we possessed as I eventually collapsed on top of him.

27

'I love her and that's the beginning and end of everything.'

F. Scott Fitzgerald.

"I'm not leaving you here alone," Zach whispered in my ear.

"I'm not alone," I whispered in return, rubbing my face along his shoulder.

"You shouldn't be here among the beasts. It's too dangerous," he said, scowling at me.

I could see in his eyes he was furious at the situation. That the angels thought I was in need of judgment infuriated me too, but I had come to the conclusion that realistically, I probably deserved it. I had killed hundreds of creatures with my own hands, and been the catalyst to cause the death of many more. Sure, they were mostly all evil and had tried to kill me first . . .

"Make me feel safe then," I whispered, turning his face with my fingers so I could kiss his neck.

My blood began to sizzle as his huge hand gripped my neck while the other pushed all of my hair to the side. He bent forward and kissed my neck softly at first, his thick lips lingering, his breath warming my skin, before becoming more savage, biting and licking. He pushed me down to the floor and straddled me, pinning my hands above my head.

He used one of his hands to stroke the exposed the skin of my abdomen, the cold air causing goosebumps to rise. He leaned down and traced my belly button with his tongue, nipping at my flesh with his teeth. He trailed his fingers between my legs, gazing into my eyes.

He groaned as he felt the moistness and stroked harder, delving his fingers between my lips, digging into my flesh. I wiggled, needing more. I would never have enough of him. I needed to lose myself in him.

I knew how huge he was. He had the thickest and longest cock I had ever seen; Greek gods were nothing compared to him. I needed to him to sink into me and ram me as hard as he could—like I knew he would. I knew the pleasure that would soon wash through my body. Even the mere thought of it sent floods of desire coursing through my veins. God, I ached.

I couldn't bear the teasing any longer. "Fuck me," I groaned. "I need more."

When our lusts were sated and we were thoroughly exhausted we lay still, entwining our fingers. Death, loss and sex seemed to have a sedative effect and I felt almost delirious, lying there. We talked nonsense for hours, until Zach told me there was an uproar about the location of the Falchion of Tabbris. The Grigori had reported there were factions of Fallen angels searching for it. Its existence was well known, and there was much speculation over where it was hidden.

"Where do you think it's kept?" Zach grinned.

I sat up, leaning on one arm, and turned to face him, smiling at the game he proposed. "Somewhere heavily guarded. Somewhere with top security and intel."

At the look he gave me I guessed I was along the right track.

I continued, my brain spinning out ideas. "Somewhere with limited access."

Zach grinned and folded his arms behind his head. "And where would *you* hide it?"

I pursed my lips thoughtfully. "Based on those ideals—somewhere with limited access, top security and intel—I would probably pick either a top secret army base, or a really high up government building, you know, like the White House."

Zach's eyes flicked up as he smiled broadly.

My face dropped. The *White House*! It was hidden in plain sight, yet was in the most heavily guarded location in the world.

"The Falchion of Tabbris is in the White House," I said.

Zach nodded slowly.

"Why isn't it hidden in the Heavenly realm? Surely that would be the safest place for it?"

He shrugged, "If I were looking for an angelic artifact which would open the gates to Heaven, the Heavenly realm is the first place I would look. Or at least, it would be the first place I would send a traitor to look."

I nodded my acquiescence at his conclusion. Clearly that had been my first thought too. A flicker of suspicion began to seep through my veins, heating up my insides. I was very well aware that my anger had just been triggered with that same thought, and I struggled to mask its influence.

“Why did you tell me where it was?” I asked suspiciously, ordering myself to stay calm.

Zach paused. “I know you won't tell anyone.”

“That’s not it,” I hissed at him, jumping to my feet. I began to pace. “You don’t think I’ll get out of here, do you? You told me because you don’t think I’ll be able to do any damage if I let it slip!”

Zach groaned and climbed to his feet, glaring at me. “I figured there wouldn’t be any harm in telling you because you’re one of us!”

“Because you don’t think I’ll ever get out of here,” I said angrily.

He ran his hands through his hair and turned away. “We will find a way, but at the moment we haven’t come up with anything. It might take longer than we expected.”

I shook my head in disbelief. “I knew it. You aren’t even trying to free me! That’s why you’re here, instead of working on an escape.”

“For fuck’s sake, Jasmine!” Zach cursed, his eyes flashing. “I’ve approached the Thrones. I’ve approached the Principalities. I’ve even requested a meeting with the archangels and no one will meet with me! Haamiah has tried, Elijah has tried - even Maion has tried to get in contact with them!”

"Oh! *Maion's* tried to get in touch with them. How incredibly unsurprising that he didn't manage to help get me freed."

"Ahhh!" Zach exclaimed. "Would you get over your issue with him? Maion's been in my life a hundred times longer than you have, and he's proven his loyalty to me a thousand times over."

"What the h*ell* is that supposed to mean?" I growled. "You don't think I'm loyal to you? You prefer him over me? Well, fine. Why don't you go back to him then and continue your bro-mance, because you're certainly not wanted here."

"Why would you think I'm not loyal to you? I'm sick of your crap, Jasmine," he bellowed.

"*My crap*?" I shrieked. "I've found out more about you in the past week than I ever wanted to!"

"What the hell is that supposed to mean?" he snarled.

My rage took over completely. I was beyond furious. "I saw all the Nephilim you killed. Thousands of them, their throats ripped out by you and Maion. You're monsters!"

Zach's face paled. He took two steps back while shaking his head then turned, spread his wings, and flew off.

28

'People don't leave because things are hard. They leave because it is no longer worth it.'

Unknown.

I immediately set off again. I couldn't sit still; I needed to clear my head. I walked for hours, replaying the argument in my head over and over again. I was shocked when I came to a stop and realized where I was—by the mermaid pool.

I sighed and cried into my hands again, frustrated and angry, lonely and hopeless. I was so tired, and so lost. I wanted to go home. I sobbed even harder, knowing that even if I did go back, I'd have everything to deal with there.

As the minutes passed my tears began to dry. I stiffened when I heard my name.

"Jasmine," voices whispered.

I peered at the water, my heart pounding as I made out at least a dozen pale faces.

"We have something for you," a male voice called out.

I rolled my eyes. "Yeah, right. You just want me to come near you so you can murder me." I sniffed. "Why don't you just get in line."

“No, it’s important. There’s something here for you.” The voice called. It seemed to take on a tranquil quality. I felt drawn to it, as though I had no option but to listen very carefully.

I licked my lips and inched closer. “What is it?”

“In the water! Look!”

I nervously leaned toward the water, trying to see. My mind felt a little foggy, my anger and misery vanishing and leaving only curiosity.

“Back away and I’ll look,” I suggested.

The mermaids exchanged long looks of humor.

“Very well,” one said. They all pushed back through the water, ripples dancing across the surface toward me.

I gulped and stepped forward. I forced myself to continue, putting one foot in front of the other through the grass, water droplets splashing up on my ankles with each step. I searched the faces of the mermaids, noting their nonchalance as I approached the water. I knew I needed to do this; I needed to see what they were hiding. For some reason it was very important. A part of me knew that this wasn’t right; I could feel the slice of fear stabbing at me. My whole body was tensed, ready for a fight, aware that someone or *something* could jump out of the water at any second and pull me under. The only thing that numbed the fear was knowing that the last time I was attacked in water my fury and rage had enabled me to be more powerful than I had ever been before.

Briefly, an image of Blue Eyes entered my head. I knew he would never back away; *he* would do exactly what I was doing. Probably with a few more sarcastic comments thrown in. With Blue Eyes’ strength fresh in my mind, I edged closer with more focus. I paused just a step away from the edge and leaned close, trying to keep the mermaids in my line of sight even as I peered into the water.

At first I couldn't see anything through the murky depths, only my own reflection interspersed with little waves. Though the Mermaids looked relaxed and calm, I could imagine that below the water their tails were working with a vengeance.

As I was about to give it up as a lost cause or possibly a trick, a shape began to take form. It seemed deeper than I had expected, only the faintest outline visible. I scowled, quickly checking the mermaids remained where they were and stepped up to the very edge, staring down intently.

The shape almost looked like a body. My heart began to pound furiously. Who was it? Had the mermaids killed someone, or drowned them? No, that didn't make any sense. Why would the Thrones allow it? Who was in the water? Was it someone I knew?

"Who is it?" I called out. Was that *me* talking? My voice sounded thin and weak.

"Who do you love most of all?" A soft voice floated over the water to me. "Come closer...*see*."

"Oh my God, *Zach*" I whispered, my eyes filling with tears even as my body began to fill with rage. Thoughts of Zach began to bombard me. Images of his face, his smile, his eyes, replayed over and over again while the rest of the world faded into a twinkling mist. I was unable to stop myself from releasing my grey cloudy power, as it began to pour from my body. My vision obscured.

"You," I snarled, narrowing my eyes at the blond-haired Mermaid smirking at me. "You killed him. You killed . . . " I couldn't say it. I couldn't say his name. It couldn't be true. I wouldn't believe it until I had his body in my arms.

I shrieked. Lightening split the sky above me, casting shadows in its wake. The love of my life—gone? I would never survive the loss. I needed Zach like the air I breathed. I couldn't live without him. Even now, the air was stuck in my throat, choking me. I hadn't even told him that I loved him last time we spoke. We had argued and he'd left angry, furious at me, and I at him. I would never get to say all of the things I wanted to tell him. I would regret that last fight forever. As I felt the rage ripple through me again, I leaped into the water.

29

'Our attitude towards life determines life's attitude towards us.'

John. N. Mitchell.

Instead of hitting the water as I had expected, the air turned into a thick viscous atmosphere and I felt my gravity shift as I fell through a portal. I gasped and winced as I landed in a crouch. I snapped my head up and clapped my hand over my mouth in shock. I was in a huge room. Was it a warehouse? Pallets and crates were stacked up, with rows of boxes. It was dark, the only light coming from narrow windows placed intermittently around the top of the walls near to the roof.

What one earth had just happened? Had I just opened a portal? I grinned, even though I felt an overwhelming urge to flee as quickly as possible. How long would it take the Thrones to realize I was no longer confined? I admit, I felt a little thrill at the thought that I had got one over those up-themselves angels. Who the hell were they to lock me up like a criminal?

The memory of what I had been doing before I left quickly surfaced, pushing away the pleasure I was feeling at having escaped. *Zach*. I stood up, wavering in my indecision. Did I open a portal and go back with the presumption that I would be able to escape again?

"Shit," I muttered. What on earth should I do? "Think, Jasmine, think."

I rubbed my temples as I pondered my options. Did I *actually* see what I thought I saw? Everything seemed clearer now. The mermaids had tricked me, drugging me with their voices.

Emily and Tanya had been adamant about not trusting the mermaids. In fact, they had been incredibly vocal about disbelieving anything the "manipulating bitch-fish" had to say or show. If I was to follow that line of thinking I should count my lucky stars I had opened a portal at the last minute, and not been dragged down to the bottom and drowned, and therefore should get off the floor and make a run for it.

However, on the flip side, if what I saw was true, then I was abandoning him to the mermaids. I frowned with doubt. Surely there was no way the mermaids could have captured a warrior angel in one of the angels' realms! I knew how strong Zach was. I seriously doubted anyone could defeat him, let alone a bunch of fish. No, I hadn't seen him. I probably hadn't seen anything and they had just been drawing me closer to kill me. I closed my eyes for a second as I flushed with embarrassment. How stupid was I?

That decided it. Now that my mind was clear, I would have to run and pray I wasn't wrong to do so.

I staggered to my feet, giving my ankle a rub as I felt it throb tenderly. I jogged around a pile of crates, looking for an exit. There had to be one somewhere, unless this was another trick dreamed up by the Thrones.

I skidded to a halt as I almost ran straight into a group of men. No . . . make that a group of demons. With yellow eyes flashing, they spotted me immediately. I spun around to run for cover, ducking under shelving and rolling across the next aisle. Another demon blocked my way so I rolled again, and then jumped to my feet.

A blow to my face sent me reeling. I dropped to my knee, my vision turning hazy. I ducked another blow and spun on the floor to face the demon just in time for another attack.

The kick aimed at my head was stopped prematurely. The strong, tanned arm that held it was soon joined by another, and the demon was thrown back into a pile of crates. I gasped as I stared up at the beyond beautiful woman fighting them off. I was stunned, and frozen in place. With each punch and kick the woman's long blond hair was tossed over her shoulder, her fists flashing with a speed I could only dream of emulating. She seemed to almost fly as she jumped from crate to crate, running up walls to catch the demons surrounding us by surprise. They didn't seem to have any idea what was happening and roared their anger so loudly I could feel the noise reverberating through the ground.

With a twist, the woman snapped the neck of the last demon and dropped him to the ground. She glanced at me, approaching slowly.

I crab-crawled backwards away from her. I could only hope she was on my side, because there was no way I could take her after that show of strength.

She paused in front of me, letting me see her clearly. I guessed her species. She had to be an angel. There was no other category I could fit her in to. She looked innocent, young. Her skin was flawless, with a soft almost pearlescent look to it. She had deep blue eyes, tinged with purple, and long golden hair hung loose, and was in disarray post fight. She wore light denim jeans with designer rips and a zipped-up thin black jacket. Blue and white Converse shoes topped up her wholesome, university student look. Or some kind of student with the most beautiful hourglass figure I'd ever seen.

She held out her hand to me. I took a deep breath. Seeing as she hadn't killed me already I guessed I could trust her for a few more minutes until I ditched her, when I knew where I was. I grabbed her hand and let her help me to my feet before taking a few steps away to allow a safe distance to defend myself.

I tossed my hair back. "Who are you?"

She smiled, the softest of smiles. "A friend."

A friend of whom? "Why are you here? Why did you help me?"

"No daughter of mine will be killed by demons!"

30

'Spend your life with only people who will lift you higher.'

Oprah.

My mouth dropped open and I let out a strangled gasp.

The woman . . . *my mother* seemed oblivious. She screwed her nose up delicately and toed one of the bodies on the ground. "Ew. Rotteo demons, at that."

"You're Lilith?" I demanded.

She turned and smiled at me, her white teeth sparkling. I could see the jewelry adorning her teeth, blue and white crystals decorating her pearly whites.

"The one and only," she said.

"How are you here? How did I even get here?" My mind was so befuddled, a thousand questions clamoring to be asked.

"You think I would let my daughter be imprisoned by the Thrones?" she asked incredulously.

"You helped me escape? The portal," I wondered out loud, "you opened the portal, not me."

Lilith winked at me. "The Thrones didn't count on my coming to your aid. They should have put stronger wards on their realm." She turned away from me as a disheveled looking man loped over.

"They're gone, there's nae more," he informed her in a Scottish brogue.

"Good. Let's go." She turned to me and held out her arm, gesturing for me to follow.

Seeing no better option available to me, I jogged after her as she ran to a tall iron door and wrenched it open. As the sunlight streamed in I ducked, covering my eyes. I hadn't been in direct sunlight for what seemed like weeks. I looked up at the man beside us, flinching as I noted the lewd way his eyes rested on Lilith. This was just too weird.

Lilith peered out of the doorway and dashed outside, running down the street. I followed automatically, grimacing at the noise and smell of heavy traffic. The narrow street we were on soon led to a busier road, and then again to a bigger one. As we turned yet another corner, Lilith led the way onto the sidewalk, grabbing my arm to pull me along with her roughly, her nails digging into my skin. The Scot followed behind us, scowling for all he was worth. I felt swamped by the crush of people, the car horns, the high-rise buildings that loomed over us.

I fought to keep up with Lilith, my shoulder aching from the hordes of people shoving past me. Scents and smells of food, cars, people, and the overwhelming stench of garbage layered with perfume assaulted me, making me nauseas.

Lilith pulled me across the road abruptly. I grimaced as cars screeched to a halt, beeping as we dashed in and out of the traffic. The Scot pulled me out of the way of a taxi, almost yanking my arm from its socket. Lilith took hold of my other arm, and between the two of them, they dragged me through the busy streets of what I presumed, from the billboards for shows on Broadway and the slow-moving traffic, was New York. As we fled through the streets as though the Hounds of Hell were after us, I tried to look up and take in my surroundings. Besides the fact that Haamiah had told us to always remember where we go in case we have to find our way back, I had the creepiest feeling that something was very wrong, and that knowing my way through these streets might well save my life.

It wasn't much longer until we had entered an apartment complex. Lilith smacked the doors open with such force a crack appeared in the wall behind. I flinched, and ran to keep up as we headed to the lift. Lilith stuck her hand in between the doors just as they were about to close. As they opened again she pulled me in after her, the Scot following close behind.

Lilith grinned at the elderly couple who glanced at us nervously, their eyes darting from Lilith to the Scot. The atmosphere for the entire short, ten-second ride was awful. My power fought to rise the entire time, and my whole body screamed danger. I breathed a sigh of relief when the elderly couple got out on the fourth floor and we continued up to the twelfth.

When the doors opened we were in a tastefully decorated hallway with plush pink carpets and cream walls. I followed my mother down the corridor, noting the numbers as we passed the doors. Stopping outside 114, Lilith pulled open a small rectangular box at the side of the door and pressed her thumb to the blue pad. I heard a loud click, and Lilith pushed open the door to the apartment.

If I had thought about it sooner, I guess I would have expected the Queen of the Damned to live in a dungeon or, at the least, an apartment filled with whips and chains, with a torture chamber behind door number three. What I wasn't expecting was clean wooden floors leading through an open plan, light and airy stylish apartment, complete with a white kitchen and a huge white sofa facing a forty-two inch plasma television. It was the kind of luxurious apartment I had never even known to dream of, like a million dollar show home.

I scowled at the man as he pushed me forward roughly to close the door behind me. Lilith sauntered over to the kitchen table and flipped open her laptop. The man disappeared into one of the rooms.

I turned to Lilith. "So, umm . . . who was that?" I asked nervously, glancing towards the door.

She looked up. "Oh, that's Lachlan," she said vaguely. At my raised eyebrows she added, "Werewolf."

I nodded, my anxiety shooting a few notches higher.

As Lilith tapped away at her laptop, I nervously walked around the apartment. Spotting a cordless phone my heart went into overdrive. I reached for it, closing my hand around it.

"Do you mind if I make a call?" I called over my shoulder.

With a wordless cry, I jumped as Lilith plucked the phone out of my hand.

I swung around. "Oh, sorry, I was just going to . . . "

“Call the very people who imprisoned you in the first place?” she asked mockingly. “What a *great* idea.”

“Whoa!” I exclaimed, stepping back to put some distance between us. “Zach didn’t do this.” I belatedly wondered the wisdom of telling Lilith his name.

“Zach?” she hissed. “Zach . . . as in Zacharael, of . . . ” she trailed off looking thoughtful.

I bit my lip. “It’s okay, I don’t need to call them right away.”

“Them? Oh, right . . . Haamiah, Zacharael, Maion . . . I never could remember the others.”

“You know them?” I asked, slightly amazed. How would a Fallen angel come to know Zach and his friends?

She smirked. “Haamiah—the most boring of all angels, and the most self-righteous nerds there ever was? Maion—with the smoking hot body that I would love to rake my nails down, but with no finesse for anything other than the most brutal of killings? Then Zacharael.” She turned to walk away, squeezing her fist tightly to shatter the phone into pieces on the floor. “Yes, I know them. You know, I’m going to help you with your little problem.”

I frowned at her, tensing. “I don’t have any problems.”

She crooked an eyebrow at me. “Yes. You do. You’ve got plenty of problems, but I’m going to start with this one.”

I swallowed painfully, grimly wondering what psychotic plan she was cooking up. How could this be my mother? I didn’t even like her.

"Let me tell you a little story," Lilith began, sauntering toward the kitchen. She opened the fridge and pulled out a bottle of beer, offering it to me. I declined, with a shake of my head, and watched as she emptied the entire contents in her mouth, pulling another off the shelf. "Once upon a time there was a handsome, if rather dull, angel called Zacharael."

I bit my lip and tried to hide my scowl. Zach was *not* dull. He was anything but.

"Zacharael and Zanaria roamed the worlds together, side by side, for a thousand years. They were everything to each other: best friends, family, comrades . . . *soul mates*."

I felt my body freeze, an icy shiver running up my spine as I stared at her. *Soul mates*? That wasn't possible. *I* was Zach's soul mate. What game was Lilith playing? How did she even know about either of them? God, did everyone else know that Zach had had someone before me?

I shook my head, trying to clear my thoughts. It was ridiculous. The whole thing was ridiculous.

"They couldn't be soul mates," I blurted out, cringing as Lilith ran her eyes over me speculatively.

"Oh, but they were. Not only did they look like each other—beautiful and enchanting, they thought alike, their very essence complemented each other's perfectly. They never disagreed and they loved each other dearly. Not even Maion, Zacharael's closest friend, could get between them.

I cringed. This was all hitting a little too close to home. Could she be telling the truth?

"Then one day," she continued, "Zanaria told Zacharel she had a problem to take care of. A holy mission, as it were. She travelled to the human plane where a young helpless Nephilim boy needed rescuing. She saved his life, and the very same Nephilim sliced her head off, brutally, and irreparably murdering her before Zacharael's very eyes. Zacharael swore to enact revenge on any and all Nephilim he met from then on. He has killed thousands in her name over the centuries."

I couldn't breathe. My chest felt constricted, my throat blocked. I felt so utterly humiliated and betrayed. I cringed as I thought of how we had kissed, how our passion had overflowed even in front of Zach's friends. They knew. They knew there had been someone before me. Someone who mattered more. This perfect person had meant so much to Zach he had slaughtered thousands of Nephilim because he had been so devastated by her loss.

Then again, could I even believe a word Lilith said? She was Queen of the Damned, for heaven's sake! She was a murderer of children and the leader of the Fallen armies, if Haamiah was to be believed. And . . . my mother? Would my being her daughter actually mean anything to her? Did it mean she felt some semblance of loyalty toward me? Is that why she saved me from the Thrones? Or was there another reason?

History told me not to trust anyone, that everyone was a liar and out for their own gain. Bit by bit, the angels had begun to influence me, enough now I had friends, and someone I loved. Was that all folly? Was it all meaningless rubbish? My heart ached at the thought that I had been betrayed yet again, the thought that I had been so stupid to open myself up one more time. But my head told me to think this through, something wasn't right, and I needed to work it out. Ultimately, I guess I needed to decide if Lilith was to be trusted. If not . . . well, then I could work out what game she was playing.

“She wasn’t his soul mate,” I denied. “This Zanaria, she wasn’t his soul mate.”

“No? And why is that?” she asked with an air of surprise.

“Because I’m Zach’s soul mate,” I answered with as much of a glare as I could manage, given the circumstances. Having a conversation with the Queen of the Damned *A.K.A my mother* about soul mates wasn’t really a conversation I’d ever imagined having.

Lilith paused for a second, appraising me. Somehow I felt that I came off poorly. “You aren’t even the same species.”

I shrugged. “It doesn’t matter. I know I am.”

“There would be one way to know for sure. A *test*, if you like,” she suggested with a smile.

“A test?” I echoed. I didn’t like the sound of this. I couldn’t think straight, I just kept hearing the story Lilith had told me in my head over and over again. I needed to get away from here.

“We could bring back Zanaria, and let your beloved Zacharael tell you which of you is his one true love.”

31

'This is the year I will be stronger, kinder, unstoppable. This year I will be fierce.'

Unknown.

I stared at her in horror. "You can bring back a dead angel?"

Lilith stepped closer, reminding me of a snake: poised and coiled, ready to strike at the first sign of weakness. She ran her fingertips down my cheek, ignoring how I cringed away. In fact, though I had taken a heavy step backward, she seemed to have somehow glided with me.

She stared into my eyes, seeming to see into my soul. "I can't, but you can."

I looked at her blankly before letting out a strangled laugh. "You think I can bring an angel back from the dead?"

"I know you can." She twirled the glass bottle around her fingers. "Your angel side will allow you to open a portal to the netherworlds, and once inside, your goodness will simply coax her out."

"This is crazy talk," I gasped. "I need to think." I backed away, sliding over to the window. I pressed my forehead to the cool glass, staring down at the street below.

"What is there to think about?" Lilith sidled up to me. I tensed as she lay a hand on my back. "Bring back Zanaria and earn the respect and love of your guardian."

"And if he chooses her over me?" I tensed.

"Then it's his loss," she said casually.

That was certainly easy for her to say. She wasn't me, though. I had gone through my life meaning nothing to anybody. Zach was everything to me. We had taken a few hard knocks, yes, but we had found our feet again, and were stronger than ever. I was his, and he was mine. *Forever*. Unless I brought back some long lost lover of his, and he chose her over me. Would he really do that? I couldn't be certain.

I blew out my breath and tried to think logically. If there were someone out there that Zach preferred to me, wouldn't I prefer to cut him loose and make a life for myself with someone else? I frowned.

No.

I wouldn't. I didn't want there to be anyone out there more perfect for him than me. Surely there couldn't be someone else out there for me?

Was that a gamble I was willing to take? Did I really have any choice? If I refused, what would Lilith do? I cringed at her nearness. I was beginning to think I was safer in the waiting room. I felt out of my depth with Lilith. Just because she said she was my mother, that didn't mean I could trust her. It didn't mean she wouldn't use me for her own gain, as a lot of other people seemed to have done. In fact, I didn't even have proof that she was telling the truth. What if she wasn't my mother? Zach had told me of another Fallen angel who had the ability to open portals.

I shook my head imperceptibly at my own reflection in the glass. No. This was my lot. It was no good thinking about what could be or what may not be; I was up against one of the most dangerous and powerful of Fallen angels, and I needed to decide whether I would agree to her plan . . . for the time being.

Did I really have a choice?

I arched my back and slid away from Lilith, turning to face her with my chin held high.

“I’ll do it. I’ll bring Zanaria back.”

With a grin, Lilith had flounced off. At some point during our conversation Lachlan had come back. He nodded at me slowly, a glint in his eye flashing at me before he followed Lilith.

The rest of the day went by in a blur. Lilith left the room whenever she took a call, glancing at me slyly to check I wasn’t nearby. Lachlan lazed about, staring at me with narrowed eyes when he thought I wasn’t looking. A few other werewolves came and went, never saying much. I watched some television, gazed out the windows, and thought things over in my mind until my brain hurt.

I was jolted awake when Lilith touched me. I leaped off the sofa to my feet when I realized a small group of werewolves, including Lachlan, were gathered near the door, whispering.

“It’s time to go,” Lilith said almost joyously.

“Where?” I asked, my mind still foggy from sleep.

"We're going to get that tramp your lover wants." She slipped an arm around my shoulder. I cringed as much at her nearness as the harshness of her words. I tried to mask my discomfort by beaming at her.

"Great," I agreed, smiling so hard my jaw ached.

I followed as she left the apartment, the wolves trailing behind. We entered the lift silently and descended to the ground floor, exiting the building. Once we were on the pavement, Lilith pushed past people, sending them crashing into each other and, occasionally, the ground.

If I had been any less preoccupied with my current situation I would have been embarrassed, but, as it was, I couldn't care less about the strangers on the street, and knew that I would likely never see them again.

How would this play out? When would the Queen of the Damned confess whatever secret she was hiding? I felt stupid for getting into this position in the first place, but what choice did I have? Lilith was by far stronger than any angel or Fallen I had ever seen . . . what chance did I have of taking her if it came to a fight? That was another reason for bringing back the dead angel, and there was no way she was going to let me back out now.

32

'When you look back on life will you say 'I wish I had' or 'I'm glad I did'?'

Zig Ziglar.

I followed Lilith and Lachlan as they wound their way through the crowds on the street. They paused outside a café and glanced at each other wordlessly. Lachlan quickly disappeared among the people, pulling a phone out of his pocket. Lilith turned to me with a smile.

"There are a few loose ends I need to tie up. Wait here." She flashed her teeth in a scary semblance of a grin. "Don't go anywhere, though of course, I'll find you if you do."

With her words ringing in my ears, she turned and followed the werewolf into the crowd. I stood shaking, outside the café. My feet felt like led, as though I were rooted to the spot.

I tried to take a step, finding the movement impossible. Had she cast a spell on me? Had she done something to make me immobile?

I took a deep breath and focused, letting my power drain into my legs, to my feet. I willed myself to move and sighed with relief as my limbs sluggishly crept forward a couple of inches.

The first thing I needed to do; find a phone.

The first telephone box I saw was in a place that was too busy for me to do what I had to do. I weaved through the crowds of people who seemed to walk in large groups at a snail's pace specifically to get in my way. I crossed the road, noting a small park further down the street. My theory being that surely at one end of the park there would be a telephone box.

I was right. I ran down the middle of the beautifully landscaped park, noticing nothing, my eyes fizzed on the telephone box at the far right corner near a semi-circle of park benches and a rubbish bin.

I forced myself to slow as I neared it, belatedly thinking that even if someone didn't care if a young woman was running in a park, they would probably notice someone racing at the speed of light. I slid into the box and pressed my fingers to the coin collector underneath the dial. I shook it, trying to dislodge it from the wall, to open it somehow. It didn't work. *Damn*. I needed a coin to get the phone to work, and the only way that was going to happen would be to break it open. I had done it before, plenty of times, before any of this angel stuff. I had easily broken into telephone boxes, letter boxes—I was even a little proud at the amount of cars I'd hotwired and fenced for money. Surely now that I actually needed one particular bad-girl skill, it wouldn't fail me.

I closed my eyes and pressed the tip of my forefinger to the lock itself, my last resort coming up. I didn't even know if this would work. I channeled my power through that one finger, specifically thinking of the words *hot, heat, combust, flame*. Surely I could do this.

"*Incendia,*" I whispered.

To my disappointment, nothing seemed to be happening. I tried again . . . still nothing. Why wasn't it working? I tampered down my anxiety and tried to control the rage I felt at the situation. I hated feeling helpless.

Maybe it hadn't worked because I wanted to *melt* the lock. Maybe my conflicting thoughts and words had somehow stopped the spell from working. This time I tried to imagine *I* was on fire. I smiled as I smelt the charred smell of material. I kept my eyes closed, not wanting to know if I was now standing in broad daylight, completely naked. I pressed harder against the little metal lock, grinning as I felt liquid drip down my fingertip.

With the loudest clatter and jingle I was brought back to reality as the entire collection box melted, and the coins fell through the base to the floor.

I scooped up some coins and quickly dialed the number for the safe house.

"Pick up! Pick up," I urged. I waited with anxiety streaming through me.

"Yes?" a low voice grumbled.

"Maion? Shit!" I swore. "Maion listen to me—"

With a click the phone disconnected.

I growled under my breath and threw more coins in, redialing.

"Maion listen to me, it's important."

"I see you found a way out," he said. He paused. "I'm waiting."

I froze, my resolve wavering. What should I say? I hadn't thought this through. If I told him where I was, would I be leading the Thrones straight to me? I was fairly certain Lilith had something planned. At the very least, I knew I couldn't trust her. I had the feeling there was more to bringing Zanaria back from the dead. There was something else, and I was just waiting for the other shoe to drop. What did she want?

I groaned. What was I doing? I pressed my forehead on the glass and forced myself to concentrate.

"Is Zach okay?" I asked. That was the first thing I needed to clarify.

"He would be better if you had remained where you were," Maion replied dryly.

I bit my lip, feeling the usual swirl of hatred in my abdomen. What else did I need to know?

"Are Trev and Sam back?"

I heard a sigh. "No."

Fuck. I tapped my fingers on the window. Could I somehow barter with Lilith and get her to rescue Trev from Castle Dantanian? As a Fallen angel, she would be safe enough going there. As Queen of the Damned, wouldn't she be welcomed with open arms?

I groaned. Sam was with Lilura. I could only presume he was safe with her. We didn't know for certain the sorceri were working against us. My goals for the moment—I needed to find and rescue Trev, avoid recapture by the Thrones, and find out what Zach was keeping from me. So far I had found out he had massacred thousands of Nephilim and promised to murder every last one, and potentially he had another soul mate just waiting in the wings. If I ever had the right to feel overwhelmed—it would be now.

"Are you done?" Maion growled.

"Wait a minute!" I screeched.

To find and rescue Trev I needed Lilith. To figure out Zach's secrets I needed Lilith, and I needed to bring back Zanaria. There was nothing I could do to avoid recapture, although seeing as Lilith hadn't been carted off yet I could presume the safest place to be was by her side. The problem was; how could I let Zach know I was safe when I didn't even know if I was? If he didn't know where I was, then how could he help me if I got into trouble? Did I even want my soul mate anywhere near the leader of his enemies?

I closed my eyes. Did I trust Maion? No. Emphatically no.

"Tell Zach . . . tell him I'm out, but not to look for me just yet." I shook my head. "Tell him I'll be okay, and I'll be in touch when I can." I paused, wondering if I should say something else, wondering if I had done the right thing.

"Whatever."

Click.

My blood began to boil. I hated that *arrogant* dickhead. I scowled at the phone for a second before slamming it into the cradle. I had another thought. I picked it up again and slotted in a coin, aiming to ring Gwen's mobile.

A hand passed in front of me and pressed the button, ending the call. Fearing the worst, I spun around with my heart in my mouth.

I gasped, frowning in confusion at the stranger who stood too close for comfort. I shoved past him, not wanting to be blocked in.

"Who are you?" I demanded.

I glared up at him, at this latest intruder in my life. Why did I attract so much trouble? Trouble in an incredibly delicious package only meant one thing—supernatural creature. He was tall, broad and bulky like Zach, but he had dark hair that would have fallen to his shoulders if it hadn't been held out of his face by a clip. With a silver ring through his nose and the faintest of stubble showing, he was your typical mystical beast. What was he? Werewolf? With his piercing blue eyes I didn't think so. Perhaps he was something else. He could be Fallen, though I didn't get the evil vibe from him.

I scowled at him and repeated my question.

He pursed his lips. "That's no' important," he said with a thick Scottish brogue.

"Maybe not to you," I retorted.

He huffed out his breath, "I'm Drew. We have—"

"What are you?" I cut him off.

"Are ye serious? There's no time for this!" he groaned.

"*What are you*?" I repeated. The rage in me was creeping up, and the more this *Drew* tried to evade my questions, the more I wanted to rip him a new one.

He stared down at me with his blue gaze and uttered one word: "Lycan."

I froze, my eyes seeming to widen of their own accord. A thousand questions popped up in my head. *Lycan*? Emily and Tanya had said the lycae could be trusted. Did I trust the word of a witch and a harpy? What did I even know about lycae? What was he doing here?

At my silence, Drew jumped in. "We need to get out of here *now*." He reached forward to grab my arm. I knocked him away.

"Why would I go anywhere with you?"

"I promise I'm no' your enemy. Things aren't what they seem."

"What is *that* gibberish?" I snorted. "If you've got something to say, then say it."

He shook his head, clearly frustrated. "Ye dinna understand."

"Then explain it to me."

"There's too much to tell ye," he groaned. "I dinna ken how much ye ken about any of this. I dinna want to freak ye out . . . although ye seemed to handle me being a lycan okay." He frowned.

I stared up at him. "What?"

"Okay, I have to tell ye something," he hissed. He leaned closer. "Promise me ye'll hear me out."

"Go ahead," I said.

I watched as he gulped nervously. "The world isn't what it seems. There are other creatures besides humans. And I don't mean animals. Lycae, witches, and a hundred other supernatural beings walk around ye. Don't be afraid, I've been sent to keep ye safe."

33

'Your future is as bright as your faith.'

Thomas S. Monson.

I frowned at him. I couldn't decide if he was being serious. He looked serious. He even looked quite anxious about my response.

I held back my smile. "You're a bit late."

"What?"

I shrugged. "I know all of that. Whoever sent you is a little behind the times. I've had more contact with the mystical creatures in this world than I could ever have imagined."

He paused and then copied my shrug. "Then that just makes this easier. We need to go."

"No! Why would I go anywhere with you?"

He ran his hand through his hair. "There's wars going on all around ye, ye need to pick your allies carefully."

"I don't have any allies."

"Exactly. Ye need to pick them quickly. I promise ye I'm a friend, please believe me. Please come with me, ye don't know how close ye are to the beast."

“The beast?” I echoed. That sounded ominous, and I certainly didn’t like the sound of it.

He reached out again, and this time I let him grip my arm. I was too absorbed by his grim tone.

“The beast is close, and is infiltrating and influencing everyone. Everyone has an end game; you need to look at the people around you and work out theirs, *then* you will see what is really happening. You need to pick a side.”

I lifted my chin up. “I’m on the side of the angels.”

He stared down at me, his piercing blue eyes seeing into my soul. “Are you sure?”

I nodded grimly. “I think so.”

“Then what are you doing here?”

I frowned. “There are a few things I need to take care of.”

He shook his head. “You’re running out of time to pick your allies, and if you’re left standing on the wrong side the repercussions could be catastrophic.”

“I don’t understand.”

“I swear we’ll do everything we can to help you, but there’s a war going on here and you can’t see the players. But you will.”

My mind immediately flicked to Maion. Was he evil? That question had haunted me since I had first met him. Everything within me recoiled from him, but I still didn’t know the answer.

I shook my head. “I need to go.”

He nodded sadly. "I know. Please think carefully before you do anything. Yours might be the action that could bring about the end."

Well that sounded just awful. I backed away from him and then, when I was a safe distance away, I turned and jogged back to where Lilith had left me outside the café. When I didn't see her I counted my lucky stars. I felt exhausted.

My brain was so full of information that didn't make sense, and little snippets of secrets that I couldn't piece together. I just couldn't think straight with all of that going round and round my head.

I leaned forward and buried my face in my hands, trying to block everything out. I didn't want to hear the city, the traffic, the cars beeping at each other. I didn't want to hear people chatting and laughing, and I certainly didn't want to think the thoughts that were streaming through my head like a news bulletin.

Who were the players the lycae was talking about? Was it Maion? I had always thought there was something off about him, but I trusted Zach and he trusted him. Or did I really trust Zach? Those visions I had seen . . . that angel . . . the way he'd killed the Nephilim so heartlessly. He had been a monster, hunting down the helpless Nephilim and slicing them apart, but then I had seen the most recent vision of him arguing with Haamiah about looking for me. He had seemed genuinely upset that I was missing, so surely that showed that he had changed.

What about Haamiah? He was a Principality angel—he plotted and directed to his whim. Didn't that scream out 'player'? Lilith and Lachlan—I was perfectly aware they had an alternative agenda. I just needed to work out what it was.

I groaned. Where did the lycae fit into this? Drew had said someone had sent him to protect me . . . I couldn't imagine Zach ever sending someone else to keep me safe. Was it Aidan? That made more sense. He had done it before; had protected me countless times. Yes, it had to have been him. I sighed, pleased that I had figured out at least one riddle.

I kept my eyes closed tightly and concentrated on keeping the noise of the city at bay. As I listened, I began to hear voices, quiet at first then louder and louder, until it felt as though they were flooding through me. I squeezed my eyes tight to block them out, and they gradually faded until just one whisper broke through.

Soon, I'll have the Dagger of Lex.

I dropped my hands and span around to come face to face with Lilith.

"Let's go, the coast is clear," she said. She paused. "You can move now."

I nodded, sure now that she had tried to use magic on me. I was too confused about what I had heard to do anything other than follow her. I had no strategy, no plan. I had absolutely no idea what to do.

Without waiting, she spun away from me and rushed off down the pavement. I ran after her, struggling to keep up until I almost slid into her a few minutes later. Up the steps leading from the pavement, Lachlan stood with his back to a partially open door. Lilith lightly stepped up the stairs and brushed past the werewolf, entering the building.

Once inside, my eyes took a moment to adjust to the darkness. I screwed them up, trying to see where Lilith had gone. I saw a flash of movement at the back of the room, past the staircase, so I walked forward slowly.

“Watch for the hole in the floor,” Lachlan’s voice grumbled behind me.

I glanced down and cringed at the gaping hole leading down into an even deeper black, just a foot or so away from where I was standing. Feeling queasy, I edged around it, finding sturdier floorboards to stand on, until I had almost reached another doorway. I held one hand out to the wall, grimacing at the dirt and dust that masked it. This place was filthy. It was beyond run-down and clearly unsafe to be in. What was here that Lilith wanted so badly? And what on earth did this have to do with bringing the angel back from the dead?

I pushed on and turned the corner leading into the next room, stopping in my tracks at what I saw. Bodies . . . dozens of them were scattered across the room. Most were ripped to shreds, their mouths open in silent screams, and their blood streaming up the walls and dripping down the ceiling. These people had been *destroyed*.

I glanced at Lachlan, noting his smirk as he saw my discomfit.

“What were they?” I asked.

He shrugged. “Gatekeepers.”

I looked down at the nearest body, now seeing a dark blue triangle complete with swirls and a circle in the middle tattooed onto his forehead. His chest had been carved open so wide I could see his organs, lying there lifelessly.

“Were they evil?” I asked, fighting to keep my voice steady.

He shrugged again.

"Of course they were evil," Lilith called, sliding up to me. "They kept me from what I want, so how could they be good?"

There was the truth. Lilith . . . *bad*. It was all beginning to unfold now. I could see it all quite clearly. The gate these men had died protecting was the gate I needed to use somehow to bring back the dead angel. Lilith wanted the angel back to find this Dagger of Lex, whatever *that* was, so really the death of all these men was my fault. Without me, she wouldn't have killed them.

Heavy despair sat with me now. I still couldn't see a way out. I could try to fight them, but I would lose. How could one woman fight off numerous werewolves and the Queen of the Damned? I could open a portal to send them away, or jump through myself but again, Lilith could do the same, and she was stronger and older than me so she would be able to just transport right back, or close it down altogether. My fire? She came from Hell—as if my little flames would even singe a hair on her arm. I could only hope that an opportunity would present itself soon. I couldn't help but think back to what Drew had said about being close to the beast—had he been talking about Lilith?

I cringed as Lilith put her arm around me and pulled me past the bodies and body parts into the center of the room. I couldn't help but compare what I saw to a Stargate on the TV show of the same name. A tall black metal archway with designs etched all around stood in the center of the room with an odd blue haze in the middle. It looked like some kind of portal, not exactly like the type I could make, but I was pretty sure it led somewhere.

Lilith pulled me closer to it.

"All you need to do is open your own portal inside it," she urged.

"Where to?"

"To the Pool of Kali."

I shook my head, "I don't know where that is. How can I open a portal somewhere I've never been?"

Lilith stared into my eyes. "You're strong. You can do it."

I sucked my breath in. There was no other option I could see. They were waiting. They expected me to do this. I bit my lip and prayed that I didn't send myself to Castle Dantanian.

"What do I do?" I asked.

Lilith grinned wickedly. She pulled me forward until I was standing mere inches away from the gate. I closed my eyes for a second then began to pull on my power. It spiraled up and blasted out from me, a misty cloud covering my body. I thought the words over in my mind, not thinking for a second that it would work. *Pool of Kali, Pool of Kali*, I chanted.

My gravity shifted and I forced myself to step forward into my portal, praying for God knows what.

34

'Never sacrifice who you are just because someone has a problem with it.'

Unknown.

I staggered, righting myself at the last moment. I looked up and gasped. Had I done it? Was this it?

I was now standing in a large room with grey stone flooring, stone walls and a large glass window, from floor to ceiling, at the far end. The room was empty, and there wasn't a thing there; no pool, no pond, nothing that looked even remotely like the "Pool of Kali." Maybe I had come to the wrong place?

"I knew you could do it."

I turned, seeing Lilith.

"This is it?"

She nodded and threw her arms wide, spinning around while laughing loudly. "Finally! Everything I want is almost within my grasp."

I paused. "So, you admit you're not here just to bring back the angel?"

She stopped turning and advanced on me. "I'm absolutely here to bring back the angel. She has something I want."

"I thought we were bringing her back for Zach?" I asked, shaking my head. I knew that wasn't the case. I had known for a while, but hadn't been able to find a way out of it. Maybe I should have tried harder.

Lilith smiled. "We *are* getting her, and Zach can certainly have her if he wants her. Come on, we're not finished."

I shook my head. "What will you do to her?"

She shrugged. "Nothing. She has something I want, or she knows where it is. She'll tell me, and you can both be on your merry way."

"What is it?" I asked.

"None of *your* business," she snapped, her demeanor instantly changing.

I flinched. "I'm not doing it if it's something evil."

Lilith grabbed me by my throat. "You don't have a choice," she growled.

I flew through the air with a force I had never felt before. There was no time to do or think anything—before I knew it, I was crashing through the glass window and had landed on my back on the stone. My body ached. I knew from the crack as Lilith had hit me that she'd broken more than just my ribs this time and as I landed on top of the shattered glass I anticipated many more injuries.

I choked as Lilith reached over me, grasping me by my throat again. She squeezed tightly, her fingers digging in. I grabbed hold of her hand, trying to pry her fingers away. They were unmovable.

“You’ll do exactly what I say,” she snarled.

I couldn’t say anything. I couldn’t even move my head. She gradually loosened her grip, just as I thought I was going to pass out. My body dropped to the ground heavily and I spluttered, gasping for breath. Lilith wrapped her hand in my hair, and dragged me up to my knees.

“Get up,” she growled.

I held on to my hair and rose to my feet. Lilith pulled me to the edge of the verandah we stood on. Stones covered the floor from the shattered glass window to the stone wall wrapping around it. Lilith forced me to lean over the edge.

“Reach out and bring her back,” she said, once more pleasant and excited, her white teeth sparkling in a sweet smile.

“I don’t know what you mean. Reach out to what?” I gasped.

There was nothing there. Past the wall was just air. There was no portal, no pool, nothing of substance to actually reach into, so her demand didn’t make any sense.

“Do it!” she screamed.

I was so frightened. Zach would hate me for this. It was clearly wrong. If the Queen of the Damned wanted me to do something, shouldn’t I do the exact opposite?

“I can’t! I won’t,” I moaned.

Lilith dropped me. I leaned against the wall gasping, trembling with fear. This Fallen angel . . . she was a maniac. She was psychotic! How could I ever have gone along with this? How did I get here? Surely somewhere along the way there had been an opportunity for me to escape.

I pictured the lycae. *There* had been my chance at escape. I should have taken it. Why hadn't I?

Lilith paced beside me. "What if I said I had something that belonged to you, and I would give it back if you gave me what I wanted?"

"Why can't you do it yourself? Why do you need me for any of this?" I asked.

She crooked an eyebrow at me. "Duh! I'm evil. The Fallen can't open a pathway to the Pool of Kali, and the Fallen can't retrieve squat from inside it. But you . . . you can get it for me."

"I'm half Fallen," I croaked. "Why would you think I could get it?"

"Because you're mostly good," she sighed. She dropped to her knees beside me and ran her fingers through my hair. "Don't you want to know what I've got?" She pouted.

I bit my lip. Did I? "What?"

She leaned in. "I've got one of your boys."

I stared at her in horror. She had either Sam or Trev? She had one of my best friends?

"Which one?" I gasped.

She shrugged, "I didn't exactly stop and ask for names. Get me what I want, and I'll give him back to you."

This changed everything. I wouldn't sacrifice my best friends for anything. There was no way I would leave either one of them in Lilith's clutches.

"I'll do it," I whispered.

She stood up and let me do the same, forcibly turning me to face the wall. I bit my lip and reached forward into the air, my hand feeling nothing, no breeze, even. I closed my eyes and pictured her face. I pictured the way Zach looked at her, so happy and content. Had he ever looked at me like that?

I withdrew my hand. Lilith gave me room to move back away from the wall now. I fell to my knees, still holding my hand out. In my palm I held a glowing light. It was a shiny, silver sliver, a little glittering mass. It coiled around my hand as I stared, open-mouthed. Even Lilith seemed entranced, unable to move. The beautiful sliver leaped up from my hand and vanished.

I looked up at Lilith. "What just happened?"

She clapped her hands together and giggled. "You did it! You brought the soul back, and she'll wander around for a while before manifesting herself back into her angelic form. Then I will get what I want at last."

"That was it? I did what you wanted me to do?" I asked.

She grinned. "We're finished here."

She turned to go but I stopped her, grabbing her arm and spinning her back to face me.

"You promised you would give whoever you have back to me," I said, my voice shaking.

She paused. “Fine. Let’s go get him.”

I nodded and wobbled after her, climbing through the shattered glass into the stone room. I staggered as she waved her hand, making a portal. Without even thinking, I fell through it with her. I landed on my front, almost passing out with the pain shooting through my ribs.

I looked up, seeing Lilith and the Werewolves standing beside me. I inched away, cowering, as a knelt up. I wanted desperately to flee, but I needed whoever it was she had.

“There’s your boy.” I heard Lilith say.

I stood up and searched the room with my eyes. Where was he? I frowned as I realized we were back in the warehouse I had found myself in when Lilith had pulled me out of the waiting room. I stared toward the far end, seeing a figure chained up by his arms. Blood ran down his body.

I gasped, my jaw dropping. It wasn’t Sam or Trev. It was Aidan.

35

'You are never too old to set another goal or dream another dream.'

C. S. Lewis.

"Aidan?" I turned to face Lilith. She stood with her arms crossed, and the slightest of smiles on her lips. "What's going on?"

I took a few steps backwards away from her, my whole body yearning to run to Aidan and protect him, to release him from the chains holding him still. My head snapped up and my eyes searched the room as werewolves emerged from the shadows all around us. Some were in wolf form, and some in human form, their eyes glowing, fixed on me. As I surveyed the scene, I could see that Lilith was in control. She was the pack leader.

"Jasmine . . . run!" Aidan croaked, the words barely reaching my ears.

Those words made up my mind for me. I ran for him, skidding to a halt. Glancing behind me where Lilith remained still, I clasped Aidan's face in my hands, staring into his eyes earnestly. I ran my hands up his body. He was cold, though sweat made his body glimmer. Puncture wounds and bite marks covered his skin, while blood had dried in trails from his lacerations and cuts. Blood ran freely from his wrists where he had obviously ripped open the skin in his attempts to free himself from the chains.

I reached up and wrapped my fingers around the chain, looping the metal around my fist. I pulled hard, using all of my weight in addition to my muscle. The chains didn't budge. I loosened my grip and went to try again, instead feeling an agonizing wrench as my arms were pulled apart and stretched as a metal cuff clamped onto my wrist tightly, and chains strung me up beside Aidan. I gasped, shocked, and now very much afraid. I looked up, seeing that the chains were wrapped around a beam running the length of the warehouse. Unfortunately it was made of steel—definitely not as breakable as wood. I gripped the chain and pulled, only succeeding in slicing open my right wrist.

I closed my eyes and let my power rein free. I felt my power embolden my arms and I yanked again, screaming as I did so.

I was stuck. Were they mystically enchanted or something? I looked to where Lilith stood, smiling as the werewolves snickered all around her.

"Lilith! What's going on?" I shouted.

I watched, helpless to do anything else as she strutted across the room, grinning as she picked up a metal skewer. She twirled it around her arms, beautiful and terrifying at the same time.

"You haven't figured it out yet?" she laughed, high and long. "You really are clueless, aren't you?"

That annoyed me. With pleasure, I felt anger stretch through me, turning my insides hot. I lifted my chin and scowled at her. I let myself feel the betrayal and shock. I let my anger feed on the anger I felt at myself for not having found a way to escape from her clutches sooner. I had known there was something very wrong with the situation, and had carelessly presumed that though she was a Fallen angel, as my mother she wouldn't harm me. Only . . .

"No. I'm not. You're not my mother, Lilith," I said calmly, belying the rage that surged through me with every word.

"Ding ding ding!" she laughed.

I tensed as she launched the skewer at us, shrieking as Aidan groaned when it embedded in his thigh. My hatred boiled over as Aidan dry heaved, coughing and spitting saliva onto the floor.

"Took you long enough," she screeched with laughter.

I scowled. "Trust me, I had some serious doubts."

She faked looking shocked, one hand at her mouth and another at her heart. "What? You didn't believe me? Didn't I seem motherly to you?"

I raised my eyebrows. "Actually, given my past experience with *mothers*, you played the part perfectly. I guess it's the fact that you didn't know who my father was. Or, at least, what species he was."

"What species?" She narrowed her eyes. "You're a Nephilim! Last time I checked, that makes your father an angel!" she stepped closer, her heels clicking on the floor. "What are you?"

I refused to answer, now regretting that I had said anything at all. Me and my big mouth.

I screamed as she threw another skewer at Aidan, catching him in the same thigh, just a few inches lower.

"What are you?" she yelled manically.

“I’m valkyrie!” I shouted. “I’m half valkyrie.”

She wrinkled her nose. “Ew! Valkyrie? A harvester? How . . . cheap and disgusting.” She waved her hand in the air, dismissing the subject. She seemed fond of doing that, and this time I guessed it was for the best. “I admit I’m disappointed you didn’t really think I was your mother. I think I would have been an excellent mother.”

I ignored her as she turned away, babbling to herself.

“Are you okay?” I whispered to Aidan. His whole body trembling. He met my eyes, saying nothing. “She’s a maniac,” I hissed.

The ghost of a smile appeared on his mouth. “What gave it away?”

“You’re not even listening to me!”

I whirled around just in time to lift my legs out of the way of the metal pole being chucked at them. It crashed into the wall behind me and clattered to the floor.

“I’m listening,” I cried. I looked from Aidan to Lilith. “What do you want from us?”

“I want nothing from *him*!” She twirled a lock of hair around her fingers. “He’s just a bit of fun. You, however, are the prize.”

At the thought that Aidan had been caught up in this for no fault of his own, my rage singed me from the inside. As I breathed, mist actually came out of my mouth.

“What do you want?” I shrieked.

I flinched as lightning lit the room up before plummeting us in shadows repeatedly. It was almost like strobe lighting in a nightclub. Again and again and again we were lit up. Thunder growled outside, like monster trucks doing battle.

"What is this?" Lilith scowled, turning in a circle to watch as the room dimmed again.

I looked around nervously, still testing the chains with little tugs. I wasn't sure what was going on either—my only explanation being a freak lightning storm, but I didn't see any harm in stalling her.

"So what? You're going to torture us?"

She rolled her eyes. "Why would I torture you?"

I frowned in confusion. "Why else would you want me here? I can't get you anything. All you're going to do is have the angels come crashing down on you, and if you think you can beat an army of full grown warrior angels, even with a pack of werewolves, you're about to be proven very wrong."

"Pfft!" She waved her hand, dismissing my words. "As if I'm even remotely concerned with your angels. No one cares about the involvement of *angels*. Besides, they left you to rot in that hell hole, there's no way they even care enough to come looking for you. They probably don't even know you're gone."

I prayed that Maion had ignored what I had said to him and had revealed my phone call to Zach. Though we left things with an argument, there was no way he wouldn't come looking for me.

"There's no one else who would care that you have me," I said, refusing to show how that comment actually stung a little.

"You're wrong. There's someone who has been searching the world over for you, *someone* who was getting incredibly frustrated that you didn't seem to be on this plane of existence after he fought to get here. Yes, I'm going to trade you for something that I want. And *he* will pay anything for you."

I could feel the color draining from my face. I knew who she was talking about. The subject of my many nightmares. The beast of my dreams. She meant Asmodeus. She was going to give me to him, in exchange for something. I felt so tense that I could fracture into a thousand pieces. *Asmodeus*. Rapist, torturer, kidnapper, murderer . . . Fallen angel. Lightening split the sky again.

"What are you exchanging me for?" I asked calmly, coolly.

She snickered. "Why would you care?"

"Maybe it's something I can get you in exchange for my freedom."

She smirked. "I doubt it. I want the Falchion of Tabbris. Do you have it hidden in your sock drawer at home?"

I froze. I knew where it was. Potentially that information could see my release. It could also mean the beginning of a Heavenly war, as it could be used to create a portal into the Heavenly realm. If I didn't tell her where it was, then chances were before the day was out I would be raped savagely by Asmodeus. Even just the thought of being bent over his table as he rammed himself into me over and over made me gag.

I vomited, choking and spitting as it fell to the floor.

"If you know where it is, tell her. You'll not survive Asmodeus again. There'll be no one to help you this time. Please . . . Jasmine . . . if you know, please tell her," Aidan pleaded, his eyes wide, horrified.

I bit my lip, and flinched when Lilith appeared inches away.

"Well? Do you know where it is?"

"No," I said, looking her in the eye.

I heard Aidan sigh next to me, and I watched, anxious, as Lilith narrowed her eyes on me, drawing closer. She hissed out her breath and turned away, leaving me to sag in my chains as her warm breath remained with me.

"Lachlan!" she screamed. "Where is he?"

Lachlan appeared from behind the werewolves and ran to her, holding out a mobile. Lilith glared at me and then snatched the phone and strode through the wolves, disappearing through one of the doors at the back of the warehouse.

"Aidan!" I hissed. "Aidan, we need to get out of here."

Aidan grunted in response. I anxiously looked around. I needed to get out of these chains.

With a howl, a body was thrown to my feet. A werewolf scrambled to his knees, spinning to look at me. With glowing amber eyes he snapped at my feet, his canines clicking together. He lunged for me, jaws open. I lifted my legs and wrapped them around his neck, snapping it with a loud crack. His body dropped to the floor by my feet. I sucked in a breath as the pack closed in, growling and snarling.

"Aidan, you have to help me. I can't hold them all off!" I shouted.

I desperately searched for Lilith. She couldn't let me die, or she wouldn't have me in exchange for the Falchion. Another wolf lunged, earning him a kick in the face. He fell back, only to be replaced by another and another. As a particularly gruesome werewolf, with one eye missing, lunged for my neck, he was ripped away from me with a snarl.

To my relief, Drew stood in front of me, and in one swift movement he snapped the werewolf's neck. With his forearm he wiped blood from his face.

“Jesus, ye havenae made it easy, have ye?” He grinned, looking as though he was enjoying every minute of the fight.

“What are you—” I grimaced. “Scrap that, get me out of these *now*!”

Drew looked up to where the chains were wrapped around the bar above us. He reached up to grab the chain and pulled. I winced as it pulled on my skin.

“Canna do it,” he wheezed.

Before I was able to berate him, he was knocked to the ground with a savage growl. I cringed and lifted my feet up, booting another wolf away as it took a swipe at Aidan. I took a second to survey the room, realizing for the first time that the werewolves were fighting each other. No . . . I glanced at Drew who still struggled with the wolf on the floor, then up at the two men who fought on the bar above me. I shook my head and turned to Aidan.

I desperately wanted to tell him what was happening. To tell him that Drew’s lycae pack were here. That they were going to save us. That for whatever reason, they were going to get us out of here. But he hung there beside me, unconscious, blood pouring from his thigh.

I silently rooted for the lycae, egging on the huge beasts as they tore the werewolves apart. The noise was deafening. Metal clashing, flesh being torn apart, growls and howls . . . and all I could do was remain still, chained as I was to the metal bar above me.

"Lass, ye owe me one for this!" Drew hollered as he shouldered a wolf out of the way, swinging a dagger at another.

Over the din, I could hear a whisper of sound; directions, thoughts. I focused on the thread of sound, amplifying it as loud as I could. I turned my head, trying to match the voice to the person. Who was muttering?

As a small but lithe wolf sidestepped Drew, I heard the voice in his head as clearly as if he had spoken it out loud.

"He's going for your arm," I screamed.

Drew's face screwed up in pain as huge white canines sunk into his forearm. He howled in anger and shook the wolf off.

"He's coming again from the left," I shrieked, praying he would listen to me. Drew turned, dagger poised, ready to defend himself against – air. "Your *other* left!" I screamed.

Drew spun around, dropping to the floor to catch the wolf by his legs. Sending him crashing to the ground, he quickly snapped its neck. As he glanced up at me I closed my eyes in relief. I opened my eyes again as a pair of amber eyes zoned in on me, inches away. I could do nothing but scream. The amber faded and the expression took on a vague, unpleasant look . . . before dropping to the floor.

Drew stood inches from me, blood coating his mouth, and his eyes glowing blue.

"Well, I've had a canny bit of fun, but I think it's time tae get goin'," he drawled wryly.

I frowned at him, suddenly anxious that he was going to leave me here. Instead, he winked and lifted his arms to the chains above my head.

"I'm thinkin' that ye are stronger than ye look," he said, his eyes seeming to narrow at me.

I nodded quickly and wrapped my own fingers around the chains.

"Are ye ready, lass?"

36

'Every love story is beautiful but ours is my favorite.'

Unknown.

Together we heaved, my power flowing through my arms into the metal itself, bending and tearing it. With Drew's additional and substantial strength, the bar above us groaned and creaked, eventually giving in and snapping in half. I slid my chains off the jagged edge and went to free Aidan. Though I was now free of the bar, unfortunately I was still stuck in the chains. Still, despite the fighting going on around us, it was definitely an improvement.

My attention was dragged back to Aidan when he groaned. Drew had pulled him out of the way of the falling bar but he now sat slumped over, clutching his thigh.

I ducked under his shoulder and pulled him to his feet. Supporting his weight, I guided him as we ran for the warehouse doors. It was incredibly difficult keeping on in the right direction with wolves and lycae snapping at us every which way. We reeled away from them as quick as possible, but even so we ended up with swipes and bites. After dashing to the side for what seemed like the hundredth time, Aidan moaned and collapsed to the ground.

"No!" I screamed. "Get up. We have to move."

His eyes rolled back, and his head dropped.

"Aidan!" I shrieked. My screams seemed to be punctuated by the bolts of lightning that flashed outside.

As I was about to kneel beside him, I was knocked to the side roughly. It felt as though I had been hit by a truck. My body screamed in protest as I hit the floor, suffocating under the weight on my chest. I wondered if I was having a heart attack before my brain reassembled itself and noted the pain flooding my body through the wound in my side. I shut off the agony that roared through me when my senses returned to me in the nick of time as narrow, amber eyes closed in, giant white teeth snapping at my face. I pulled a leg up under me and booted the werewolf off my body, leaping to my feet.

I instantly hit the floor again as I belatedly felt a stinging backhand across my face. I scrambled up and darted backwards, putting some distance between us. Lilith had entered the fight, and she certainly didn't look pleased.

While I moved into a fighting crouch with blood running down my face, my fists ready and my weight neatly balanced, Lilith stood with one hand on her hip, the other clutching a mobile phone. She gave me a smug look tinged with amusement. It was that arrogant look you got when someone disregarded your attempts to do well, a distinctly superior expression. Only she wasn't superior to me.

I saw red. My Fallen angel side reared its head and I narrowed my eyes. Focused on her, I swept my right foot out high and to the side, knocking loose the phone from her hand. I smiled as time seemed to still, the phone spinning out of her reach and splintering into pieces on the ground.

Lilith turned to face me, looking seriously pissed off. "*That* was expensive you little bitch!" she roared.

She leaped forward and gripped me by my shoulders, heaving me through the air. I hit the brick wall and crumbled to a heap on the floor, plasterboard and brick falling down all around me. I gasped, pain radiating through my chest and gazed up at her in horror as she approached me.

I staggered to my feet as she closed in and ducked below her first swing. I jumped, using my power to elevate so I could run up the wall and backflip away as she aimed a kick. She pulled her foot out of the wall and ran, sliding towards me. With a grin, she spun, knocking me off my feet. I gasped as I hit the floor on my back.

She quickly straddled me and punched me again and again. I could feel my left eye swelling; I could barely see, and my eye felt as though it was about to explode. With a crack, I felt my jaw give way under her pounding. Blood coated my face, and I had bitten through my lip so I was also choking on the blood that filled my mouth. If it had occurred to me to give up at this point, I probably would have.

Unsure how the idea came to me, or even how my brain was able to function under the onslaught, I recalled my power, letting it heat and burn through me. Within seconds I was alight, flames reaching out from my skin, yet not burning me. Each flickering flame seemed to envelop me, almost making me feel safe.

Lilith howled and quickly threw herself off of me, slapping at the fire burning through her clothes. Lachlan appeared behind her and smothered the flames with his hands before turning to me with a savage snarl. I scrambled back on my hands, having no time to do anything other than cover my face as he launched through the air, morphing into his wolf form midflight.

I shrieked, the sound so loud it was almost unrecognizable to my ears. The fire still raged through my body even as a grey mist obscured my vision.

As I cringed, waiting for Lachlan to reach me, I heard an echoing shriek nearby. The pain didn't come as I expected it to. There was no savage biting, no ripping off of body parts . . . nothing. I opened my eyes, my heart pounding erratically, and tried to will my mist away. The glittering mass remained, despite my efforts, so instead I concentrated on dimming the flames and scrambling away - or at least in a direction I thought was away from Lilith and Lachlan. I rolled forward to my knees and pushed hard to stagger to a stand. When I opened my eyes to take stock of the situation I gasped, forcing my eyes so wide they stung.

A man stood in front of me, shielding me from Lachlan. He fought him, kicking him back, again and again. Every attack Lachlan made was avoided with ease and was returned in kind twofold. The wolf eventually darted back, cowering behind Lilith, panting as he recovered his breath.

"And who the fuck are you?" Lilith spat. She held up her hand. "Actually, no, I don't care. *She*," she pointed at me, "is my payment, and you have no right interfering with my business transaction!" she screeched at the end, losing her composure.

The man chuckled in response. While Lilith worked herself up in a rage, I took the opportunity to gaze at the man who had saved me from a severe face chomping. He stood between Lilith and I but had turned so that I could see his face while he mocked her. He was ruggedly handsome. He was tall and muscular, perhaps a little bit shorter and a little bit stockier than Zach or Aidan. He had short blond hair, piercing blue eyes, and a curved, smiling mouth that seemed to hold genuine warmth. He was dressed in ripped, faded jeans and a grey T-shirt with blood smeared across it. Though all signs pointed to him having already been fighting here—sweat making his T-shirt stick to him—he had an air of relaxation, and nonchalance. He seemed perfectly at ease with the situation, even though fighting roared all around us.

That was when I realized I had been frozen to the spot, gawking at him, when I should have been looking for an escape. I didn't know who this guy was! He probably wasn't even helping me; knowing my luck, he was probably some kind of assassin sent to rid the earth of half valkyrie half Fallen angel hybrids. Also, I belatedly thought with a grimace, I *should* have been checking if Aidan was even still alive. There was just something about this man that was oddly mesmerizing.

I looked to where Aidan lay in a crumpled heap, a meter or so away from me, and I felt my eyes sting with tears as blood began to pool underneath him. I staggered to my feet, thinking to myself that I must have lost a lot of blood, too. I was so cold, freezing, actually, despite having been on fire a short time ago. I looked down, expecting to see a gaping wound with the breezy air wafting through, and let out a horrified yelp as I realized my clothes had mostly been burned away.

I regretted it immediately as my yelp distracted the stranger, allowing Lilith to take advantage of him. She mashed him in the side of his face as he whipped his head around to look at me. He staggered, surprisingly able to remain on his feet. He returned the punch, skimming her face as she whirled away. She spun closer, chopping him in the throat, using the flat of her hand to slam him in the sternum. He flew back, landing on his feet in a crouch. She followed him move for move and leaped up, scissoring him with her legs, kicking him to the ground.

Lachlan ran at me. Unable to do anything about my partial nudity I met him head on, and tossed him to the side. I unleashed my inner bad-ass and went so crazy on him I would have made Emily and Tanya proud. I ripped his fur, digging my nails in deep enough to shred strips of skin from his back, shrieking all the while.

I stepped back as Lachlan wrenched his body free of my ravaging fingers. I turned my head, realizing that the stranger and I stood side-by-side, facing Lachlan and Lilith. I could only hope he wouldn't turn on me just yet. Three on one would be a bit much. I bit my lip as I scowled him.

He gave me an unreadable look, one that had me masking my scowl.

"Go for the wolf, I'll take on this cheap, skanky whore," the man advised with a wide grin.

I could feel the happiness emanating from him. It was the strangest feeling, as though I was getting a sneak peek into his psyche. I pushed the thought away, thinking I was being ridiculous.

"You'll pay for that," Lilith was snapping in response to his dig. She gestured to her charred clothes. "These are *not* cheap! These are designer!"

The man sniggered. "Yeah, well now you've got custom made *designer* burns."

I looked at him in amazement. I couldn't believe he was joking at a time like this . . . and with *her*! This was the Queen of the Damned, and he'd called her a skanky whore, insulted her clothes . . . and I had smashed her mobile. I felt the corner of my lips tug up. I *was* a bad ass.

She curled her lips up in a savage smile. "Make your jokes, fool. The dagger of Lex will be mine in a matter of days and when I exchange this little creature for the Falchion, you'll all kneel before me."

I readied myself to take on Lachlan, focusing on him as he ran for me. At the last moment I had an idea. Oddly, I had no doubts about my ability, and no concern if it would work or not. I turned and threw all of my power into my thighs, forcing it down to the ends of my toes, and I made contact with Lachlan's chest. I felt the raw power running through me as he flew back through the air at an impressive speed. In the split second that followed I let my power churn through my abdomen, and unleashed it even as I fought nausea when my gravity shifted. I beamed as a portal opened up behind him, like a giant net. I laughed out loud as he sailed right into it.

The man next to me gasped, quickly recovering enough for the next blow Lilith aimed at him. She hadn't seen the portal yet and I struggled to keep it open, my body trembling under the drain of power pouring from me.

I watched, amazed, as the man copied the high kick I had given Lachlan and sent Lilith into the portal. I let the portal lapse and dry heaved, nausea and dizziness making me sway. I turned and groaned at the ensuing faintness the slight movement caused. I felt partially mollified that the man seemed just as exhausted. He leaned forward on his knees and panted. He straightened and stretched his arms up over his head before turning to me with a glint in his eye. From where I stood, bent in half as I heaved, my stomach rolling, his feet come into view in front of me. I quickly straightened, grimacing as I did.

I needed to be sure Lilith wouldn't come straight back through the portal. Had we injured her enough to be sure she would need time to recover? Or would she reappear back here in mere seconds?

The seconds ticked by, each one heavy with tension. Nothing happened. I began to release some of the pressure I was holding inside and let myself stare at the man now in front of me.

The man grinned. "I've dreamed of meeting you for years . . . I just never thought I'd see so much of you."

My mouth dropped open. "What?"

"I'm Caleb. But if you want, you can call me Dad."

37

'Don't waste time on jealousy. Sometimes you're ahead, sometimes you're behind.'

Mary Shmich

Without waiting for me to give him a reply, he heaved Aidan up over his shoulder and weaved through the remaining werewolves. Most had fled after seeing Lilith hurled through the portal, but some remained, only to be torn apart by the lycae.

I was stuck in place. *Dad*? This was my Dad? This beautiful, deadly man was my father? Somehow I could begin to believe it. He certainly showed similarities to me in his features, more so than Lilith, that was for sure.

I yelped as something tightened around my wrist and yanked me backwards. Caleb spun around to face me, and within seconds had freed my arm and was leaning toward Drew threateningly. Drew didn't back down, instead snarling viciously and looming over the man who claimed to be my father.

"Caleb . . . " I stuttered. Did I call him Caleb, or Dad? Caleb was probably the wisest choice until I had verified his claims. "It's okay, he's a friend . . . I think."

Caleb glanced at me, his confusion evident. "You *think*?"

I shrugged. I didn't know if Drew was to be trusted. Everyone seemed to be surprising me these days. Someone would save your life and claim to be your ally, only to betray you a moment later and vice versa. Emily had tried to trick me, playing the part of evil witch well, only to become a good friend to me later.

Drew growled. "And who the hell are ye? Bit late, are ye no'? The lass comes wi' me."

I stepped between them as Caleb flushed with anger. I needed to stop this before something happened. "Drew, this is my dad . . . I think."

"Ye think? Ye aren't a quick learner like, are ye? I was listening in while ye were talking to that bitch. Didn't ye think Lilith was your bloody mother a wee while ago?" He rolled his eyes, "I'm no' letting ye out of my sight."

At this point I became uncomfortably aware that we were surrounded. The lycae pack had dispatched of the remaining wolves and had blocked the exit, waiting for their leader to give them orders.

"I didn't invite you to come with us, *dog*, so take a hint and leave," Caleb threatened.

I couldn't believe this was happening again. What on earth was wrong with the men in my life? And since when was I the peacemaker? I was the one with out of control emotions and rage that could blow people up and decimate armies, yet I seemed more irritated than irrationally angry.

I flinched as lightening flashed, accompanied by high-pitched shrieks. The sound didn't bother me as much as it did the lycae, judging by their howls.

When the flashes stopped my eyes slowly adjusted to the gloomy light again. I couldn't move a muscle. Instead, I was only able to flick my eyes around the room to view the newcomers and judge the threat they posed. All around us, perched on the beams above our head, on top of crates and cartons, some even halfway up the wall clinging onto cracks, were beautiful woman, aiming their weapons at us. Some held guns, others a bow and arrow, others clutching throwing knives and stars, and some even more simply held their palms out, ready to throw their magic into the mix.

Drew scowled and backed down reluctantly, stepping slowly away from me. "Doona think this means ye've won. It just means I dinnae want tae see the lass hurt if ye unleash your nest of psychos."

Caleb grinned, the insult amusing him. His eyes seemed to twinkle with merriment.

Drew jutted his chin at me. "I'll be in touch."

I watched the lycae file out, snarling and growling their disapproval. Caleb looked at me, appraising my reaction. When I simply stared back, unamused at the show of male dominance, he flashed a smile. With one hand holding Aidan still on his shoulder, he threw the other out wide to encompass everyone.

"Jasmine, meet your family."

I hissed in a breath. I had suspected it, but actually hearing it said out loud was another thing entirely. I whipped my head around at the approaching women. "Valkyrie."

He nodded. "Come on, we need to get going. We can do introductions later."

I nodded absently. How could these women be related to me in any way? They were . . . amazing.

I could tell the difference between them and the other mystical females I'd encountered. Witches were much more earthy, voluptuous and smooth, almost hippy-like, and mercenaries, like Emily had said. Elves were quiet, thin and obedient with an almost pixie-ish look to them, their features delicate and sharp. Angels were ethereal, soft and small, their very essence seeming to flow peacefully around them. *Valkyrie* were warriors. Yes, they were beyond beautiful as all mystical seemed to be, but they packed on lean muscle, their eyes were sharp and *seeing*, every movement a threat. I could imagine that a single one would make a lethal assassin.

I watched as they swiftly moved in toward us. One, a tall, muscular woman, with eyes as black as coal, stepped closer than the others, and withdrew a vial of grey liquid from her jacket pocket. She tipped it onto the floor and stood back, staring down at the puddle. Seemingly of its own accord the liquid began to move, swirling round faster and faster like a whirlpool, no more than a meter wide.

A witch's spell. It had to be. I glanced at Caleb, who simply waited patiently. One by one, the women sat on the edge of the pool and lowered themselves in slowly. I counted fifteen drop in until it was just myself, Caleb and Aidan left.

"After you," Caleb said softly.

"Where does it lead to?" I asked.

"Does it matter? More than likely the werewolves will be back here before long." At my insistence he lamented, grinning ruefully, "You're just like your mother." He didn't seem to notice when I tensed. "Home. It leads home."

I took a deep breath. "Whose?" I wouldn't mind being taken to the Nephilim safe house right about now."

"Yours . . . mine. I'll take you to the valkyrie colony. There, we can talk."

I nodded. I figured a valkyrie colony would be the safest place to be besides home. I hesitantly stepped toward the pool. I turned back to Caleb.

"Promise me that Aidan is coming with us, and you're not going to dump him here." I paused. "He means a lot to me."

Caleb looked at me solemnly. "I swear to Odin."

Yeah . . . and there was that. I bit my lip and slid into the pool, not seeing any other option. I took a deep breath before I let my head go under.

I landed on my feet, not expecting the long drop, and a little unprepared for it. It was always quite unsettling going through a portal of any kind, never knowing if you were going to land in water or on solid ground, or how high up you would be. I had learned to just take a deep breath and go with it.

I quickly shielded my eyes from the light. It was bright, really bright. Had we gone to a different dimension, or a different country?

As my eyes gradually adjusted to the light I shielded myself for an entirely different reason. I was standing with the other valkryie in the middle of a street, just a normal suburban street with a pavement on each side of the road and houses lined up opposite each other.

I gasped in shock, covered my half-nudity, and turned to Caleb who had just dropped in next to me.

"You brought us *here*? Where humans can see us dropping out of thin air?" I hissed.

Caleb smiled, seeming completely unconcerned.

"This is our house," he said.

"What, you own a whole street?" I asked sarcastically.

"No," he conceded, "but the mystics do. This whole suburb is pretty much filled with witches, harpies, elves, valkyrie, and demons, of various sorts. There are still quite a few humans, but none on this particular street." He pointed to a huge grey and white double story house protected by a tall iron gate.

I stepped closer and looked through the bars of the gate, my mouth dropping open as I saw the huge, immaculate lawn leading up to the imposing building. There was a double garage beside it and a white sports car parked in front. It was a Saleen S7, or at least, it looked like it. It couldn't be. They were, like, six hundred thousand dollars!

"Is that . . . ?" I pointed to the car.

"Sure is," Caleb replied, pushing open the gate and squeezing through with Aidan. "Touch it, and Izzy will kill you, though." He swung around to face me. "I mean it . . . don't touch it."

I nodded my agreement and silently followed him in, flanked by the other Valkyrie. This whole moment seemed surreal. The house, the place, the people . . . it was everything I had never known to imagine. This was my family? That's what Caleb had said, but did he mean that literally? Did I have cousins here? Aunties and uncles? Or did he just mean that these were valkryie, like me?

I sidled past the car, almost drooling at it as I peered in the window. It was beautiful. Definitely the sexiest car I had ever seen. I could totally see Zach driving it . . . if he didn't have wings, and actually had to drive places.

One of the other valkyrie darted in front of Caleb and opened the front door, rushing in.

"We're home," she screeched, before disappearing into one of the rooms.

I followed Caleb in, trailing him into the kitchen where he lay Aidan down on the table. Aidan groaned and turned his head, oblivious to everything that was going on. I leaned closer and lay my hand on his forehead. He was cool to touch, no obvious signs of fever, and the wounds on his leg had ceased to bleed, so that was also a good sign. I was pushed out of the way as a red head jumped in and ripped Aidan's clothes off, leaving him almost naked on the table. I hissed in my breath as I saw the wounds covering his body. He had more injuries than just the leg wounds Lilith had made when we had been chained up together. She must have had him for days.

I frowned, feeling edgy and irritated as the valkryie gathered round, ogling him. It wasn't as if he was *mine*, but still . . . he could have been. I felt my anger rise swiftly and tried to push it down. There was no need to get on the bad side of everyone as soon as I arrived.

I couldn't help it. I felt my mouth open and heard the snarl come out of my mouth before I knew what was happening. Whereas the Nephilim would have jumped away, completely freaked by my show of aggression, the valkyrie simply ignored me and continued to stare at him.

I looked around amazed, turning to look sharply at Caleb as he said to a black-haired girl beside him, "She's definitely one of us."

I edged closer to Aidan, feeling the need to not exactly protect him, but protect my place with him.

"What do you mean by that?" I snapped at Caleb.

"Territorial much?" a blonde said from the other side of the table.

"Yeah, we thought the angels might have influenced you too much, you know, being *good* and all . . . " A punky looking pink-haired girl with studs all over her face laughed. " . . . but *you* will fit in just fine."

I frowned, unsure whether to be pleased by that or not.

"Is there a healer here?" I asked.

The valkyrie shook their heads.

"We've sent for Anna," the pink girl said.

"Who's that?"

"She from the coven across the street. She's pretty cool."

Coven? I frowned. "She's a witch?"

The girl rolled her eyes. "Don't freak out. We know the angels don't approve of witches or whatever, but she's a friend of ours."

"No," I shook my head. "I don't . . . " I took a deep breath. "I'm not like that. I had a friend who was a witch."

Collectively, they seemed to be surprised by this. Judging from the curious expressions on their faces, they didn't seem to know what to make of me. Was I a disappointment? Were they expecting someone else?

Caleb held out a drink beneath my nose. It took me a second to realize, I was so involved in my thoughts. I took it, and watched him take a drink out of the glass he held.

"We need to talk. Leave the Fallen to be healed and come with me," he said, turning to leave the kitchen.

"No. I'm not leaving him here," I growled, biting my lip when I realized my rage wasn't quite tucked away.

"Is he your boyfriend?" a petite blonde girl asked from the other side of the table—where it was probably safer.

I scowled. "No."

"Then there's no reason to stay. He'll be fine when Anna gets here," Caleb said.

I hesitated before meekly following him to the kitchen door. I did want to know more about him and my family. I had a million questions for him, but I felt strangely hesitant to leave Aidan's side. I wanted to know how Lilith had gotten hold of him. There had to be a whole back story there, and I didn't want to miss any of it. Still, he was unconscious at the moment, so there was no harm in leaving him just for a few minutes.

I left the kitchen behind Caleb, who walked through a small study area and into what must be the living room. It was huge, at least double the size of the open plan kitchen-diner in the Nephilim safe house. There were four large sofas, covered in throws and cushions, bean bags, and floor rugs everywhere, all vaguely aiming in the same direction—at the huge television on the wall. A stand beneath it held a Playstation and an Xbox. Trev and Sam would *love* this place.

My heart ached at the thought of them. I hoped they had been found. I hoped that Gwen had convinced the others do go looking for Trev, and that Maion and Zach had found Sam before Lilura could do anything to him. When I thought of Zach, my whole soul cried out for him. Why hadn't he come for me when Lilith had a hold of me? What would he say when he found out about Zanaria? Would he leave me for her? Why had I ever agreed to bring her back? I was such an idiot.

"Can we make this quick? I need to get home. There's a lot of stuff I need to sort out," I said as soon as Caleb sat down.

He looked up at me, his mouth dropping open in surprise before handing me a jumper. I quickly pulled it over my head, relieved when it covered my knees.

"I'm serious, there's stuff I need to do," I advised him.

"More important than learning about who you are? Who your family is? I can't imagine the angels have been very forthcoming about our history."

I frowned. "I know you worship the god Odin. That you're warriors and you—" I shuddered. "—harvest the souls of soldiers, and abilities of other creatures. There's a final battle you're all preparing for . . . "

"Ragnarök," Caleb supplied.

I nodded. "And I know that you're all demi gods and goddesses, that you count Odin as a parent."

When I fell silent, Caleb stared at me for a moment. "So you know something of our kind, only the basics though." He sighed. "I can tell from what you've said, and the way you've said it, how you feel about the valkyrie—the influence of the angels." He shook his head.

I scowled. "Those *angels* have taken care of me these past few years. They fed me, clothed me, trained me and protected me. Where the hell were you?"

Caleb looked at me sadly. "I thought you were safer with them."

"You knew where I was?"

He shook his head. "No. But I was told they had you."

"What about when I was little? Where were you then?" The conversation hadn't exactly gone in the direction I had wanted it to, but I needed to know.

"Your mother took you away from me when you were only a baby. Not only away from me, but from all of this. She said she didn't want you to grow up with this as your life. She wanted you to be human. She abandoned you at a hospital where you would be taken in and protected, treated as a human."

"Only that wasn't the case," I spat.

He looked up, shocked. “What do you mean?”

I hesitated, biting my lip. Did he really not know? Maybe it was better not to tell him then. “I was fostered, but my mother . . . she wasn’t exactly mother material.”

“What happened?” he asked stonily.

I shook my head. “It’s too long a story to tell.”

“I want to know everything,” Caleb said, his eyes flashing with anger.

I glared at him. “My childhood was crap, my mother was a crack head and my step-dad a rapist. I hated school . . . I got into trouble *a lot*. I was just falling through life when, all of a sudden, Fallen angels started coming after me, trying to kill me. I ended up being rescued by the angels . . . by Zach, and he took me to the Nephilim safe house. Only then I ended up in Castle Dantanian, where I encountered Asmodeus.”

Caleb went white. “Asmodeus?”

I forced back the tears and fear that always threatened to overwhelm me when his name was mentioned. “Aidan helped me escape.”

“That Aidan?” Caleb asked, pointing towards the kitchen. When I nodded, he looked grim. “Then he will always be welcome in the valkyrie colony. I will tell him when he wakes.

I shrugged, though I felt stupidly pleased at that. I had always wanted Aidan to have a home. For him to belong somewhere. At least here he would have somewhere to go to if he was in trouble. Somewhere he would be welcome, unlike with the angels.

"Anyway, I escaped and ended up meeting James." I paused, waiting for some sign of recognition. "You don't know him. He's not . . . "

"Who's James?"

I swallowed hard. "My brother. Or, maybe my half-brother, seeing as you don't know who he is."

Caleb scowled. "He's not mine."

"Anyway," I said, brushing over the tense silence, "I ended up entering the Tournament of Accession to try to save him, but it turned out he was an asshole anyway."

"You survived the tournament?" he asked in shock.

I bit my lip. "I won it."

38

'A real friend is one who walks in when the rest of the world walks out.'

Walter Winchell.

Caleb . . . my *dad* stared at me open mouthed, beyond confused at what I had confided.

"The Star Mist?" he breathed.

I grimaced. "They made me drink it."

For the longest moment he just stared at me, then a grin spread across his face. He began to whoop loudly, causing the other valkyrie to come running. He jumped up, fist pumping the air.

"The tables have turned!" he yelled. At the questioning look of the others he began to laugh. "Jasmine won the tournament of Accession. The Star Mist is on the side of the valkyrie!"

The valkyrie turned to me, amazed. I cringed away from the attention. I might as well have had a spotlight shining on me.

The pink girl with the piercings approached me. She stared, appraising, before pulling me in for a hug.

"I'm Sarah, but call me Shmaz, "she introduced herself.

My eyes widened as the other valkyrie now approached, introducing themselves to me. I didn't have a hope of remembering their names but I thought I'd caught a few. Pink girl was Shmaz, the blonde who had ogled over Aidan was Kathleen, the tall, black-haired beauty was Izzy, who Caleb had warned me about, and the owner of the Saleen on the driveway.

With a roar, a further three girls piled into the house, screaming and hollering. I flinched away, returning to stand by my dad as the valkryie embraced them with equally raucous cries. Shmaz pulled one of them, a green-haired, black-eyed woman towards me.

"Anna, Jasmine. Jasmine, Anna," she introduced.

I gave a little wave. This was the witch who would heal Aidan. I needed to keep on her good side.

"Hey, hon," she greeted me.

"Jasmine is the newest inmate," Shmaz continued.

Inmate? I glanced at my dad.

"Really? Awesome," Anna squealed. "I hope you like karaoke, 'cause there's no escaping Thursday nights!"

Karaoke? I felt as though I'd just fallen into a chick flick. This was probably what everyone else at school had been doing while I'd been getting high . . . a *lifetime* ago. This was way out of my league.

Focus, Jasmine. I told myself. Focus on the achievable. One, I needed the witch to heal Aidan. Two, I needed to find out what my dad meant when he said the tables had turned—though I didn't intend to be dragged into any more mess, I needed to know if there was a fight looming. Three, I needed to get back to the safe house, check on Gwen and Trev, who I presumed would be back there by now, check that Sam was still safe with Lilura, and deal with the aftermath. Four, I needed to find some way to avoid recapture by the Thrones.

When I zoned back in to the present time and place the whooping and shrieking was still going on. If anything, it had gotten worse. It was also accompanied by lightning strikes outside.

I turned to Caleb. "The lightning . . . ?"

He nodded. "Our emotions set it off."

"Oh," I breathed in and out. Make goal number five—do not trigger any lightning.

Focus. I turned to the green-haired witch, who was for some reason belly-fiving one of the valkryie.

"Anna, my friend is injured. Can you heal him?" I caught her attention.

She nodded and was ushered into the kitchen where Aidan remained unconscious. She poked and prodded him, conversing with the two witches who had accompanied her.

She nodded and clucked her tongue, turning to me. "It's gonna cost fifty thou."

I gasped. Fifty thousand dollars? Where would I get that kind of money? I could just imagine Zach's face when I asked the angels to cough up.

"Or . . . " she considered.

Thank God there was an *"or."*

"You could deliver me Racumbin."

"Who?" I gasped.

She shrugged. "if you don't know him, you'll not be able to get him. It was wishful thinking." She stroked her chin while appraising me with her eyes. "An alliance?"

I gulped. "What kind of alliance?"

She tilted her head. "The witches and valkyrie are long-term buds, but what of you? You're new. You're clearly powerful, if you took the Star Mist. That could be worth something."

"You want an alliance with me?" She wanted something that I probably would have given for free anyway?

Anna glanced at the other witches, all nodding in agreement. "Will you form an alliance with us? A bond that would last . . . um . . . .at least one hundred years."

I gasped. A hundred years? As if I would even live that long! That would make me 126-years-old, or more than likely a rotting corpse by then.

"You do realize I'll be dead by then?"

Collectively, the valkyrie and witches gasped.

"Why?" Shmaz shrieked. "Are you ill? Is it the plague?"

"Are you diseased? We can cure it," one of the witches cried.

I frowned. "Are you kidding? I'll be a hundred and twenty six!"

They continued to stare at me in silence. I was lost. So, completely lost. I turned to Caleb, who frowned at me for a moment before seeming to understand something.

"Oh! Jasmine, you didn't know?" He laughed.

"What?" I demanded. What was wrong with these people?

"You're immortal."

I froze. "What?"

He raised his eyebrows at me, his eyes and mouth laughing. "You're half valkryie, half Fallen—both immortal creatures. You're immortal. You can still be killed, but you won't age and die like humans."

I didn't know what to say or do. I just stared at him. The valkyrie seemed to understand my predicament and began to laugh, hugging me and stroking my hair.

"Oh she thought she would die of old age."

"Poor thing, what a shock."

"What a wonderful day, finding out you're immortal."

The voices and shrieks of laughter seemed to echo around me. I turned slowly to face Aidan, noticing his eyes trained on mine. Furrows between his eyebrows and on either side of his mouth told me he was in agony, yet he held himself still. He had heard. He knew I was immortal.

I pulled my eyes from his and focused on the witch. "You have my alliance. Do it. Heal him."

One of the other witches left the house for supplies, returning within minutes with a backpack stuffed with herbs and potions. I bit my lip and leaned against the counter, watching what was going on.

Within the hour Aidan was fully awake, his wounds completely healed, though he was severely weakened. Not surprising, really, after being tortured by the Queen of the Damned. When he was able to, he stood and limped toward the door, looking back at me repeatedly. As he left he said only one thing . . . "Thank you."

That was one of my tasks completed. I turned to Caleb.

"Caleb . . . *Dad*, why is it so important that I took the Star Mist? The angels were freaked by it, and I mean *freaked*, so why are you all celebrating!"

He ran his hand through his hair, ushering me into the next room. "That's angels for you," he muttered. "Jasmine . . . " He glanced at the other valkryie as they surrounded us. "Ragnarök is coming. It won't be long. The oracles are predicting it, the seers are channeling the powers, and every supernatural creature in existence is allying themselves to ensure they see it through. The game is in play, but the angels can't see it. They don't believe, and they won't believe until it's too late."

If ever there was a cue for apocalyptic music it would be now. My skin crawled, my heart ached and my head thrummed with a thousand questions.

"Someone told me I needed to find my allies," I confided. "That I needed to work out everyone's end game before I made my move."

Caleb nodded. "Our endgame is to survive. We are an army of talents and abilities. We can do what every other creature can do, and then some. We have an army of warriors waiting to be dispatched. They've been waiting for centuries for the moment we will release them into the final battle."

The *souls*. He was talking about the souls of warriors the valkyrie had harvested.

“Of what importance is the Star Mist?”

Caleb bared his teeth in a grin. “You are our secret weapon. The valkyrie learn and adapt other abilities. You will harness them exponentially and make us all unbeatable, unkillable, unstoppable.”

39

'One loyal friend is worth ten thousand relatives.'

Euripides.

I felt dizzy, dazed. Instead of just finding my dad, I had found a war, an army, and unwanted expectations and duties. Maybe I shouldn't have asked him what the valkyrie end game was. Battle just didn't seem to be the one I would choose.

What was my end game? I flinched. What was the angels' end game? Wasn't I on their side? If war was the valkyrie, then what was the lycae? A deep pit of sickness settled in my stomach as I remembered that I had already promised my alliance to the witches, and therefore to the valkyrie.

I looked up at Caleb. Before I did or said anything more I needed to speak to Zach and Haamiah.

I gulped. "I need to go home."

The valkryie began to file out as my dad looked at me with a thunderous expression.

"Jasmine, you *are* home."

I shook my head. "I am really happy to have met you, and I'm really grateful for you getting me away from Lilith and . . . I'll come back, I promise, but I need to see my friends."

Caleb huffed out a breath. He gestured around. “You’ve only just got here. You’ve spent years with the angels, yet you can only spare a few hours for the valkyrie?”

I shook my head. “No, it’s not like that. My friends are in trouble. Two of them are missing. I need to sort the mess out first then I can come back, and we can discuss this some more.” There, that sounded reasonable.

Caleb glared at me. “Are you not listening to what I’m saying to you? Ragnarök is coming. If you’re caught elsewhere we might not be able to get to you. Do the angels see you as family? Will they take care of you the way your *real* family will?”

My rage slithered free. I was so sick of being manipulated. Was it me? Did I look so weak that everyone around me thought I could be influenced so easily? Did they know me at all?

My power slipped from me, mist beginning to circle my body. I began to growl, low at first, until I snarled freely. Lightning shook the house, scorching the garden, narrowly missing the Saleen on the driveway. Caleb took a step back, before grinning.

“There you are, *Yasameen*. You’re just like your mother. Always have to have your own way.” He shrugged. “Go, I’ll be here waiting for you when you return with your questions.”

His unexpected response took the edge from my rage. Was that all it took? A show of power? Is that all I needed to do to get what I wanted?

Anna slid back into the room. In her hand was a vial of clear liquid. She held it out to me.

“Take it. It’ll help you get to wherever you want to go,” she said.

I took it from her hand, glancing at Caleb, then back at the witch. “How does it work?”

“Drink it,” she said. “Drink it, and think of home. Clicking your heels isn’t necessary.”

I nodded, and before I could change my mind I downed the contents, dropping the vial on the floor as the sweet yet spicy flavor ran down my throat. I blinked, anxiety rushing over me in a wave as Caleb, the valkyrie and the house faded away, leaving darkness.

I stumbled forward, falling to my hands and knees. Grass, I was kneeling on grass. I looked up, squinting in the darkness. Why was it so dark? I crawled forward, trying to contain my fear. What had the witch done to me?

I pushed through what seemed to be plants or bushes until my knees sunk into mud. I crawled quicker, dreading the thought of sinking into it.

I sat up, covering my face, as a light suddenly lit me up. I peered round my fingers, my heart in my mouth.

I was home. I squealed and jumped to my feet, running through the flowerbeds and up the garden, thanking God for the movement sensor and security light that had lit up the yard. I ran up the steps and along the verandah to the kitchen door, heaving it open, spilling into the kitchen.

Nephilim turned to look at me. They froze with their mouths half full of food, some with forks raised up in the middle of their dinner, while the television blared out, announcing the latest evictee of *Big Brother*. I looked down at myself, grimacing as I realized mud was coating my clothes—not that I was even wearing much, burnt off as they were.

I sidled through the kitchen, no one saying a word to me as I ran toward Haamiah's office. I didn't bother knocking but forced my way in, skidding to a stop as Zach, Haamiah and Elijah stared at me in shock. At least, Zach and Elijah stared in shock. Haamiah simply crooked his eyebrow. I could have sworn he mouthed, *It took you long enough*, but I had no time to question him as Zach pulled me up into a hug. Relief slithered through me as I realized that he had forgiven our argument back in the forest.

He squeezed me so tightly I could barely breathe. And I was glad.

"Where the hell were you?" He put me down and shook me by the shoulders, furiously glaring at me. "You weren't there."

I pulled away from him, Yeah, I . . . um . . . I got out."

"How? No one gets out of the waiting room," Elijah asked incredulously.

I rolled my eyes. "You know, that's what everyone said about Castle Dantanian. It happened, get over it."

Elijah glanced at Haamiah, trading surprised looks.

I turned to Zach. "Something happened. I know you're going to be mad, but it just happened."

He reached out to touch my jaw. "I know."

"You know?" I echoed.

"I've seen her."

I glanced at Haamiah. "The angel?"

“Zanaria,” Zach supplied, beaming at me.

I nodded. "Can we do this in private?”

“Why?”

“Because if you’re going to leave me for your real soul mate then I don’t really want to have an audience.”

Zach flinched. "My real soul mate? What are you talking about?”

I shrugged, chewing the inside of my lip. “Zanaria. I saw your past, Zach. I saw her, I saw you with her. Lilith said—”

“Lilith?” Haamiah thundered.

I cringed at his tone and glanced at him. “Lilith rescued me from the waiting room.”

“Sit down,” Haamiah shouted, pointing at the seat in front of his desk. With a look that clearly demanded my obedience, I slunk into the seat, preparing myself for a grilling.

40

'Nothing is perfect. Life is messy. Relationships are complex. Outcomes are uncertain. People are irrational.'

Hugh Mackay.

One and a half hours later I had learned three things. Firstly, and ranking most important on my list was that Zanaria was Zach's twin, *not* his lover. Her soul had found her way to Maion who, *get this*, was her actual soul mate. The thought of Maion getting naughty with anyone was enough to give me the heebie-jeebies, but as the tale went, he was such a dickhead to me because his brother and his soul mate had been murdered by Nephilim. I guessed that would make anyone a tad pro-vengeance. It also explained why Zach had been so hateful to me when he had first met me. Zanaria and Maion were currently elsewhere catching up.

The second thing I had learned was that Zanaria hated me. Zach had cringed when he told me he had confessed, telling Zanaria he was preparing to marry a half Fallen angel half valkyrie hybrid. Apparently she had majorly lost it, and demanded he break it off with me. I didn't delve too deeply into the answer he had given her. To my relief, the entire time spent in Haamiah's office was one spent with him stroking my hair and shoulders. At one point he had actually lifted me onto his lap. We were definitely okay.

Thirdly, we had clarified that Lilith most certainly wasn't my mother, but that Caleb was most definitely my father. Haamiah confirmed what I had learnt about valkryie, yet refused to consider the possibility that the end of the world was near. Zach also waved that piece of knowledge aside—just as Caleb had said they would.

Haamiah promised the Thrones wouldn't take me back, telling me he had extracted a promise from them, provided he was responsible for my actions. I rolled my eyes at that, despite his glower. Exhausted, I told them I needed to find Gwen and Trev and, ignoring Haamiah's worried expression, I left his office. Zach followed. Intent on finding Gwen I ran toward the stairs. Zach planted himself firmly in the way.

"Zach, I need to check that Gwen's okay."

He halted my words by licking my lips seductively. I gasped as he grasped my hair, pulling me into him as he began to devour my mouth, my body melting at every nip of his teeth, every lick of his tongue. He pressed me up against the wall, ignoring as two Nephilim giggled and ran past us.

"We can't do this here," I murmured, distracted by his soft lips nibbling at my ear.

"Yes we can." He nuzzled into my neck, inhaling deeply.

"Not when the others are so near, they'll see us," I protested.

Zach pulled back and up to his full height, towering up over me. In that moment all uncertainty was gone, all doubt and worry vanquished. I ached for him. I *yearned* for his body to be in mine.

“I don’t care if God himself is watching us; I need to see you right now, I need to be in you, watching you come around me as I fill you.”

I gasped as a flush of desire rocketed through me. I could feel tingles all over my body, from my toes to my ears. I could do nothing other than sink into his eyes as the black pits swallowed me whole. He suddenly descended on me; his lips crushing mine, his tongue demanding entrance. I opened to him, inhaling his scent through my nose even as my teeth gently nibbled his lip. I leaned closer, folding into his body, kissing the corner of his mouth. Shivers ran up my body as his hands trailed slowly down my spine before resting on my bottom. He began to knead slowly, an intense massage that I could feel through my flesh right to my clit.

I had placed my hands on his chest but they quickly became fisted and tangled in his T-shirt. I reached up, standing on my tiptoes and pulled as hard as I could on his clothing. I needed him to get rid of it. I needed to be able to feel his skin, to feel the hardness of the ropes of muscle across his abdomen. I wanted to press my lips to the expanse of muscle across his chest and lick my way down to his hips, where the muscles remained defined, leading the way beneath his black trousers.

Zach lifted his hands from me, leaving me feeling bereft of his touch. As I began to frown, he reached back and ripped the T-shirt from his back, flinging it to the ground. He towered over me again and pulled up my own top, being much more careful as he removed it.

When I would have fallen into his arms he stopped me, leaning down to press kisses to my breasts, removing my bra quickly, and discarding it as he had done my top.

He sucked my nipple into his mouth and I moaned in renewed pleasure as I felt myself dampen. I became acutely aware I was pretty much naked in the central corridor of the house, right outside Haamiah's office.

"Not here," I gasped as his mouth laved my breasts, breathing in my skin as he bit and sucked.

"I need you. I missed you," he groaned.

I was helpless to his onslaught. It was only when a Nephilim exited one of the nearby rooms and froze, his gaze on my bare chest that Zach picked me up and stormed off down the corridor. With super speed he had me in my bedroom, slamming the door shut behind us. He reached to what remained of my trousers and ripped them off completely. I leaned back, my bottom just reaching the top of the dresser, as he dropped to his knees before me, spreading my legs. He groaned as he spread my lower lips with his fingers, stabbing his tongue deep.

I moaned, bracing myself with my arms behind me. He ran his hands down my thighs, pulling me closer, flush against his mouth. I couldn't move, couldn't do anything but stand there, my legs trembling. With each suck of his mouth, each nibble on my clit, I lost a piece of myself. I moaned loudly, unable to be quiet despite knowing that others in the rooms either side of mine would be able to hear me as I was pleasured.

As the swell of orgasm raised up, spiraling through me Zach pulled away and turned me, leaning me across the table with my bottom bared to him. He filled me completely, instantly. He pressed his palms to my shoulders, holding me still beneath him as he forced himself into me again and again until I writhed with pain and pleasure. I felt him grow harder, impossibly thicker right before he exploded into me, the hot stream of come sending me over the edge. My core throbbed, vibrated around him. He withdrew from me and turned me around. He picked me up and gazed into my eyes.

“I'm not even nearly done with you.”

With that, he threw me onto the bed and began all over again.

* * * *

When I woke up I showered, smiling the whole while, even as I winced while cleaning the come that had dried on my thighs. I was sore, but deliciously so. I didn't think I had ever been taken so thoroughly. Not once had Zach allowed me to set the pace. The heat was on him too badly, his strength bruising me all over.

Now I needed to find Gwen. I slipped out of my room and ran down the corner to where hers would be. I tried the handle, locked. I knocked gently. The door swung open immediately and she stood staring at me, as though she'd seen a ghost. Her dark brown hair was a mess, her makeup tear-marked. Instead of her usual designer outfit, she wore jeans and a baggy jumper—was this how I'd looked when I'd escaped Asmodeus?

“Gwen,” I whispered. I ran into her arms, pulling her into a tight embrace. “I missed you. I'm so happy to see you.”

She squeezed me tightly, refusing to let go. Eventually I stepped back, extracting myself from her arms. Her eyes were full of fresh tears, some trickling down her cheeks.

"Gwen, what is it? You can tell me." I pushed my way into her room, closing the door behind us.

She sniffed and bit her lip, her chin trembling. She shook her head. "Jas, they're not here," she whispered miserably.

"Who?" I racked my brain to think of who she meant. Who were *they*?

Gwen shrugged, trying to restrain her tears, trying to hold them in. "Trev wasn't there when they went to look for him, and Sam's missing."

I gasped. "How is Sam missing? He's with Lil."

Gwen shook her head. "The angels were wrong. Haamiah admitted that he was wrong to ally with the sorceri. They've vanished with Sam."

"Vanished?" I repeated. I stared at her, open mouthed. What was she talking about? How could Sam vanish? He was with Lilura, and they loved each other. The other sorceri may not be exactly trustworthy, but I knew Sam loved Lil.

"We called him and he said he was having some problems he needed to work out, that he was with Lilura and the sorceri for now."

"So you left him there?" I shrieked. A bolt of lightning flashed outside.

"No! We went there. We flew to him, but he was gone. No one has been able to track any of them. The bar is closed, the sorceri are gone."

"Who's we? Who actually went there?" I demanded.

"Jasmine . . . "

"I'm serious. Who has tried to find him?"

"The Oracles, the Principalities, the Watchers."

I stepped away from her. I couldn't prevent the flash of doubt. I wondered if anyone had even looked for him or if this was another endgame that I had stumbled upon. *Just another game.*

"The witches can find him," I suggested.

"Witches?" Gwen gasped. "Witches, Jasmine? We're with the angels. Don't go allying yourself with other creatures."

I shook my head at her. "You're the same as the rest of them. You can't see what's happening."

"You're changing," she cried. "We are with the angels. Forget the witches or harpies, the Fallen, the sorceri, we need to be loyal to the angels."

I glared at her, desperate to swear and scream. It just wasn't worth it, though. I needed to find Sam. I needed to know he was safe, and then I would sort out whatever was wrong with Gwen.

"They'll keep looking. Haamiah loves Sam," she tried to soothe me.

"I need to go," I said.

"You should rest," she agreed. "Please don't be mad at me, Jas, the angels will deal with this."

I left the room, pulling the door closed with a click. I paused as I surveyed the corridor; Haamiah stood patiently outside my bedroom door, staring at me. I sauntered up, giving him a challenging look as I opened my own door and stepped inside. I paused.

“I’m having a lie down.”

“You should rest,” he agreed. I could have imagined it, but I was sure there was a knowing look in his eyes. As if he knew what I was about to do.

Surprisingly he stepped into my room, sitting on the window ledge.

I waited for him to say something but he didn’t. Instead, an awkward silence reigned. “I have an idea. I can’t promise it’ll work, but it’s worth a go,” I whispered.

Haamiah nodded. “Why didn’t you say anything to Zach?”

I worried my lip. “There are so many things going on at the moment. I need to sort them out in my head, first. But you know . . . don’t you?”

Haamiah looked away, refusing to answer.

“Something has been happening to me over the past few years. I’ve learned things, things that didn’t seem to make any sense at the time. Now they’ve accumulated, and they’re starting to mean something. I might be able to find Sam.” I waited for a reaction. Maybe I shouldn’t have said anything.

Eventually he sighed, running his hand through his hair. Was it me, or did his dreadlocks seem untidy today? His shirt a little rumpled? He looked tired and . . . older. He looked beyond stressed.

I moved forward and lay on the bed in a ball, resting my head on the pillow. I knew I could do this. I had done it before, albeit unintentionally. Now, though, I had reason to believe in myself. I had thought all along that these crazy things were happening to show me my heritage. I had never looked at the bigger picture—selfishly, I had never for a single moment considered that this could involve more than just myself. I had thrown myself into finding my family, finding somewhere I belonged, but it had taken a lycae to point out that everyone had an endgame, and even longer for me to even accept and understand that. I felt beyond selfish. Though I couldn't see what was unfolding before me I could touch it, smell it, I could taste the tangy spice of anticipation just on the horizon. This wasn't about me discovering my abilities; it was about the endgame that incorporated every single one of us.

I closed my eyes, smiling as Haamiah came to sit on the edge of the bed.

"That's the thing. Everyone belongs because no one belongs. Change the dynamic, change the game. To look ahead is to look behind. You must learn, but you must be the teacher," he whispered in his gravelly voice.

I tightened my eyes, his words filling my ears. It sounded like soothing nonsense to me, but I would work it out later. I reached for my power, a triumphant glow spreading through my body as my mist poured out, adrenaline streaking around my body with every beat of my heart.

I could do this. I could definitely do this. I began by clearing out my mind, picturing a blank wall—well, not entirely blank. I couldn't help the glittery shimmer in my mind. Then, I imagined

Sam. I pictured his face, his soft brown eyes and light hair. I drew him in my mind, his tall, slender but defined body, his ready smile, the good-natured glint in his eye.

Sam stood open mouthed, anger contorting his face. He was cast in a pink and red glow. Lights—pink and red lights highlighted him, making him glow. He looked fierce, furious even.

I squinted, trying to move forward to him in my mind. I could feel a crunch beneath my feet. I looked down; broken glass littered the ground, making a textured glittery carpet. I reached out my hand to Sam, calling his name. I saw his lip curl up in a snarl. I paused. If he was angry, maybe distracting him wasn't the best idea.

I stood next to him, turning to see who he was directing his glare at. Lilura . . . he was glaring at Lil? She stood, screaming at him, though this channel seemed to be on mute. I could only see her mouth moving rapidly, and his, replying. I frowned at him. What was happening? I peered around, seeing other sorceri standing in huddles, glancing at the raging argument.

I screamed as a gash opened up across his cheek. What on earth had just happened? Sam didn't move, despite the blood pouring down his face. Why didn't he move? I followed the dripping blood, noticing more slashes on his arms and chest.

I spun around, looking for whatever had attacked him. Lil remained in place with a bitter expression on her face. She spat words I couldn't hear. This wasn't getting me anywhere.

I turned to Sam, willing him to move. He couldn't. His wrists were held in place with steel manacles, chained to the floor on either side of him. What was happening? Was Lil torturing him? I didn't get the feeling that I was dreaming this, more like I was actually here with him. I felt as though I was in his mind, and if I was in his mind, then he should be able to hear me.

I leaned in close, willing him to hear me. I stood on my tiptoes and placed my mouth to his ear.

"I'm here. I'm going to help you. When I free you from the chains, run for the door," I shouted.

He winced. Damn, all I'd probably done was give him a headache. I needed to keep it short.

I placed my fingertips at the manacles, cringing as the metal began to melt. I whipped my head around, my rage evolving into the mother of all fury as Lil leaned over, laughing as Sam screamed when the molten metal scalded his hands. She thought one of the other sorceri was doing it. As much as I detested hurting Sam, this could work to our advantage.

I released my glittering mist, completely obscuring Sam from their sight. I leaned in again, trembling.

"Sam! Run!" I screamed with as much force as I could muster.

Sam whipped his head around, looking for me. My heart froze then pounded erratically—he had heard me! I waited, but he didn't run. He was ignoring me.

"Move it, now," I shrieked.

That got him moving. He bellowed as he ripped his arms from the molten manacles. I kept him shielded with my mist as he leaped through the sorceri, making it to the door. Once he'd pulled it open, the world flashed white and I was abruptly ejected from Sam's mind.

41

'Falling in love and having a relationship are two different things.'

Keanu Reeves.

In the days that followed Haamiah kept my secret. Neither of us spoke a word of what had happened. Neither did he do any more than assist me into the bathroom, leaving me sitting on the side of the bath, when I had come to, my face and wrists covered in blood.

There was no word from Sam.

Zach and Haamiah had exhausted all of their sources to locate him and the sorceri but they seemed to have truly vanished. I was wracked with guilt, questioning if I could have done something more, something differently. Had I done enough? I had attempted to enter Sam's mind again, but had been blocked out.

Sam seemed to have vanished off the face of the earth, and as there were a hundred other dimensions out there, our chances of finding him didn't look promising until a few days later.

The house phone rang while we sat in the lounge. I was closest to the mobile handset on the coffee table so I reached over, groaning to ensure my unwillingness was known.

"Yes?" I answered rudely.

"Jasmine?"

It was Sam. I sat up straight, clutching the phone to my ear.

"Sam?" I shrieked. "Where are you? Why haven't you come home? Are you hurt?"

"No I'm okay," he slurred. "God, Jasmine, everything's fucked up. Everything's totally fucked up."

He sounded so despondent, beyond devastated.

"Sam, I know what happened. At least some of it."

"I knew you were there. I heard you," he said, sounding amazed.

"Please come home," I pleaded.

"I can't, I just wanted to call to make sure Haamiah knows the sorceri can't be trusted. They're fucking bitches, Jas,"

"Are you drunk?" I asked, unable to keep the shock out of my voice.

"*Wasted*. I seriously messed up. I should have known," his voice broke.

"How could you have known? Sam, come home," I begged. I stood up, paced, waving my hand as Gwen peppered me with questions.

"I can't come back. Not after what I've done. You don't understand," he wailed. I could hear the misery in his voice and it broke my heart.

"Tell me where you are, we'll come and get you." I stared as Gwen began nodding her head enthusiastically.

"No, I can't be near anyone right now. I'll just cause more trouble. Just make sure you tell Haamiah."

Click.

I held the phone to my ear for a second longer before dropping it on to the sofa.

"Well?" Gwen jumped up expectantly.

"He hung up," I said.

"But he told you where he was, right?"

I grimaced.

"What did he tell you?" Gwen asked, her eyes wide. She looked scared.

I shook my head. "Not much. The sorceri have betrayed us. He told me to tell Haamiah not to trust them."

"Did you say he was drunk?" she gasped, her hand covering her mouth as her eyes filled with tears.

I nodded. "Yeah. He said he couldn't come back, that he'd messed up."

"Jas! We can't leave him wherever he is. We need to get him," she cried, tears now running freely down her face.

I bit my lip. "We don't know where he is. Maybe Haamiah can tell the Grigori to look for him again."

Gwen marched up to me and glared. "It didn't work last time, it's not going to work now. You can find him, you're just too chicken."

My jaw dropped. What was wrong with her? Gwen was a feisty bad ass, and now she'd turned into a dripping, crying mess who was seriously pissing me off.

"What?" I demanded, glaring back at her, my temper flaring.

"You know you can do it, you're just too scared."

"How exactly can I find him if no one else can?"

"You can open a portal to him. You've done it before, focus on him and just do it," she shouted.

I gave her my best withering glare. "It doesn't work like that. God, what is your deal?"

She bared her teeth. "It could work. You're just too scared to try."

I snorted. "Yeah, I *am* scared. You know what of? I'm scared I'll open a portal to the bottom of the sea and drown. I'm scared I'll open a portal into the middle of a war and be killed. I'm scared I'll appear in the middle of the sky and plummet to earth. But do you know what I'm most scared of? I'm scared of appearing right beside Asmodeus, and being raped and tortured for months on end . . . again! Tell me, would you do something that risked going back there?" I screamed. "What the fuck happened to you there, Gwen? You're being a bitch."

She flinched, paling. She clamped her mouth shut and gave me a look of betrayal before stomping away, slamming the kitchen door behind her.

I threw myself down onto the sofa. What a bitch! How dare she speak to me like that? She was so . . . so . . . I buried my face into my hands. She was right. I was a coward, though I would never admit it to her. She'd seriously got my back up.

When I thought of what Sam meant to me—how could I *not* risk it all for him? He'd do it for me. Ideally I would have liked to have a practice first, but I wouldn't even know where to begin.

I glanced around. The kitchen was empty. It was either now or never. I would just have to do it and pray to all the gods—both angelic and valkyrie—that I didn't end up in the clutches of Asmodeus . . . or at the bottom of the sea. I briefly wondered if I should tell Zach what I was doing. I quickly cancelled out that idea, knowing very well that he would try to talk me out of it, and when that failed he would insist on coming with me. I wouldn't be responsible for his torture again. *I wouldn't.*

I took a deep breath. There was no time like the present. I relaxed my power, letting it cover my vision and speed up my heart. The ground tilted and swirled, my stomach heaving in the process until I found myself falling.

I landed face down in the sand. It was certainly not my best moment. I cringed as I scrambled up, frowning as my knees caught on the material of my white, billowing dress.

White dress? I scowled. I haven't been concentrating enough, or I had at least been concentrating on the wrong thing—a wedding, anyone? Now my tracky bottoms and my comfortable hoodie were gone and I was bare foot in the most inappropriate floor-length angel-like gown I could have imagined. At least I wasn't in a sex outfit, I realized with relief.

When I eventually moved myself to my feet whilst holding my dress low enough so that the wind couldn't whip it over my arse, I surveyed my new location.

I was standing on a beach. The sea was roaring in, and thunderclouds overhead turned everything into shades of grey. At the top of the beach a road held a few convenience stores, what looked like a café and a hairdressers.

And there was Sam, sitting on the sand, a hundred or so meters away from me. While congratulating myself on getting here, I pulled my dress down, jogging across the sand to him. Though I shouted his name, the wind ripped the words away. Reaching him, I knelt before him, my hands on his knees. He really did look wasted. A half-empty bottle of Jack Daniels sat beside him, half buried in the sand. I flinched as I noticed the deep fresh burns across his wrists and hands, the skin pink and blistered. He took a swig of the bottle then put it down again.

"Are you really here?" he muttered.

I nodded. "I'm here. I'm going to take you home with me."

Sam shook his head, refusing. "I don't have a home. I don't belong there."

I clutched him, forcing him to look at me. "You *do* belong there. That place is just a house without you. You made it home for me."

Tears began to pour from his eyes. I worried my bottom lip. I'd never seen him like this before. Sam *never* cried. Out of all of us, I was the crier!

"Sam what happened?" I begged. "Please, tell me."

He shook his head miserably. “They’ll hate me. They’ll never forgive me. God, Jasmine what did I do?”

He looked grief stricken, terrified of something.

“I can’t help you if you don’t tell me what happened,” I said in my most soothing voice. He was so distraught it actually hurt me to see.

“They wanted the Falchion. I couldn’t hold up against them. They hypnotized and tortured me until I told them.” He dropped his head.

I froze. “How did you know where it was?”

“I’m telepathic, remember?”

“Oh,” I said, biting the inside of my cheek. I could taste blood. “The Falchion of Tabbris?” I clarified. I needed to be sure that we were as completely screwed as I thought we were.

He nodded.

Suddenly everything started to click into place. “Sam, I think Asmodeus already has it. There’s so much I have to tell you.”

He lifted his eyes and frowned at me. “What?” he choked.

“I don’t even know where to start.” I ran a hand through my hair, thinking. “The Thrones imprisoned me in the waiting room for being dangerous, so much went down there, and I’ll tell you everything another day. Anyway, Lilith broke me out and made me bring an angel back from the dead because she knows where the Dagger of Lex is.”

“The Dagger of what?” he asked incredulously.

"I don't actually know what it does, but there it is. Anyway . . . she then tried to trade me for the Falchion with Asmodeus. I was rescued by the lycae . . . and returned home. In the meantime, Gwen and Trev had been kidnapped by the Fallen. Gwen was rescued by some unknown demon and Maion," I rolled my eyes. "Go figure, but Trev is still missing."

I took a breath, and winced at Sam's shocked expression. He stared at me with eyes so wide they must have stung.

"Are you serious? Are you sure Asmodeus has the Falchion?" he asked, seeming to thrum with anticipation.

I shrugged. "I'm pretty sure, otherwise why would they trade me?"

He frowned. "But Asmodeus wants you so he can get into the Heavens, right? The Falchion does the same thing, well . . . it will *accomplish* the same thing, so what's the point?"

I paused. "Huh . . . I don't know. I didn't think about that." I shrugged. "I don't know, Haamiah can figure it out when we get *home*."

We sat in silence for a moment.

"If he'd taken you I would have killed him. I swear it, Jas," he said seriously, cupping my face.

I bit my lip and continued to smile at him. "I know you would," I said. I knew he would try . . . it was kind of the same thing.

I grinned as he took another swig of the J.D. "Hand that over," I said, reaching for it.

He groaned. "The party police are here."

I rolled my eyes and twisted the cap off, chugging some down. I winced at the burn that followed, my eyes watering. "No one *ever* accused me of being the party police."

"Alright." He laughed, clapping his hands together. He paused and pointed his finger at me, accusingly. "No drink driving Jasmine."

I grimaced. That was a good point. I needed to be stone cold stone sober if I was going to get us home.

"You're coming then?" I asked with a grin.

He nodded. "I suppose so."

I stood up and held my hand out to him. He took it, almost pulling me over as he struggled to stand. I looked down at his wrists.

"I'm sorry, Sam."

"For what?" He leaned heavily on me, the whisky fumes making my stomach roll.

"Your wrists, the metal chains—I melted them. It was the only thing I could think of doing," I said.

"Hey, that's pretty cool. Fuckin' hurt, but like you said, it was the only way." He shrugged.

I grimaced at the burn marks then grabbed hold of him, burying my face into his chest, all the while covering us with my mist, willing a hole to open up in the right place.

42

'If you think you can do a thing or if you think you can't do a thing, you're right.'

Henry Ford.

I wasn't too far off. We landed in the wooded park near to the safe house, only a few minutes walk away. Close enough for the trip to be a success, in my books. Of course, if I'd landed a short distance over I would have likely appeared out of thin air in someone's bedroom.

Sam kissed me on the cheek and took my hand, interlinking his fingers with mine. I smiled at the mere pleasure of having him near, knowing he was safe.

We hobbled the short distance, Sam occasionally stumbling even while continuing to drink from the bottle. Taking a shortcut, we climbed over the wall into the garden and ran up the grass toward the kitchen. Sam seemed to be almost back to his normal self. I guess the realization that you hadn't doomed Heaven to Hell would do that. I could still sense a lingering sadness among the whisky fumes though. It might have been chicken of me, but I didn't want to mention Lilura just yet.

Zach landed in front of us, his eyes furiously slashing at me.

"Where have you been?" he growled. Ignoring Sam, he stared at my dress with dawning comprehension. "You opened a portal?

You opened a portal without me?" His voice was laced with threat and anger.

I cringed. I had known this was coming. “I had to.”

“Bullshit!” he snapped. He spun on his heel and stomped off into the kitchen.

I frowned, closing my eyes lightly. Why did I always make him so cross with me? I just had to do it every time. This time I couldn’t even pretend to be annoyed at him. I had known he would be angry if I went without him and ta-dah—here we were.

Sam staggered off on his own toward the house. “Best get this over with,” he called over his shoulder.

I sighed and plodded after him, feeling pretty despondent. Once Sam had navigated the kitchen door he paused. I helped him to sit on the sofa, and went in search of Haamiah.

By the end of the day I was exhausted. Gwen had screamed and cried over and over again, seeming a little too enthusiastic at his arrival. Sam had passed out close to lunchtime, and only then could the J.D. bottle be pried from his fingers. Elijah had carried him up to his room and healed him a little, just enough to be sure he didn’t vomit. As he had put it—he wasn’t in the business of curing hangovers.

Zach had appeared with Zanaria and Maion, avoiding all eye contact with me, yet I could feel the heat of his glare when my back was turned. I struggled to ignore the way he and Maion fawned over Zanaria, and of the way she preened, basking under their adoration. I should have been happy that his sister was alive again, but instead I felt put out that she shrank away whenever I approached, never saying a word of thanks.

I could understand that Nephilim made her wary, but I wasn't even a Nephilim, for Christ's sake! You would have thought that Maion would have said something to me about the return of his soul mate, but if he hated me before, I simply ceased to exist in his eyes now.

Haamiah was the only one who acknowledged what I had done. He patted me on the back and smiled grimly—as much of a congratulations as I was going to get, clearly.

I moped with Sam and Gwen, each of us miserable for different reasons, but equally miserable all the same. Sam was devastated Trev hadn't been found, and had gotten stuck back into his J.D. the moment he woke up. Gwen and I helped him to finish the bottle before the day was done.

I gave Zach my best glare, not that he saw it, and stumbled up to bed with Gwen, praying for today to finally be over.

When I woke up the next day I took a long shower. I didn't think I would ever tire of being clean. I pulled on jogging pants and a plain grey T-shirt and sauntered out to the back porch. I took a seat on the steps and stared out into the dark garden, rubbing my arms when they were chilled.

I was definitely pleased to be back. I was even more pleased they had been able to rebuild the safe house, as I knew from the general conversation around here that the angels had considered moving elsewhere. Instead they had purchased a sanctuary spell from somewhere—I presumed from the witches, now that the sorceri had proven they had their own game plan. Now I was back here, it seemed like I was *home*. It was the weirdest feeling, as now I knew I belonged among the angels even less, but I felt like I was really a part of them now. I was happy to be back where I belonged but I was still devastated at the loss of my friends. Our dynamic was gone. Gwen was silent, sadly moping around—similar to how I imagine I'd been when I had escaped Asmodeus's clutches, and I knew from experience there was nothing I could do to help but be ready for when she wanted to talk. Sam was putting on a brave face, but it was clear he was shattered by Lilura's betrayal—as were we all. We had been completely blindsided by that, and I felt truly upset for Sam. He was such a genuinely lovely guy, he really deserved a beautiful, honest, wonderful girl. We hadn't gotten any further on our plans to find Trev. Though it terrified me, I was keen on opening a portal to go to Dantanian and find him, but Haamiah and Zach were adamant we needed proof that he was still there before we all risked our lives. Haamiah seemed to think that he would have escaped there, too.

I shook my head and leaned my forehead on my knees. I felt so contradictory. I was thrilled to be back, but worried that I would be taken away again. I felt closer to Zach than I ever had before, but I was worried that the return of his sister meant that we would be torn apart again. It was no small matter that she didn't like me. I was happy to be back with my friends but we weren't whole, and I still had the feeling that Haamiah was keeping something from us all.

I looked up as I heard the crinkle of leaves further down the garden.

"Is someone there?" I called out.

When no one answered I stood up and took a few steps, peering into the darkness. Every inch of me said someone was out there. Was it Lilith?

"Whoever's out there, show yourself," I shouted.

I took a couple more steps. A familiar face appeared in the darkness.

"It's just me," Aidan said quietly.

My heart relaxed, my mouth pulling up into a smile. "I was wondering how long it would take you to come here."

"You're unharmed? You're safe?" he asked.

"I'm fine," I replied.

I heard him sigh. "I'm sorry, Jasmine. I didn't know about Lilith. I just wanted to help," he said sadly.

"I know," I reassured him. "It's worked out okay. I promise I'm not mad at you. I could never be mad at you. If it weren't for you going to Lilith, I'd still be stuck there. I knew pretty quickly that you had gone to her, and I don't blame you at all. Honestly, I'm happy you went to her, Aidan."

Aidan closed his eyes for a second, relief on his face. It was so good to see him. Like a balm on my soul. I had been so worried, wondering what had happened to him after he had gone to Lilith. Seeing his tall, muscular and gorgeous body appear like that was amazing. I grinned as he flashed his shy smile at me.

"Come out of the shadows," I called.

He hesitated, "I wanted to do something for you. So . . . "

I frowned in confusion as Aidan reached back and pulled forward a wriggling figure, hands tied behind his back, his shouts muffled by a gag. Aidan held him tightly as he strode toward me.

It was Trev.

While at first my whole body screamed in delight, I then tensed in horror as I began to see him properly. His hair was matted with blood. More blood coated his face, and his clothes were ripped and bloody.

“Oh my God,” I breathed, running for them. “What happened?”

“I went to Dantanian to find him . . . for you,” Aidan said, holding a shouting Trev.

“Let go of him,” I cried.

“He’s too dangerous, Jasmine,” Aidan said.

A commotion at the kitchen door had me spinning around.

“What’s going on?” Haamiah’s voice boomed.

Zach appeared next to me within seconds. “What the hell is going on? What do you want, Aidan?”

“Get Elijah! He has to do something,” I screamed.

“I’m here! I’m here!” Elijah shouted, flanked by a horde of curious Nephilim.

“He’s injured. There’s blood everywhere!” I told him, feeling somewhat relieved when Elijah reached my side and took him from Aidan.

“If you’ve done what you came to do then get going,” Zach said with hostility.

I turned to face Zach, my mouth open in shock. “Zach!” I chastised. How could he be so rude when Aidan had just brought Trev home?

“It’s okay, Jasmine, I’m going,” Aidan said quietly.

With sadness in every move, Aidan backed away and disappeared into the darkness.

“That was rude,” I hissed at Zach.

He shrugged and sauntered into the house, leaving me to trail behind. I ran up the steps and through the doorway into the kitchen.

“Gwen, come on,” I said as I passed by her.

She was lingering in the kitchen with the other Nephilim. Zach, Sam and Haamiah had taken Trev up to see Elijah, so why was Gwen hovering down here?

“Gwen, seriously, what’s up?” I asked when she didn’t move from her leaning position against the kitchen bench.

“I think I’ll stay here. There’s probably too many people up there already,” she said quietly.

“What? Trev needs you! You’re important to him—his best friend. What’s going on?”

She shuffled from foot to foot. “You saw him. He’s not going to have a clue if I’m there or not.”

I slid up to Gwen. “You’re his *best* best friend. He’s going to know if you’re not there.”

She shrugged. “Fine.”

I was more than a little worried, but at least she was following me up to Elijah's rooms now. I ran through the hallway, checking on Gwen as I ran. We could hear the shouts and growls from the bottom of the stairs. By the time we got to Elijah's rooms the commotion was even louder. I ran through the open doorway and slid to a stop, staring in shock as Zach pinned Trev to the floor while Elijah was letting his magic flow through his palms.

Zach snarled when Trev sank his teeth into his arm. Haamiah pushed Sam out of the way and pulled Trev's face away from Zach, blood rushing down his arm. Haamiah and another older Nephilim restrained Trev further.

"Oh my God," I breathed, my heart pounding. What had happened to Trev? I turned to glance at Gwen only she was no longer there. I tensed, ready to go after her, before another savage snarl had me spinning back around.

Trev fought against the angels, his body thrashing on the floor. My eyes were transfixed on the fresh blood coating his mouth . . . Zach's blood. Elijah continued to chant, a blue icy glow emanating from his palms as Trev snarled and growled. When he eventually fell slack, no longer fighting the angels holding him, I breathed a sigh of relief and stepped further into the room. Zach growled as he stepped away from Trev, cradling his injured arm. I ran to him and placed my hand on his forearm below the cut, trying to avoid the steady run of blood. I took a deep breath and freed my power to flow up through me and through my fingers. As connected as we were, I could feel the way my warm power soothed his torn flesh and began to knit the tears back together as a light grey mist surrounded us.

I let go when I felt the wound was closed and relaxed as the mist cleared, my power receding back inside. Zach smiled gratefully at me, his black eyes caressing my face. Our previous quarrel about my portal travel was forgotten for now.

Feeling needy, and flushed, I spun around to face the others, smiling as Zach slid his arms around me.

“So what’s wrong with him?” I asked, watching as Elijah peered into Trev’s eyes with a torch.

Elijah was silent for a moment before sitting back on his heels. His eyes met mine. It wasn’t good news.

“All the signs suggest vampirism,” he muttered.

I felt Zach tense behind me. “What signs?” I asked.

“His eyes have a red ring around the pupil, a clear sign of the hunger for blood. He has fangs—he was feeding from Zach just a moment ago. He is a lot stronger now than he was in his Nephilim state.” Elijah looked down. “I’m sorry.”

“But there has to be something we can do, right? Some way we can turn him back?” Sam burst out. He looked devastated.

“The only thing we can do is destroy him before he awakens and kills one of us,” Elijah said, standing up.

“No!” Sam cried.

From where I stood, I could see the sheen of tears in his eyes. I knew this must be harder for him than anyone here. He had lost so much in such a short period of time. This was just one more blow.

"No," I echoed Sam. "There has to be a way . . . there has to be something we can do."

I pulled out of Zach's grasp and skipped over to Sam, pulling him into my arms. He felt stiff and cold. I could feel the shivers running through him.

"We're not killing him," I said, glaring at Elijah over Sam's shoulder.

"Then what do you propose we do with him? As soon as he wakes, he will look for someone else to feed from. He'll kill his way through the entire safe house," Elijah said.

"There has to be a way to rehabilitate him. He can drink blood from the blood bank, he doesn't need blood from a live person," I suggested.

"Vampires are evil. There is no rehabilitating them. They don't want to be good!" Elijah argued.

"Trev is good. He's a Nephilim," Sam shouted, pulling away from me. "Surely there is a good part in him that we can find and bring out. You're always telling us that good triumphs over evil, so if there's good in him *and* evil, then surely the good will win."

Elijah shrugged and turned away.

I turned to Haamiah. "Okay, Haamiah. What do we do? How do we rehabilitate a vampire?"

43

'Don't find fault, find a remedy.'

Henry Ford.

"You're not alone," I said with a moan. This conversation had gone on for so long. Both Haamiah and Elijah had been useless in coming up with any ideas to cure Trev, and as a result Sam, Trev, Gwen and I were sitting in the kitchen in complete misery. The angels were loitering near us, always on constant vampire guard.

"I am," Trev said gruffly. "I'm not one of you anymore. I don't belong here. I don't belong anywhere."

This was my cue, the only chance I would get. If I didn't say something now, I would only regret it in the future. My best friend was in pain, and I could potentially soothe the ache.

"You're not the only one who doesn't belong here," I said quietly, measuring my words.

"For God's sake, Jasmine! We're not doing this again," Sam cried, exasperation in his voice. "I thought we had put all that to rest.

I frowned, irritated by the implication I was whining. "Sam, stop," I cut in. "I'm trying to tell you all something important. I don't belong here because I'm not a Nephilim."

A chorus of gasps rang out, each one of my friends frowning in confusion and shock. Even Trev looked astonished. As I glanced at Maion, I saw him smirk.

“Jasmine,” Zach warned, concern etched on his face.

I shook my head. “No, I have to tell them. It’s not right that they don’t know.”

“It’s too dangerous.”

I ignored him and turned to face Trev. “I’m not a Nephilim. I don’t even know what the name of what I am is. These past few weeks have been the craziest of my life. My real father was a valkyrie and my mother was a Fallen angel.” I winced as I saw how pale Gwen had become. “I’m sorry I didn’t tell you all sooner . . . I’ve been working through it.”

“And imprisoned on a different plane,” Zach muttered in my defense.

I smiled at him gratefully. I breathed in deeply as they all stared at me, seeming unable to speak. I waited.

“Okay somebody say something. This is driving me crazy!” I exclaimed.

“How can that be true?” Gwen burst into tears. She looked at me through her fingers. ”How can you be evil?”

“She’s not evil,” Zach growled.

“I’m not evil,” I denied at the exact same time.

“You’re half Fallen angel, Jasmine?” Sam asked, aghast.

"I'm not evil," I protested again. "It's not as simple as that. Just because something is labeled as one thing doesn't mean everything is. You can't tar everyone with the same brush."

"What?" Sam asked, his eyes wide.

"You know what I mean. Not *every* Fallen angel is evil," I said.

"Pfft! Name one," Zach said.

I glared at him. "You forgot the Fallen who helped us escape?"

He glared at me in return, "you can't say that the Fallen aren't all evil. They are."

"You're saying *I'm* evil?"

"*You're not Fallen*! You mother might have been, yes, but you aren't."

"No, not every Fallen angel is evil, and you know it. Some of them are good," I denied, shaking my head.

"Here we go," Maion muttered, turning away.

"*You*!" I snarled.

Before I knew it, my power had risen up and was churning through my chest. Sparks of glitter were shooting out around me as the floor undulated. I couldn't think straight, couldn't reason. I felt arms circle me and before I could resist, I felt strong lips crushing mine. I gasped and felt Zach's tongue sweep in, linking us.

After a moment, I was able to see clearly again and could breathe without the tight knot in my chest. I stepped back, smiling when Zach grinned at me.

“How did you know that would work?”

“I had a hunch, and I’m getting to know your quirks, babe,” he answered with a smirk.

I laughed and turned away, my eyes widening as I realized everyone was staring at us in amazement.

I sent them an apologetic look. “I’m not evil. I just have a few minor differences that I need to get a better handle on,” I said calmly, daring anyone to contradict me.

Maion snorted and left the room. I stiffened then relented, and allowed Zach to wrap his arm around me. I could put up with anything Maion had to throw at me as long as I had Zach by my side.

“I need to sit down,” Sam mumbled, throwing himself onto the sofa.

“I’m still me,” I said to Gwen, who remained standing stiffly by the doorway as if she thought I would pounce. “And Trev is still Trev. We’ve just got some . . . ” I glanced at Zach. “ . . . *quirks* to work out. But we’re still your friends.”

“I guess,” Gwen said, uncertainly.

“Trev, you belong here more than I do,” I urged.

“Yeah, you can’t leave, dude. We’re in this together, remember?” Sam said with a small smile.

“I don’t know. I’m not who I was, I’m different now,” Trev said quietly, sadly.

“Come on, Trev. Who isn’t different?” I asked. “We’re all different. Take Zach!” I pointed at him, noting his scowl. “When I first met him he was grumpy, rude, and not interested in being my guardian in the slightest! He hated Nephilim. Now look! He lives here in the Nephilim safe house, we’re engaged, and he even smiles sometimes,” I joked.

Zach rolled his eyes, clearly not amused.

“Sam has fallen in love, then—” I shot him an apologetic look. “—was betrayed, kidnapped and blackmailed. You think he’s exactly the same person he was before that happened? And the same with Gwen. We’re all different, but we’ll be okay if we have each other.”

Trev took a few steps closer to me. “I don’t want to be here if my presence will make other people uncomfortable.”

“Who . . . ?” I belatedly realized who he was talking about and glanced at Gwen, still hovering by the door.

“Gwen,” he breathed, chancing a look at her.

She bit her lip. “You should stay. This is your home, too.”

“As long as you stay,” he replied, waiting for her answer.

When she didn’t reply I grew suspicious, “Gwen?”

She shrugged, and plastered on a fake smile. “I was thinking of going to visit my dad for a while.”

Sam groaned, and dragged his body off the sofa. “Gwen, what are you doing? This is us. Us four . . . we’re in it together. Whatever happens, we can handle. So, the two of us are the only normal ones—that’s exactly the same as it was before. Yes, we have a few obstacles. Trev needs to control his bloodlust, and Jasmine needs to stop trying to kill everyone the moment she gets angry. I have my own issues to get over, and so do you. But none of us are leaving. Why would we, when we're surrounded by angels who will help us through this?"

I briefly contemplated saying that I was fairly sure all angels couldn't be trusted but bit my tongue, certain that that didn't apply to Zach, Elijah and Haamiah.

Trev nodded, and Gwen finally took a couple steps toward us.

"Will you try?" Sam asked, looking at us all.

I nodded, smiling with relief when Gwen and Trev agreed. Excusing myself, I headed up to my room, dragging Zach behind me. It had been too long.

* * * *

Hours later we convened back in the kitchen. I sat on the kitchen counter while Zach stood between my legs, alternating between kissing my lips and my neck.

A disturbance at the door had me looking away from him. A delicate exotic-looking angel stood beside Maion. I knew her immediately.

She scowled at me. "Zacharael, step away from her. She's not what you think," she snapped.

"Fuck you," I snarled, sliding off the bench.

"Jasmine, stop it," Zach growled. He stepped in front of me. Shielding me from her line of sight . . . or possibly shielding her from my power. “Zanaria, please. I’m in love with her. Jasmine and I are engaged to be married.”

“You would taint our blood line with a creature like her?” she cried softly. Her eyes flashed with distress. “It was bad enough when I thought her one of the Nephilim-scum, but to find out she’s actually in league with those who plot our downfall? Lust blinds you! She has tricked you somehow.”

“You never used to think like that,” Zach said sadly. “You wanted to save the Nephilim.”

“Well that changed when I was betrayed, and killed by one of them,” she hissed. “That you would aid my killers . . . it’s devastating to me. How could you?”

“She’s not like the others. I swear it. Wait until you get to know her. You’ll love her as I do, I promise,” he pleaded. “Please, just give her a chance. We’ll go now, and let you settle in. Maybe we’ll see you tomorrow instead and talk this over.”

Zach’s claims of love were the only thing that kept my power in check. I was furious that she dared to stand right in front of me, telling Zach I wasn’t good enough for him. How dare she?

“Zacharael! I have been dead for 600 years and you’re not even going to look after me?” she exclaimed. “I don’t know anything in this time. I don’t understand how things work here. Don’t you love me? Will you really side with one of the Fallen over me?”

“No! I’m not siding with her,” he said.

“You’re not on my side?” I demanded. “Thanks a lot, Zach.”

"Jasmine, don't make this any more difficult than it needs to be," he groaned.

"Well, then, I'll make it really simple. I'll go," I said, my heart aching.

Zach swung around immediately, grasping me by my shoulders. "Jasmine, don't do this."

I bit my lip and stared up into his black eyes. Those eyes that were usually filled with heat seemed to be in such turmoil now. I tried a shaky smile, and failed.

"I'm not saying we're over or anything. I just . . . " I swallowed. "I need to focus on everything that's happening. Trev, Gwen and Sam need me to be levelheaded, and I need to get better control over my power. With her around I don't see that happening."

"Then what are you saying?" he asked stiffly.

I shrugged, masking my pain, "Let's just take some time . . . apart. You show your sister the ropes and when she no longer needs you to hold her hand, *then* we'll talk."

Zach brushed my cheek with his fingertips. "Jasmine . . . " he whispered.

"I know," I replied, blinking to brush away the tears in my eyes.

I stepped back out of his reach slowly, and, keeping my dignity intact, stepped out of the room, making it all the way to my bedroom before letting my tears run free.

44

'A loving heart is at the beginning of all knowledge.'

Thomas Carlyle.

I woke up to a tapping at my window. I sat up and looked at my bedside clock. It was five a.m. I groaned. Why was I awake? I didn't want to face the world just yet. I rolled over, and buried my head in the pillow. I sat up quickly when the tapping at the window finally registered. With my heart hammering away inside of me I leaped out of bed and prowled around the window. Who was it?

It was so dark outside I couldn't see a thing. I spotted a dagger on the dressing table and quickly picked it up, running my fingers across the plain handle. Zach must have left it here. I gripped it tightly and approached the window slowly. Reaching for the catch, I took a deep breath and unlocked it, lifting it up with one hand while peering out.

I let out a shriek when Zach slipped in front of me.

"What are you doing?" I hissed, my whole body weak with fright.

"I had to see you," he whispered.

"And you couldn't have come to my door like a normal person?"

He shook his head, sadly. “I’m not a normal person, and neither are you.”

Now I registered his somber mood. He looked . . . miserable. I had rarely seen him like this. Grim, angry and violent, yes, even excited and lustful, but never truly upset. Had something happened with his sister? Was it really any of my business?

I scratched my forehead and sighed. “What do you want, Zach?”

He held out his hand. “Come with me?”

“I’m not climbing through the window,” I refused.

“You know how much effort it takes to keep afloat like this? Just climb out the fucking window,” he growled, his temper flaring.

I scowled at his words and peered out. His white wings were billowing out behind him. He wasn’t holding on to a thing, simply hovering outside my window.

I blew out a long breath and knelt up on the window frame, turning to sit on the edge with my legs hanging down in front of me.

“Now what?” I asked. I glanced down at the ground and back at him. If he let me fall from this ledge I’d kill him.

He didn’t. Zach reached out and plucked me from the windowsill, rising up higher and higher. I clutched at him, feeling both pleased and sad when he wrapped his huge strong arms around me firmly so that I couldn’t move an inch. I buried my head against his chest and closed my eyes, breathing him in as he rose higher, gravity falling away from us rapidly.

It was cold. Even next to his hot body the air was freezing, and damp as we shot through it. I wondered for a second where we were going before realizing that I didn't care. I was with Zach. My man. My soul mate. The only one who mattered. Clarity seemed to rain down on me with each second in his arms. He was everything. Why had I told him to be with his sister when I wanted him with me? Had I really done the right thing? I was trying to be selfless and give him what he needed, but did I actually stop to ask him if it was what he needed? Had I been a complete fool?

My questions stopped as we descended. I grimaced as my stomach rolled, protesting the speed at which we seemed to be dropping out of the air.

He landed softly, his wings slowing us at the last moment. Refusing to put me down, he swung me into his arms and stormed off. I looked around, seeing nothing but grass and sky.

"Where are we?" I whispered in his ear.

He ignored me and continued to walk a little further. He set me down on my feet facing him, and then abruptly spun me around to face away from him, his arms encircling me from behind.

I gasped. We were high up. Really high up, on a cliff side, overlooking the sea. The wind whipped around me, cold and wet. I could even taste the salt on my tongue. It was still quite dark, but I could see the sun beginning to peak over the horizon, just beginning to taint the sky, changing the grey blue to a slight pink hue. Even the sea seemed to have golden tips.

"Why did you bring me here? Are you going to throw me off the edge?" I joked.

Zach tutted. "Shh now."

I frowned. I contemplated telling him to go shove it before deciding to go with the flow, and see what it was he had dragged me out of bed for. If anything it felt wonderful to be in his arms, and rest the back of my head against his chest.

I began to feel lost in the beauty of the moment. It truly was beyond beautiful. Standing here, with my man, watching the sunrise, was a moment I wanted to go on for eternity. The moment the sun fully rose over the edge of the sea a warm glow ran over my body, the cold air heating up, the sky lightening with every second.

Zach leaned closer, his breath warming my ear.

"This is what I wanted to show you," he said.

"The sunrise?" I asked.

"Not just the sunrise. This is the way I feel about you. Every time I'm away from you I feel cold, lost in the darkness. I feel like a part of me is missing. Then I see you, and I feel as though the sun has finally come to make everything clear to me, to warm me, to make me *see*. You are my world. Sometimes I feel as though I'm drowning in you; the need I have for you is so strong it's painful . . . but it's worth it.

"You wanted to know why I was so cold to you when we first met, why I seemed to dislike you. I had perhaps hoped never to tell you, but now I will.

"Fighting had been my way of life for a thousand years; I didn't know how to be anything different. I was a warrior angel, so to be told I was now a guardian . . . it felt like a huge demotion at the time. Little did I realize, being a guardian would be the most important role of my life.

“When I first met you, I knew you were someone who would turn my world upside down and cloud my judgment. You were . . . you *are* an emotional whirlwind. I dreaded being sucked up like debris. I never could have guessed that I would pray every second of every day to be swept up by you, to pray you would never drop me.

“When I first realized you were my soul mate, I thought of you as the piece of me I didn’t need. I was content in the dark. I knew and respected the cold. You’re not even the same species as me! I railed and fought against the idea of us, holding up all of my guards against you. This seemed like it could only end in tragedy. This love is insanity, Jasmine. I know you feel it too. But despite that, despite our families, our heritage and our destinies, I will make sure mine is always entwined with yours, because you are my clarity.

“When I feel your warmth against me, I lose all common sense. I know I’ve hurt you again and again, but I’ll always make amends, whether you let me or not. I will chase you relentlessly. I’ll always fight for you. No matter who comes back from our past, you will always be my present, and my future.”

When he released me I spun around and gazed up at him, tears pouring down my face. I braved a watery smile, sure I looked terrible.

“I love you, Jasmine,” Zach said. “Whether you’re a half Fallen angel-valkyrie hybrid, or whether you’re a human, or a Nephilim, or any combination of species you can name. You’re mine, and I will always choose you.”

Refusing to close my eyes I reached up, standing on my tiptoes, silently begging him to kiss me. When his lips brushed over mine, I sighed my relief. Everything was going to be okay.

45

'Love is a better teacher than duty.'

Albert Einstein.

After watching the sun rise fully, smooching and making naughty on the cliff, Zach flew me back. After a slight mid-flight crisis, when I remembered I was in my nighty, Zach ensured I returned to my room the way I had left. I showered, dressed and ran downstairs to the kitchen where he had promised he would meet me. Before entering, I had a thought. I spun on my heel and jogged up the corridor to the opposite end of the house. I knocked on Haamiah's office door. I was sure he would be there. He was *always* there.

He opened the door, and looked at me with an expectant smile.

"Hi," I said. "Can I talk to you for a moment?"

Haamiah silently opened the door further, allowing me entrance. I ignored the seat across from his desk where I normally sat and remained standing. His office was spotless, as always. A pile of papers sat neatly next to his laptop on the desk, a couple of pens in a pot, and a steaming cup of coffee on a coaster. His window was open, and sweet scents from the garden were wafting in, mingling with the strong coffee aroma.

“Why don’t the angels have any allies?” I asked Haamiah. I didn’t look at him. Instead, I stared out to the garden, and let the light breeze toss my hair back over my shoulder.

“Who would you suggest?” he asked.

“The valkyrie are nice.”

“They harvest souls. Angels save souls, and transport them to the Heavenly Realm where they receive love and warmth for infinity. How can we ally ourselves with a species that hides souls away, ready to bring them back to war whenever the mood strikes them? Souls deserve peace.”

I shook my head. “They’re not like that. It sounds worse than it is.”

“They worship their own god, when we know *our* god to be the one true god, how can we accept their beliefs?”

I shrugged. I could see his point, though I didn’t necessarily agree with it. “The witches?”

“The witches will only assist another for monetary gain. Do you wish for us to have an ally who can be bought? Or one who is loyal to us, no matter the benefits offered?”

I bit my lip. “Harpies?”

“In the commandments, it was made clear to us all; thou shall not steal.”

“The lycae?” I asked, disregarding the werewolves. Apart from Valentina, they had proven distrustful, time and time again.

He smiled. “The lycae . . . we can consider.”

I turned to him and crooked an eyebrow. “Drew will be so pleased.” I ran a hand through my hair, picking at a knot at the end. “Haamiah, what am I doing here? I’m not an angel. I’m not a Nephilim. Now that I know other gods beside the one the angels worship exist, I’m more inclined to believe, but I can’t say I fully do yet. Why am I *here*? Why did you send Zach to me if I don’t even belong here? I’m nothing like anyone here. I’m nothing like anyone anywhere.”

Haamiah smiled. “A higher power was at work,” he said.

I groaned. “A higher power? That’s the answer you’re going to give me?”

He smiled again. “It’s the only one I have for you.

Leaving Haamiah’s office more confused than when I had entered, I ran to where I knew my sanity waited.

He was there in the kitchen waiting for me . . . as was his sister. Without pausing, I ran up to him and kissed him fully on the mouth. I ignored her when Zanaria turned away, scowling, and instead focused on the love of my life. He was gorgeous. He looked exactly the same as he had earlier—bare chested, in black trousers, but he looked so . . . .delicious standing there in the kitchen waiting for me. I grinned, unable to hold back my overwhelming excitement. I would replay everything he had said over and over in my mind until the day I died. He was so romantic, even if he didn’t want to be.

I detached myself from his lips when someone cleared their throat.

I turned around, and beamed at Sam and Gwen. The two of them grinned back at me. Maion rolled his eyes and pulled Zanaria away from us, as though I was diseased. The tension was eased somewhat when Haamiah and Elijah entered the kitchen with a couple more Nephilim. I poured some cereal and handed the box over to them, sitting down at the kitchen bench. Zach pulled out a stool beside me. When Trev entered, the tension rocketed up again.

Though Gwen and Trev had agreed to try to work through this, it clearly wasn't going to be easy. I sighed around a mouthful of cereal. Zach opened his mouth, beckoning me to feed him. I rolled my eyes and stuffed a spoonful of cereal in, giggling when milk dribbled down his chin.

Gwen pulled some toast out of the toaster, flinching when Trev passed by her. I could tell he saw, and felt the urge to cry when his face dropped. He was devastated by this, and who wouldn't be? He had been turned into something against his will, and the girl he liked now thought him abhorrent. I quickly finished my cereal then sat by Gwen on the sofa in front of the television.

"Stop it," I whispered.

She looked up, startled. "What?"

"What you're doing to Trev. It's not fair. You're hurting him."

She glanced at Trev and then back at me. "It's none of your business."

My rage flared. "Yes it is," I replied crossly. "You agreed to give him a chance! We only spoke about this yesterday, and we all agreed to try to make this work. It's not his fault he's now a vampire," I hissed, trying to keep my voice low enough that the other Nephilim wouldn't hear. It wasn't anyone else's business that Trev was a vampire, and until he chose to make it public knowledge I was determined they wouldn't hear it from me.

"It's okay, Jas," Trev muttered from behind me.

I spun around and shot him an apologetic look when I realized he had heard me whispering.

"It doesn't matter. I think I should go," he continued.

"No!" Sam shouted, startling the others. Other Nephilim crowded into the room trying to see what the commotion was about.

Gwen stood up, edging towards the door. "No, I'll go."

"Would the two of you stop it? We just agreed to try to work together on this," Sam bellowed. "I'm sick of this shit. Why does everything have to go wrong? Why can't things just go right for a change?"

I cringed, feeling sorry for him all over again. Poor Sam.

"I'm sorry, but I can't change my feelings that quickly," Gwen retorted.

"Your feelings about . . . " Sam glanced at the other Nephilim listening in. " . . . a*liens*. But there aren't any of those here, only the same friends that you know and love."

She hissed in a breath even as Trev looked at us with hope in his expression.

"You're talking out of your ass. You don't have a clue what I've been through," she shouted.

"So share it. Tell us! Make us understand," Sam growled.

I was shocked, my good mood gone. I had never seen Sam so angry. I had never seen him and Gwen shout at each other. Trev turned away, moving to the far end of the kitchen in front of the television. He stared at it blankly, clearly wishing to be anywhere away from here.

“What is going on here?” Haamiah bellowed from the doorway.

The Nephilim scattered, and Zach came to hover over me protectively.

“I asked what is going on,” Haamiah repeated.

Maion stood in front of Zanaria, who cringed behind him. I couldn’t help but feel a little sorry for her. None of this was her fault. None of it even had anything to do with her.

“Guys, come and look at this,” Trev shouted, the urgency in his voice breaking through the tension.

In a silent mutual agreement a momentary ceasefire was called, and we shuffled across the kitchen to where Trev stood staring at the TV, watching a female news reporter gesturing wildly. Sam picked up the remote from the coffee table and tapped at the volume.

“The United Nations has officially declared a state of emergency. The demolition of the White House is the sixth deadly attack today. The US army, the FBI and the Secret Service are present at the scene in Washington as we wait to be told the origin of the attacks. The country mourns for the president, with services being held across the country for those lost today.

“As the death toll currently stands at 1112, survivors are sharing some disturbing accounts. One survivor claims that the insurgents

had fangs and drank the blood of a colleague, while others claimed the attackers looked demonic. Some of the reports we are getting claim that the men and women involved had wings. As much as these reports sound incredible, we are hearing similar stories from officials in London, Paris and Tokyo, while survivors are yet to be found in Moscow and Canberra."

We stood, frozen to the spot. I looked at my friends, each with a disbelieving, horrified expression. I looked at them until my gaze rested on Haamiah. He took the remote from Sam and pointed it at the TV, muting the volume. One by one we turned to face him.

He solemnly raised his eyes from the floor to meet mine. "And so the war begins."

To be continued . . .

ABOUT THE AUTHOR

Laura Prior grew up in the North East of England, and has travelled the world while working as a nurse. She is currently living and working in Melbourne, Australia, with her partner. She enjoys snowboarding, long walks, shoe-shopping and cocktails. She loves reading passionate novels with strong female characters.

Find me:

www.facebook.com/fallingforanangel

Twitter @falling4anangel

www.laurapriorbooks.com

Printed in Great Britain
by Amazon.co.uk, Ltd.,
Marston Gate.